Playing the Field

By Jennifer Seasons

Playing the Field
Stealing Home.

Excerpt from *Stealing Home* copyright © 2013 by Candice Wakoff.

Excerpt from *The Mad Earl's Bride* copyright © 1995 by Loretta Chekani.

Excerpt from *Wanted: Wife* copyright © 2013 by Gwen Jones.

Excerpt from *A Wedding in Valentine* copyright © 2013 by Gayle Kloecker Callen.

EPub Edition AUGUST 2013 ISBN: 9780062271464

Print Edition ISBN: 9780062271471

JV 10 9 8 7 6 5 4 3 2 1

Playing the Field

A DIAMONDS AND DUGOUTS NOVEL

JENNIFER SEASONS

AVONIMPULSE
An Imprint of HarperCollinsPublishers

This one's for you, kids.
Because you love me whether I'm half-nuts,
full nuts, or anywhere in between.
Never stop shining your lights and always,
always know you're loved.

Chapter One

SONNY MILLER HATED Saturdays. Unusual, she knew. But she had good reason. In her experience Saturday was the day of doom, when everything bad that could happen, did. A long list of travesties had been compiled in her life, providing strong supporting evidence for her decision.

Given the transgressions, it was a rational belief. Saturday was the day her dad had skipped town when she was seven, leaving her with nothing but a crumpled ticket stub from the movie he'd taken her to before he broke her heart.

It was the day she'd found out she was pregnant after a three-month relationship had gone sour and the guy had refused to believe it was his. The jerk had bailed faster than the Bondo could dry on his rusted out Dodge Dart, leaving her with forty bucks in cash and a box of stale Cheerios in the cupboard.

Real swell guy, right?

Yeah. She should have seen it coming, too, but she'd been all of twenty then, about as smart as a box of rocks and up to her ears in daddy issues. So, yes, she'd picked a real winner.

Looking back, there was no doubt that it had been for the best that he'd bailed. They'd been about as functional together as a broken toaster. But he'd given her a son that she loved more than life itself, so the scale had balanced out in the end.

Still, Saturday was a serious pain in her ass. She'd been evicted from her apartment after losing her waitressing job on that awful day because she couldn't work with a broken ankle and had no money for rent.

And her son Charlie had been diagnosed with type I diabetes after a panicked trip to the emergency room.

If she was prone to superstition, she might just think that Saturday had a personal vendetta against her. As it was, she tried damn hard to avoid going out on that day, other than to her son's Little League games, preferring to use it for general housecleaning and lying low. When normal people were out partying it up, Sonny was in her sweats, ordering Chinese food, and having a date with the vacuum cleaner.

So when Charlie had asked her one Saturday to take him to a state-sponsored charity event hosted by the Denver Rush pro baseball team, she'd nearly said no. He knew the routine—knew her rule. But one look at the excitement and hope in his soft blue eyes had killed the word before it had even left her lips.

For Charlie she'd do anything.

That didn't mean that she wasn't keeping her eyes peeled like a hawk's, though. A charity event for diabetic kids sounded safe enough, but she wasn't willing to bet on it. Before they'd left their place up near Longmont she'd shoved an "emergency pack" in her oversized purse. It consisted not only of Charlie's insulin kit, but pretty much everything a person could need to survive a nuclear war short of the bomb shelter. But even that she could probably fabricate from the stuff in there if the need arose.

She wasn't taking any chances.

Some might call her paranoid, but they didn't have her track record. And *for* the record, paranoid was totally different from superstitious. Any sane person, after reviewing the facts laid out on the table, would exert the same amount of caution as she did.

And swear to God, the only reason she got the loan to start her own business last year was because banks didn't process on the weekends. If they did, there was no doubt she'd be flipping burgers at the local Dairy Queen rather than busting her ass with her organic goat cheese venture, Sonnyside Farms.

"Mom. Hey, *Mom*." Her son's voice pierced her thoughts. Sonny glanced down at Charlie's upturned face as they maneuvered the halls of Coors Field, noting his flushed and eager expression.

"What's up, kiddo?" It seemed just like yesterday that Charlie had been a toddler. Glancing at her ten-year-old boy, she took him in. School had ended for the summer just a few weeks ago and she swore he'd already grown six inches. The basketball shorts he was wearing used to go clear past his knee. Now a good inch of skin above them was bare. Where had the time gone?

"Do you think I'll get to meet my favorite player today?"

Sonny tuned back in to her son and replied, "Pretty sure, hon." The entire team was supposed to be in attendance. "And if JP Trudeau is there, I promise that we'll get his autograph for you."

Days of leisure had been few and far between since Charlie's birth. Most days it didn't faze her—she'd gotten used to shouldering the responsibilities. But occasionally it got to her and wore her down. On those days she struggled.

She took heart in knowing that everyone did from time to time. Considering she'd been raising a son all by herself for a decade—plus getting a college degree, working full time, and now starting a business—Sonny figured she kept it together better than anyone could expect.

Competency was a skill she'd had to learn, self-sufficiency a character trait she'd had to develop, whether she'd really been up to the task or not. Raising a boy into a man took practicality, strength, and perseverance. Not to mention a ton of patience and an appreciation for a boy's often gross sense of humor. Charlie had more jokes about human anatomy and its baser functions than she could shake a stick at.

Which reminded her, "You did remember to bring your mitt, right?"

Charlie lifted his well-loved baseball glove and grinned, "*Duh*, Mom. Like I'd forget it."

Sonny quipped back with a grin of her own, "You seem to forget your homework an awful lot, so I was just checking." Sometimes fear shadowed her, making her uncertain and afraid. But nobody knew. Nope. Everybody thought that Sonny Luanne Miller had it together. Including herself. Steadfast avoidance had kept that niggling fear that she was in denial at bay.

Same went for the voices that whispered at her loneliness. Those weren't meant for her, she told herself. They were for someone else.

Tossing an arm around Charlie's angular shoulders, Sonny pulled him close as they rounded a corner and stepped onto the freshly cut ball field. Next month her baby would feel different to hug than he did right now, he was growing so fast.

She took a moment to savor the now with a prolonged squeeze. "Love you, kid. Let's go get that autograph."

JP Trudeau was the new hotshot Rush player who had the media all in a tizzy. They were enamored with his cover-model looks and RBIs. And she couldn't blame them. The guy was hotter than an Arizona desert. His face was regularly plastered across the front page of the tabloids that were displayed in the checkout line at the grocery store. Last week someone had captured him trail-running shirtless down near Morrison and she'd actually bumped into the customer in front of her when she'd caught a glimpse of all those gorgeous, rippling muscles. They were that good.

The realization that she was about to see those whiskey-colored eyes and washboard abs up close and personal had a butterfly taking flight in her stomach. It'd been a long time since her blood pressure had shaken loose over a man. And Sonny found the buzz of fresh anticipation a real surprise.

Not that she had the time to do anything with it. But she had to admit it was nice to know she still had a pulse. Even if it was a weak and thready one.

Planting a reassuring kiss on Charlie's sandy blond hair, Sonny's gaze scanned over the crowd. She wasn't looking for anyone in particular. Okay, well maybe she was looking for a Denver Rush baseball jersey, number thirty-nine. Charlie really wanted to meet his sports idol.

A tidy woman with a brisk walk and a Sarah Palin smile blocked Sonny's view before she could land her eyes on the prize.

"Hi there. My name is Connie Jackson and I'm the event coordinator. Would you mind giving me your tickets and names so that I can cross you off the list?"

Giving the woman her polite stranger smile, Sonny dug into her purse and pulled out the envelope that held the tickets. "Here you are." She handed the envelope over and added, "This is such a cool thing that the Rush players are doing. Charlie here could barely sleep a wink. He was so jazzed about meeting the team."

As it was, Charlie was vibrating in his cleats—which he'd insisted on wearing. People were milling all around the outfield grass and Rush team members populated the crowd with the occasional green and yellow jersey. Photographers and reporters mingled with the guests, flashing their media passes and snapping pictures. Her son's eyes were super wide and glued to the scene; his mouth hung a little gaped.

It totally made the Saturday excursion worth it.

Score one big fat mom point for her. With a mental pat on the back, Sonny watched her son pull up on his tiptoes and crane his neck. No doubt it was killing him being so close to the famous shortstop, yet not being able to see him.

The woman crossed their names off the list and sent them on their way with another practiced smile. Sonny placed her hand on Charlie's shoulder and led them into the crowd, narrowly avoiding clipping shoulders with a photographer. She did smack his camera hard with her elbow though, sending it swinging from its braided canvas strap around his neck. "I'm so sorry!"

The guy smiled at her, not even phased—though he was now sporting what looked like a pretty decent rug burn. "Not a problem." He raised the camera and brought it to his face, focusing the lens on her. "Bill Haman. Photographer with the *Post*. Mind if I take a few pictures?"

Sonny glanced down at the media pass dangling at the front of his shirt. Sure enough, his name was in fact Bill Haman and he was a photojournalist with the *Denver Post*. Said so right there next to his headshot and everything. How very official.

She hated having her picture taken. Why anybody would put up with it on a regular basis was beyond her. "We're sort of in a rush—"

"Mom and I would love our picture taken!" Charlie piped up at the same time, all bright, excited grin and sparkling eyes.

Apparently they weren't in that much of a hurry after all. "I guess we'd love our picture taken." One of them *way* more than the other.

Snagging Charlie around the shoulder, Sonny pulled him in close and slapped on a fake smile just in time for the camera flash. When it was done the photographer thanked them and disappeared into the mix, gone as quickly as he'd arrived, leaving her with a vaguely disconcerted feeling. Though she felt a frown tugging at her brow, she shrugged it off and set about scouring the crowd again for a certain jersey.

Families milled around as they waited for their turn in line for food. Tables were set up with cloths decorated with the Rush's signature logo, a swirl of yellow lettering set to a deep green backdrop. It was timeless and classic in the way that only baseball could be.

Leading them toward the buffet tables on the far side, Sonny took in the overall casual feel of the place and sighed with relief. She's spent forever in her bedroom trying to figure out what to wear. Seeing so many families dressed in typical Colorado casual made her feel much better. There was an overall lean toward the outdoorsy and hippie side. Coloradoans kept it chill.

Even Sonny had that bent, dressed as she was in a thin-strapped white tank top and a long, flowing cotton skirt with a bold, quilt-like print. But she stopped at the Crocs—she just couldn't do it. Instead she lived in cheap flip-flops.

Since she was blessed with a rose-cream complexion and full, high cheekbones, Sonny rarely wore makeup.

Her idea of "dolled up" was eye shadow, mascara, and Burt's Bees lip balm. She wore her strawberry locks long, wavy, and natural. And she couldn't even remember the last time she'd used a hair dryer.

It was one of the many wonderful perks of living in the state. Coloradoans were laid back, active people. Especially in Boulder County where she lived. Organic earthiness was the name of the game, right there alongside outspoken earth-consciousness. It was why her organic goat cheese business was such a solid investment. Locally grown produce had a hugely supportive audience. In fact, farmers' markets were so popular, they'd even built a permanent structure on site at the Boulder County Fairgrounds in Longmont as a cover for customers if it should happen to rain.

Not that it rained often, mind you.

On a good summer, there were the afternoon thunderstorms. Those were the best. The sizzle and the pungent, primal scent of dirt and charged energy. Those storms made her think of sweaty limbs and passionate, raw, physical sex.

And that was about the extent of her intimate life. Pathetic, but what was she going to do? Charlie was her heart. Making the best life possible for him was her journey. Her dharma.

That's why she was there now, tempting fate on a Saturday.

Suddenly Charlie grabbed her arm and whispered loud enough to shout, "*Mom!* I see him!" She could feel tremors of excitement in his fingertips.

Following his ecstatic expression and completely awed stare, she scanned the crowd off to her right. At first she couldn't see the ballplayer. A very large, fair-haired Germanic family blocked the space between them. Which was saying a lot, considering Trudeau's stats put him at six feet three inches. She knew that because Charlie spouted stats at her all the time. That's why he'd been in Little League since he was old enough for tee ball. Ever since he could toddle, he'd loved the game. It just worked for him. Made sense to the core of who he was.

Sonny was absolutely convinced that Charlie was going to be a pro ballplayer someday. He had that visceral connection to the sport. Some people were just born knowing their thing—what it was and how it connected to them.

Charlie had that.

Sonny, now, she'd not been nearly so grounded. She'd flown all over the map and landed herself on the wrong side of twenty, pregnant and alone. Charlie being born had given her a path. Once she'd stepped on it she'd dedicated everything she'd had to it, including her autonomy. Nurturing her baby and building a good life had been all she'd thought about and lived since the day she'd brought him home from the hospital.

Now he was growing up and grasping at some autonomy of his own. Their relationship was changing—slowly, but still evolving into something different. Something with a little more space.

That new and exotic little bit of wiggle room had opened a fissure in Sonny, just a teeny little crack. But it was enough, and something newly awakened inside her was feeling a little restless. A little flighty. She didn't like it one bit. It wasn't safe or predictable or familiar.

It was foreign and she was domestic.

Which made it the enemy. The life that she'd carved out for the two of them was stable. She knew how to handle it and felt in charge. Anything different was not okay. It left things open to change. And if things changed then she might lose her grip on control. Status quo was good. It didn't hold any surprises.

She wasn't looking for them anyway. So when the herd of large-boned people shifted and her gaze landed on a green and yellow Rush jersey, number thirty-nine, she felt a slip—just a subtle shift of the earth on its axis. But it was enough. The world moved under her feet. And when the sin-with-me eyes locked on her from twenty feet away she felt a tremble in her grip on control.

Because she was suddenly hit with instinct and knew beyond a doubt that, from this moment forward, nothing in her life was going to be quite the same.

The sky opened up and the universe showed her a very simple and clear truth in one lightning-quick moment. It was written all over his sinner's grin and loose-hipped swagger.

JP Trudeau was a whole lot of trouble.

Chapter Two

DAYS LIKE TODAY made JP a very happy man. The sky was its trademark brilliant summer blue. He was about to play ball with a group of kids and give back to the community, and he'd just spotted one seriously luscious beauty across the way without a ring on. Life didn't get much more perfect than that.

Appreciation made its way up his chest and settled into a little hum in his throat. It wasn't every day that he saw a woman who made his mouth water at first glance. But this one did. She was sexy in such a simple, effortless way that he felt a ball of heat flare in his belly. And since he didn't consider himself a complicated guy, her natural beauty appealed to him on a couple levels.

JP was a straightforward kind of guy. He liked what he liked, knew who he was and what he wanted. All his life he'd had a clear line on what made him tick and had never doubted himself. It made for a life free of tangles.

He saw something—he made a decision. He didn't look over his shoulder. Because of that, JP knew he had a certain kind of centeredness that was rare for a guy in his mid-twenties. He possessed a clearness of sight that had guided him faithfully and gave him grounding. Right now that sight was set on a cool drink of water—and this Iowa farm boy was real thirsty.

JP tugged at the brim of his hat and flashed his best grin. Stirring, prepping to walk over to her, his teammate Drake Paulson cut him off before he'd managed a step.

"Hey, brother. Looks like we got ourselves a perfect day for playing ball." The player grinned and scratched his unshaven chin. "Course, it's a perfect day for a different kinda sport too. The horizontal sort that makes me tingly and happy. What say we have us a bet, man? First to score a phone number from a single mom gets dibs on the ice bath after practice tomorrow."

Sliding a sideways glance at the gruff player, JP shook his head and said, "Don't seem fair to bet on single moms, hoss."

"Why not? They want to get laid, same as the rest of us."

JP's eyebrow arched at the logic. They probably did want to get laid, same as them. But they had kids to consider. That made it different.

"I don't know what kind of women you've been playing tickle with lately, but they aren't right."

Drake clamped a hard, meaty hand on his shoulder and turned them both toward his fantasy woman in the hippie skirt. He tipped his head in her direction. "You telling me that you wouldn't give your left nut to have her phone number, boy?"

Through the crowd of excited children, media, and helicopter parents, he studied her. A colorful woven purse the size of a small suitcase hung crosswise across her body and her fair skin made him think of winters back home in Iowa. Pristine and flawless. Her long, wavy hair was more gold than red and her curves were the perfect balance between lanky and lush. And when she smiled at the boy by her side, her whole face lit up.

Would he give his left nut for her number?

Yeah.

Sometimes he wondered at the things Drake knew. The guy said things that bordered on offensive more often than not. But the hell of it was that he was eerily perceptive. JP had only been with the team for a season, but he'd already seen that guy's sharp observations prove correct countless times.

Pulled from his thoughts when a cleat dug into the back of his knee and buckled it, nearly making him fall, JP turned his head as pitcher Peter Kowalskin stepped beside him. He held a paper plate full of food and was chewing on something. "What's got you girls so enamored over here?"

Of all his team mates, JP liked Pete the best. Not that the other guys weren't great, because they were. It was just that he and Pete were a lot alike. They both grabbed life by the horns and bent it in whatever direction they wanted. And they both did it with smiles on their faces. However life decided to be, sideways or upside down, they were always on top.

It gave a guy a helluva lot of confidence, and it made him one ballsy son of a bitch.

Drake shoved up the brim of his cap and scratched at an itch, his eyes squinting against the sun's glare. "Trying to convince JP here to play a game of phone numbers."

A grin full of bad intentions lit Pete's face. "*Nice.* Personally, I'm hoping that a hot single mom in need of some old-fashioned attention wins that raffle to have dinner with me." The grin amped up a notch. "And breakfast in the morning."

Like magnets, JP's eyes were drawn back to the woman with the bohemian vibe. Yeah, he'd settle for that too. It wouldn't be a hardship to eat waffles with her in the morning. In fact, he bet he'd like it just fine.

Aware that he was openly staring, JP noticed her cheeks suddenly seemed pinker than they had been before. Then he realized that she knew he was ogling her because she was blushing and trying hard to avoid looking at him in return.

The boy, on the other hand, hadn't been able to take his eyes off of JP. And it gave him the perfect excuse to approach her. "We best be getting back to it, ladies. They're going to be starting the raffle soon."

There were three winning raffle tickets for the day's event. The prize was an all-expense paid dinner with a Rush player. He'd volunteered for it, alongside Pete and the catcher, Mark Cutter. It had sounded like fun, and he liked kids, so he'd signed up. Coming from a family of six of them himself, he'd long ago gotten used to the odd shit they said and did.

Speaking of . . . "I'm going to mingle. Make yourselves useful, old men, and hit the rounds."

Before they could rib him about calling them old, he was on the move. He'd made it four feet when a boy ran up asking for his autograph. Giving the kid his undivided attention, JP inked his signature and chatted up the freckle-faced redhead for a few as a photographer stood a few feet away and tried to capture the moment. When the parents arrived and ushered the boy off, he scanned the crowd.

He spotted her and her son and set off again. By the time they'd reached each other, he'd been stopped a half dozen times. Each time he'd given the kids and their families his complete attention. They deserved as much. But each time he did, it took a few minutes to find the woman again in the shifting crowd.

Now he was finally standing in front of her and his interest had doubled. She was even prettier up close, but with an approachable earthiness that hadn't been apparent from the distance. Her eyes were the color of his favorite old blue jeans, and she had freckles smattered across the bridge of her nose. Her lips were soft, plump, and naked. Just the way he liked them. And she smelled fresh and natural, with just a hint of something citrus.

He wanted to eat her up.

He gave her his most disarming smile as she regarded him with hesitation in her eyes. Instinct told him to play it slow, so he shifted his focus from her to the blond-haired boy at her side. All elbows and boney knees now, the kid was going to be tall someday. For now, he was stuck with a body that didn't quite coordinate. JP remembered the days. He'd been skinny and gangly with the best of them.

The boy had the same look about him with the nose freckles, light hair, and blue eyes. He looked about ten, excited as a pig in a parlor, and he gripped a ratty ball glove tightly in his hand. He stared up at JP with a look of hero worship in its purest form. He remembered what it was like to meet his favorite ballplayers as a kid, how it lit his world from end to end.

Now on this side of things, he knew he had a responsibility to be deserving of such high status. Which was why, even though his dream woman was standing right there, he gave the kid his all. It's what he was there for—to put face time in with these kids. To help them understand that diabetes didn't have to limit them, and that they could have full, active lives so long as they kept on top of things. And that exercise was essential for diabetics. JP had a buddy who had diabetes *and* was a professional rock climber. It didn't slow him down one bit. Kids went nuts when he shared that bit.

Besides, he figured her having to wait on him would only whet her appetite.

JP gestured to the worn glove. "That's a great lookin' mitt you have there." The boy looked at it, eyes lit with pride. "I can tell it's been well used. I'm JP, by the way. You play ball?"

Out of the corner of his eye he saw the woman shift and place a hand on the kid's shoulder, giving it a reassuring squeeze. And he also saw her gaze slide over him for a brief moment. Was that interest he glimpsed?

The mitt was shoved under his nose and JP smelled leather and the outdoors. The kid explained, "I've been playing ball since I was in diapers. Least that's what my mom says."

JP grinned at the visual and took the mitt, examining it. "Is that so? Moms always say weird stuff like that, don't they?"

The boy rolled his eyes with exaggeration. *"Totally."*

JP relaxed and cocked a hip, his cleats puncturing the outfield grass as he settled. "What's your name, kid?"

The boy's chest blew up like a puffer fish. "I'm Charlie Miller and this is my mom. Her name's Sonny. She plays baseball pretty good for a girl."

The look she gave her son had JP laughing out loud.

"What do you mean 'for a girl'? Who schooled you and your friends last week at your birthday party with a homer that shot clear over the barn into the pasture?" She waggled her thumbs at her chest and JP couldn't help scoping out her breasts for a second. "Oh, that's right. It was me."

The sound of her voice surprised him. She had one of those Katherine Heigl voices that was all smoke and sex. It sent a shiver through his belly and had him thinking naughty thoughts. If it was this husky now, what would it be like during a hot romp in the sack?

He caught her eye and their gazes connected, held. Something sparked, but before he could explore it she broke contact and looked away, her face a little flushed.

She cleared her throat and said, "It's nice to meet you, Mr. Trudeau. Charlie is a big fan and plays shortstop too.

We were at a few Rush games this spring when you'd first been traded. He watched the way you fielded and decided he wanted to try out the position. It's been a lot of fun for him."

JP reached out and ruffled the kid's hair. "No kidding? You thinking of going pro someday, Charlie?"

The boy nodded emphatically. "Definitely. What's it like? Is it as cool as I think it is?"

"It is, buddy," he said after considering how cool his job would seem to a ten-year-old. "But it's a lot of hard work and dedication too. You have to practice even when you don't feel like it, and you have to be away from home a lot during the season."

Charlie nodded seriously. "That'd be okay."

"You miss your family some. And it's hard to have a pet because you're gone so much and don't have time to take care of them properly."

With a nose wrinkled in contemplation, the boy replied, "Well, I gots my mom and she could watch my dog. We have a farm anyway, so there's lots of room."

"Yeah?" He'd loved growing up on a farm. Couldn't imagine a better place for a kid to roam. "I grew up on a farm too."

With a grin full of confidence, Charlie said, "I know. I've looked up all your stuff."

JP smiled and started to hand the glove back. "It's about time for the raffle to start, so I'd better make my way to the stage."

Charlie pushed the mitt back. "Would you sign my mitt for me, please?"

"Sure thing." He reached in his pocket for a Sharpie and wrote his name across the thumb piece. "Here you go."

"Thanks!"

JP figured he'd given her long enough and turned his gaze back to Sonny. "So you play some ball too?" he said, referring to the birthday ball game.

She tucked a strand of hair behind her ear and said, "I played softball all through high school."

Her voice was seriously erotic. "Yeah? You from Colorado?"

Sonny nodded. "Mostly." A tentative smile cupped her lips. "I know you're not."

"Ever been to Iowa?" He liked hearing her speak so much that he was willing to make small talk. Even if he sounded like an idiot.

Her beautiful hair slid over her shoulders as she shook her head. "Nope. I've been exactly two places in my life. Here and California. But I imagine it's humid and green and flat."

"Pretty much."

Movement out of the corner of his eye caught his attention and he glanced over to see a photographer settle into shooting position. Without thinking, he shifted to allow the guy an unobstructed shot of Sonny and her boy standing with him. Dealing with the media was second nature to him now and most of the time he didn't mind. They were just part of the gig. He helped them out and they gave him good press, making his agent happy. It was win-win.

Surprise ran through him though when Sonny shuffled, too, until she was almost standing behind him.

"I'm just in the way of his shot," she mumbled and turned her head to look behind her like she was searching for something, effectively shielding her face from the photographers.

Amused at her camera shyness, JP grinned as he said to her, "It's okay. I promise they don't bite." Then he winked down at Charlie and added, "Not hard anyway."

Over the sound of the boy's giggles he barely heard her mutter dryly, "That's reassuring." Then she adjusted her shoulder bag and peered around him at the half dozen media personnel hovering nearby. "I don't know why they're interested in Charlie and me."

He did. The woman was a breath of fresh air.

"Why don't I stand over here?" he said. Obviously all the attention made her uncomfortable and for some reason he didn't like the idea of her feeling uneasy. Taking two steps to his right, JP checked over his shoulder to make certain she was blocked and saw Kowalskin a few feet away. "Hey, Walskie. Toss me one of the balls you're holding."

The pitcher arched a black brow. "What do you want my balls for?"

"Ha ha, funny. For real. Give me one." He had an idea to get the attention off of Sonny—or at least try anyway. Events like these were crawling with media and there was only so much he could do.

Peter underhanded him a shiny white ball and smirked. "Play nice with it, big boy."

With a smile tugging at his lips, JP shook his head and caught the ball. Smartass. "Thanks."

Turning back around, he noted the growing crowd of photographers with no surprise. They had an uncanny ability to sense when something was about to go down. Like the time they'd caught Pete with his pants down after giving Drake a well-deserved mooning. His bare ass had wound up on the front page of a big tabloid with some derogatory headline he couldn't remember now. He just recalled how Pete had laughed hysterically and then had the thing framed and hung in his living room.

JP tried to be a little more publically reserved than that, but he still got his share of tabloid bullshit. It was just one of those things.

"Hey, Charlie. Want to see a magic trick?"

The kid nodded vigorously, "Yeah!"

Glancing behind him to make sure the photographers were watching, he held up the ball and announced, "Now you see it, now you don't."

That got their attention. Camera shutters started clicking as he went about amazing the boy with the one and only trick he knew. Even Sonny seemed to be fascinated. She kept leaning forward from her hideout a few feet away to get a better view. When he held out his hands in front of him and the ball had disappeared, Charlie's eyes went wide. *"No way!"*

"How did you do that?" came her sexy voice behind him.

Not finished, JP shot her a wink and relaxed his stance. "Magic."

She gave him a face and he outright laughed. "I don't believe in magic."

Now that was really just too bad. Everybody needed a little magic in their lives. "Here, Charlie. Why don't you take my hat for a second?" He took off his cap and handed it to the kid.

Thoroughly engrossed in the trick, the boy grabbed it eagerly and asked, "Where'd the ball go?" He'd been scanning the ground like he was hunting for Easter eggs.

Sonny stepped up beside him and added, "The real question is if you can bring it back." The skepticism in her tone implied she didn't think he could.

How wrong she was. "Thanks for holding my hat, kid. I'll take it back now."

Charlie handed it back and JP made a display of putting it on his head. "Ouch. Man, what is that?" Faking confusion, JP pulled off his hat and turned it over, inside facing up. And right there in the center of his cap was the ball, snowy white in the afternoon sun.

The boy practically shoved his face into the ball cap. "Holy cow! How did you *do* that?"

One of the guys from the *Post* piped up nearby, scribbling furiously on a tiny notepad. "Hey, Trudeau. Want to introduce us to your friends?" He glanced up from the pad and adjusted his eyeglasses. "You know, for the byline."

JP flashed his best grin. "Sure. This here is Charlie Miller, shortstop for . . ." He trailed off and glanced down at the kid in question. "What's your team's name?"

Charlie puffed out his chest and stood as tall as he

could. To the reporter he boasted, "I play for the Long-mont Hawks."

Sonny spoke up, her voice soft and kind of tense. "Is this just your normal? I mean, all these photographers and stuff?"

Glancing down, he noted she looked tense too. He was so used to being in the public eye that he forgot how un-comfortable it could be to some. "Yeah, it's pretty much just part of life. You get used to it."

She looked up at him and her gorgeous eyes shut-tered. "I couldn't do it." He opened his mouth to respond when a *thump thump* on a microphone turned his at-tention toward the low stage. The event coordinator was almost ready to give her speech. That was his cue to get moving.

"Hey, I have to go. But it was great meeting you, Charlie."

His gaze slid to Sonny. A lazy smile curved his lips. "It's been a real pleasure."

He watched color bloom in her cheeks and couldn't stop the heat that started to coil in his belly. Didn't partic-ularly want to, if truth be told. He'd never dated a single mom before, but then again he'd never encountered one like her either. It was more than just her looks and the fact that he was seriously attracted to her.

She had something.

And he had the rest of the event to figure out what he wanted to do about it. Because she had a kid and if, deep down, he was just after a piece of ass, then he'd have to find it somewhere else. Unlike Drake, he couldn't mess with that just to get naked with a woman. Guess he was old-fashioned that way.

Turning to leave, JP stopped when a slender hand touched his arm. He felt the zing of connection clear down to his toes. It was like a thread of electricity snaking a path through his body.

Beautiful blue eyes were waiting for him when he looked up, sparkling and a little cautious. "Thank you for taking the time with Charlie. It means the world to him."

Just to test the waters, JP placed a hand on top of hers and squeezed a little. He let it linger before he slowly slid it away. Then he leaned in close. His gaze slid down to her kiss-me mouth and held. He felt his arousal grow with every passing heartbeat.

JP let it show. Let his interest be clear as day. And he saw the moment it registered with her, because her eyes went wide and unfocused.

That's what he thought. "Any time."

Chapter Three

"I STILL CAN'T believe I won the raffle, Mom. It's so awesome!" Charlie yelled from his bedroom across the hall.

Neither could Sonny. But after her little run-in with JP Trudeau last week at the charity game it was all she could think about. And she was seriously irritated with herself about it. The guy was a friggin' sports star. Flirting with women was probably just one of his favorite pastimes.

Man, he was *such* a celebrity too. The way he'd smiled and played to the media had made it glaringly obvious that he enjoyed the limelight. Not that it should have surprised her. JP was one of those incredibly gorgeous, gifted people that were all confidence because they had the world on a string. Rightfully so, in his case. But, still. Just thinking back to what it'd felt like having all those media people surrounding them, wanting to know their business made her skin crawl. Bad.

Privacy was essential to Sonny. Like breathing.

Still, the way those bedroom eyes of his had looked at her lingered in her memory. Thick, long eyelashes framed eyes a deep honey brown, and when he turned them on you there was such singular focus in them that it was totally disarming. Sonny'd been completely off balance after their exchange for a good two hours. And for the next forty-eight she'd marveled at her response. She wasn't even in the market for a man, so why was she so fixated on him? Especially since she'd never even consider dating him with his lifestyle?

But if she wasn't in the market for a man, why had it taken her over an hour and ten rejected outfits before she'd settled on one to wear to dinner?

Ugh. Snapping the lid on her eye shadow box, Sonny huffed and placed it on the dresser with more force than necessary. She'd just put *eye shadow* on, for crying out loud. So what if it was a soft, neutral shimmer? It was the fact that she'd just *had* to put it on in the first place.

JP Trudeau was just a guy. Maybe an extra hot one. But a guy all the same. He didn't merit all the fuss she'd put herself through. Besides, she had Charlie and her work and that was all she needed in the world.

Sonny took stock of her reflection in the mirror above her dresser. That's right, she thought. She didn't need anybody.

But why the heck wasn't her hair cooperating?

Shoving a tousled mass over her shoulder, she hollered back at Charlie, "We're leaving in five minutes, kiddo. It's going to take an hour to get to the restaurant."

The Mexican eatery they had reservations at was a

landmark in Denver. Casa Bonita was everything a kid could want in a restaurant and more. Part theme park, it housed a thirty-foot waterfall, cliff divers, and good ol' gunfights. One time she'd even watched a swashbuckling sword fight between pirates scheming for booty.

Shows were long enough to entertain, but not so long they disrupted the eating. And to cap the evening off, there was a gift shop to empty your wallet and leave you with an authentic imitation of *La Mexicana*.

Because it culminated in such an expensive evening out, Sonny had only taken Charlie there once before. The budget was always super tight, so she had to space out their big outings and rotate through the approved list of children's venues. The only thing she indulged in more than she should were Denver Rush ball games. Charlie loved going to them so much that she'd made it a point to get them out to at least three during the season.

For a single mom with a mountain of school loans and a hefty business loan to repay, those games were an extravagance. But they made him so darn happy that she didn't mind the crimp it put in her finances. Some things were just worth sucking it up for.

Still, it was nice that she got to give Charlie a night out at no expense besides the gas. Breaks like that were few and far between for a single mom all alone in the world.

Well, technically she wasn't alone. Her mom was somewhere down in Guatemala living in a hippie commune, last she heard. They hadn't spoken or seen each other since she'd dumped Sonny on her grandmother's front steps twenty-four years ago.

That'd been just a few months after her dad had divorced her mom and left. One day she'd had both parents. Then one parent. Then none. Before Sonny could blink, she'd found herself living in rural Colorado with a grandmother that she'd only seen twice before in her life and who considered her a real inconvenience.

And, yes, it'd been a Saturday.

When she turned thirteen she got a letter, postmarked Brazil, belatedly explaining that her mom had realized she just wasn't cut out to be a parent. That it tied her down and she needed to be free to follow where "the spirit" led her.

Then, after her grandmother had died and she'd inherited the small four-acre farmette, Sonny'd received a one-sentence letter from Guatemala demanding to know about her mother Grace's share. As executor of her grandmother's will, she'd packed up the shoebox worth of her mother's "share"—which had amounted to a few dozen old photos and an ivory barrette—and sent it on its way.

That'd been over eight years ago, and she hadn't heard a word from her since. Not that she wanted to. The last time they'd been face-to-face had cured her of that. Even at the tender age of seven.

Grace had shoved a small blue suitcase into her hands, the scent of nag champa clinging to her overly bronzed skin. Sonny could still recall the smell if she tried.

She didn't try.

Then her mother had turned to go, the sob that ripped from Sonny's chest stopping her. Behind her some guy that wasn't her father sat in the driver's seat of a red convertible, tapping his thumb on the steering wheel impatiently. He'd been around for a few weeks by that point, but he still felt like a complete stranger.

She'd cried out, "Don't leave me, Mama! Don't go!"

Her mother had turned back and wrapped her up in a tight incense-filled hug. "You'll be fine. I promise. Your grandma will take good care of you." Then she'd cupped Sonny's cheek and kissed her tenderly, almost as if she felt bad that she was abandoning her kid. "Make your own destiny, honey. And always, always follow your heart—just like I'm following mine."

Pulling herself back to the present, Sonny took one last perusal in the mirror. Hearts led a person astray. She'd learned fast to use her head instead. Then she pushed the memories aside and studied her reflection. The outfit she'd finally settled on was simple and casual and she was totally annoyed that it'd taken her so long to choose jeans, boots, and a dove-grey peasant top.

Charlie appeared in the doorway, hair combed and his best shoes on. "I'm ready, Mom. Let's get this show on the road."

Sonny blew out a breath. Right.

JP WAITED IMPATIENTLY at the fountain in front of Casa Bonita. Glancing at his watch for the umpteenth time, he sighed and raised his gaze to scan the crowded parking lot. Sonny and her son should be there any minute.

Smiling at the families who passed him on their way

to the towering pink stucco entrance of the restaurant, JP clamped down on the antsy feeling and forced his body to relax. He'd been thinking hard about Sonny ever since the charity last Saturday, and he'd come to a few conclusions. Though he was in the middle of a season and he was still new to the team and should only be focusing on that, it simply wasn't going to happen. Sonny had lodged herself firmly in his thoughts. It'd been almost a week since he'd first seen her and he'd thought about her as much today as he had then.

Being a thorough kind of guy, JP had sat on things without formulating a conclusion. But when he'd still been fixed on Sonny and her incredible smile after almost a week of games and life trotting by, he'd made up his mind. For him to be so caught up thinking about her meant something significant.

He wasn't only out for a piece of ass.

It didn't mean it was going to be simple. She had a kid and he hadn't shrugged that off. If he wanted Sonny— which he did—then he had to want Charlie too. They were a package deal. And he didn't take that lightly. But he had just turned twenty-six and wasn't sure he was ready to lock down with an insta-family. He wasn't really sure how he felt about it all yet, truth be told. He just knew he was interested. But he wasn't completely opposed to the idea. It all just depended on how things went.

It had crossed his mind that Sonny might already be in a relationship. If that was the case, then he'd have to reassess, shift angles, and try harder. JP didn't mind thinking he might have some competition ahead. He played ball—he was competitive that way.

All he knew, and all that mattered right now, was that he was seriously interested in getting to know Sonny better. To be able to do that, she and Charlie needed to get their butts to the restaurant. He'd glanced at his watch again. It was already five past seven. They were late.

JP was about to push away from the fountain when he a noticed an older Honda minivan whip into the parking lot, nearly taking out two pedestrians. Catching a glimpse of gold-fire hair, he grinned and shook his head. Sonny had arrived, and it just figured that she drove like a madwoman.

Another minute went by and then she and Charlie were hustling toward him, Sonny apologizing and looking frazzled.

"Sorry we're late. There was an accident on I-25 and we got hung up." She looked embarrassed and sheepish and so damn fine in her snug-fitting jeans.

Charlie waved his arms in front of him and exclaimed, "There was this huge pile up, cuz a big semi truck rolled over and smashed a lot of cars. It was nuts!"

JP took them in and pushed away from the fountain, unfolding to his full height. Yeah, they'd see how it went all right. Because one look at her and he was back to feeling buzzy, like he was jonesing for something.

That something was standing in front of him with legs a mile long and a smile that could melt the Arctic.

With a smile of his own, JP notched his head toward the front door and said, "No worries. Shall we head in?"

They fell into step with Charlie chatting a mile a minute. Though he tried hard to follow, the kid was talking about things completely foreign to JP. Whatever they were, they involved creatures called Pokemons. He nodded and glanced over Charlie's head at Sonny for help, but she wasn't paying any attention.

She seemed nervous. It wasn't until they were seated at a table surrounded by palm trees and the scent of refried beans and fajitas that she started to relax. The giant waterfall was off to the left, and the sound of rushing water seemed to calm her. She kept looking from it to Charlie and back. Him though, she tried not to look at so much. He figured it meant she was on the shy side. Wasn't that sweet?

Charlie turned his attention when he pointed toward the waterfall. "Look! Some dude's going to jump off the cliff."

Sure enough, when JP looked over his shoulder, a guy was standing on top of the replica of Acapulco's waterfall getting ready to hop off. While they watched, he flung his arms wide and proceeded to swan dive off the cliff to the great entertainment of the restaurant goers.

He had to admit the place was pretty cool, but he'd dived off the *actual* cliffs of Acapulco and it didn't compare. Still, for all the landlocked citizens of Colorado, this was the next best thing.

JP noticed Sonny working the corner of a coaster and decided to let her be for now. It didn't hurt anything to let her settle in and get comfortable. If things went the way he planned, they'd be spending time together soon enough. There was no hurry.

He turned to Charlie, "Tell me about yourself, slugger."

The kids sat up a little straighter and looked at JP in all earnestness. "Well, I'm gonna be in fifth grade this year and I play Little League. Me and Mom live up near Longmont and I go to a charter school. My best friend's name is Sam and I got a dog named Vader, cuz I love Star Wars." He took a deep breath and continued, "I'm allergic to peanuts, and I hate Language Arts in school, but Mom makes me do it anyway."

JP chuckled. "Language Arts can be rough, kid. I hear ya. When's your next ball game?"

Charlie looked at Sonny. "It's on Saturday, right?" She nodded and he turned back to JP. "My mom hates Saturdays."

Really now. That was interesting. "Why do you hate Saturdays, Sonny?"

Before she could answer, Charlie piped up. "Cuz she thinks they're cursed."

Sonny stopped tearing the coaster and pegged her son with a hard stare. "I do not."

The blond-haired kid grinned at JP. "She so does. It's funny too, cuz she talks all the time about it, and swears she's not superstitious. But my games are the only things she ever does that day. When it's not Little League season she doesn't go out at all. It's our cleaning day."

JP leaned back in his seat and signaled a waitress, his eyes on Sonny the whole time. "Is that so?"

He heard her mutter and shuffle under the table. Charlie let out a yip and scowled at his mom. "What'd you do that for?"

She scowled right back. "Because you weren't supposed to say anything."

The kid rubbed at his sore shin. "Why not? It's hilarious, Mom. You're totally weird about it."

JP watched the interplay with amusement. Sonny's face had gone bright red and Charlie was mortally offended that she'd kicked him under the table. Mothers and sons. That was some funny shit right there.

He tried again. "What's wrong with Saturdays?" He really wanted to know.

Sonny slumped a bit and sighed heavily, giving Charlie one last good glare before answering. "Bad things happen."

"Do they now?" He wondered what kind of bad things happened to a woman like her. She was beautiful and sweet and perfect. Like a ray of sunshine.

She straightened in her seat and shoved a lock of wavy hair over her shoulder. "Yes."

The waitress showed up and they all ordered, Sonny making sure Charlie picked something acceptable for his diabetes. When they'd first been seated, they'd excused themselves to check his glucose levels and give him an insulin shot. Now he was ready to rumble and ordered from the adult menu.

Because it seemed like she could use it, JP ordered two margaritas and pondered when the last time was that Sonny Miller had cut loose and unwound. She was bound tighter than a new book. To hate Saturdays was damn near sacrilegious.

He knew a real good way to help her out with the relaxing, but they'd get to that later. For now they'd start with the margarita.

The waitress headed off with their orders and Sonny tipped her head to the side, studying him. "Did you just order for me?"

"Only a drink, sunshine. You need to relax."

Her lips puckered in protest, but then the wind seemed to go out of her some and she gestured with her hand. "Oh, what the hell."

The food and drinks came and as soon as the margarita was set in front of her she scooped it up and took a long pull through the straw. The way her lips wrapped around the red plastic had his gut tightening with arousal. But since Charlie was right there, he kept it under wraps and continued talking good-naturedly with the kid. Every so often someone stopped at their table and asked for his autograph and his opinion about the Rush's run for the pennant this year. He signed and chatted and waited for the right moment to pounce.

Once Sonny had downed about half her drink and had settled in more comfortably, he decided the time had come to do some probing. He wasn't the least bit subtle. "What's your story, Sonny?"

She looked up from her drink. "What do you mean?"

"I mean, what's your story. What do you do, what do you like, what are your hobbies? Are you involved?"

Suspicion crept into her gaze and she hedged, "Why do you want to know?"

"Because I'm interested." He absolutely was. In her.

"Cuz we're sharing, Mom," Charlie added.

He could tell she was considering how much to divulge because she stared at her hands and then over his shoulder. But she'd been sipping steadily on tequila and sugar. It was truth serum. He'd get it out of her.

And after a suspended moment, she caved. "I own an organic goat cheese business."

JP leaned back in his chair and crossed his jean-clad legs at the ankle. Lacing his fingers together behind his head, he settled in and prepared to listen to her tale. "Do you own goats or buy the milk?"

She seemed surprised by that question. "Own. You're the first person to ever ask me that. Nobody ever thinks about the work that goes on behind the cheese. All they want to know is where they can buy the finished product."

That's because most people weren't farm kids. JP knew all about livestock and what it took to run things. Just because he chose to play ball for a living didn't mean that he failed to appreciate the hard work of farming. Every time he went home to see his folks, he got a personal reminder about it. His dad still rolled him out of bed at the ass-crack of dawn to feed the cows and collect eggs. Last Christmas he'd been out breaking ice in the water trough with a pick-ax before Santa'd finished filling the stockings hung over the fireplace. He liked it a whole lot that Sonny shared that same background. It meant they already had some common ground.

JP snagged a tortilla chip and popped it in his mouth. "I know jack about cheese-making, but I know about goats. We had a few growing up. Believe it or not, I lost my baseball jersey to the appetite of one." That still kinda ticked him off. He'd just moved up from Triple A and it was his first uniform in the big leagues. He'd had to tell management that a goat had chewed a damn hole through the crotch of his pants.

Sonny let out a low laugh. "I know what you mean. I've got six and they've eaten stuff I didn't think was possible. That's why I built a custom fence last March to keep them contained."

She added, "I've been at this business for almost two years and it's going well. Some local stores carry my product and I've just been picked up by Whole Foods, which is huge. Hopefully in another year I'll be making enough profit to breathe easy."

JP eyed her, noting the way her eyes lit when she talked about her work. Obviously she loved it. "What about the rest? Is it just you and Charlie?"

Since his name was mentioned the kid decided he should answer. "Yep, it's just us. Always has been. She says we're exclusive."

Pinning her with a stare, he replied to Charlie, "Sure you are, slugger. But when the right person comes along there's always room."

She must have read the challenge in his eyes because her spine snapped straight and her expression became shuttered and withdrawn. "Charlie and I are a two person team, JP."

He thought about it for a few moments, turned it over in his mind, and made a decision. His next words made his intent clear. "For now."

Her eyebrows shot up in surprise and then pulled

down in a frown over her clear blue eyes. Then she leaned across the booth toward him like she wanted to say something, but must have changed her mind because she fell back against the seat and shook her head instead. Her hand waved dismissively and knocked her fork to the floor. Apparently his words had flustered her. Amusement sparked in him and he leaned forward to retrieve the utensil at the same time she did. They nearly bumped heads, making her release a slight gasp. Their gazes locked, held. But before either of them could speak, a flash came from their right and nearly blinded him. Blinking hard, he turned his head and searched for the person responsible for the intrusion.

When he spotted the culprit his jaw tensed. It was the same skinny, black-haired emo twerp from that trashy tabloid *The Beat* that had taken to dogging him the past few weeks. Damn paparazzi. They sure knew how to ruin a moment for a guy sometimes.

He looked back at Sonny, who'd melted back into her seat and was rifling through her purse like it was the most important thing in the world. Yeah, the moment was over all right. Now she wasn't even looking at him.

With a sigh he settled back and mentally flipped the tabloid shooter the finger. Sometimes his lifestyle could be damn inconvenient.

Chapter Four

THE NEXT MORNING Sonny was way out of sorts. *For now, her ass*, she thought. She still couldn't believe JP had the gall to say something like that to her. Did he actually think she would just flop on her back and croon, "Take me now, hot stuff?" over such an arrogant, utterly ridiculous statement?

Padding barefoot into the kitchen, Sonny beelined for the coffeemaker and poured a cup of the strong brew. She was tired and cranky and on edge this morning. JP's words had played over and over in her mind all night, making good rest impossible. Between that and the unwelcome paparazzi visit, she hadn't slept a wink. After tossing and turning endlessly, she'd finally given up and climbed out of bed before the sun rose to make coffee and shower.

It was then that she'd realized her phone was missing. That was the second phone this year she'd lost and it majorly irked her. Now she couldn't call her best friend Janie when she needed someone to talk to. Lovely.

Through the windows in the kitchen she could see the sun just starting to peek from behind the horizon. The sky was turning a stunning deep pink. Leaning her butt against the counter, Sonny took a long sip of the bracing coffee and watched the sun rise. Most of the time she only had tea in the mornings, but she'd needed something more potent this time. Her brain was mush and there was too much to do. She needed to get it together.

It was hard, though, when every thought turned back to dinner with the cocky shortstop. The whole way home Charlie had gone on and on about how awesome JP was while he hugged the souvenir the ballplayer had bought him from the gift shop. And the whole time she'd barely listened, stuck as she was in a mild state of shock and feminine outrage.

Even now she bristled at his high-handedness. JP Trudeau didn't get to choose what she got used to, or didn't, and when things happened. Just because he was confident and charming and gorgeous didn't mean she was going to do what he wanted at the drop of a hat. She'd come to terms with her singlehood a long time ago and wasn't giving it up now that Charlie was half-grown. He still had a lot of growing up to do and she couldn't afford any distractions. It still mattered and he still needed her one hundred percent.

Taking her eye off the ball was something she simply couldn't do.

The way she'd carved out a life for herself and Charlie had taken so much determination and focus. Messing that up now would be like throwing away all those years and sacrifices. She'd worked too hard for that.

Their life had a predictable, steady rhythm. Nothing much came by that threw the beat off. And that's the way she needed it. Raising a kid alone was hard. The less clutter and complications, the easier it was, and Sonny was determined to keep it that way. Charlie was only a kid once and she wasn't going to screw it up for him. She wasn't her mom.

Sonny tried damn hard not to be her mom.

The sun had risen higher and the sky was now vivid orange and fuchsia. The white light of morning bathed her kitchen in soft glow, warming the golden oak floors and pulling out the grain in the old cupboards.

A lot had changed in the old ranch since she'd inherited it. Most of it was simple cosmetics, but still. She'd done her best to update the brick rambler and bring it into the modern age. Overall Sonny was happy with what she'd done. Sure there was more—there always was—but for now it worked. Charlie had a roof over his head and that's what mattered.

And she'd become the thrift store queen of Boulder County. What had started out as necessity had evolved into a darn fun hobby. Turned out that she had a knack for finding the gems of the secondhand world. Sonny's style was definitely eclectic, with a dash of global funk. The result was an open, airy house in bold colors set to a neutral background and dotted with warm wood accents and unframed canvas prints everywhere.

And she liked it just fine. Because the truth was she was okay with where she was now. It beat the hell out of the alternatives. She and Charlie were doing okay. It may not be the most exciting life, but she loved it just the same.

The clock on the wall signaled the new hour and Sonny cringed. It was time to get the day started, and first up was feeding and milking the goats.

Sonny dumped the last of the lukewarm coffee down the drain and put the ceramic cup in the dishwasher. Vader must have finally noticed her rustling around because he showed up in the kitchen and whined at the door to be let out. Most of the time Charlie followed close behind him, bleary eyed and cheerful. It was his trademark expression in the morning. It was one of the things she loved so much about him. The kid was upbeat and always happy to experience another day.

It was a good reminder to her to be thankful of the process and not get so caught up on the finished product. One of the most surprising aspects she found about parenthood was how much she learned from her own kid. Charlie was her mirror, for sure. What she saw wasn't always pretty. That was the other thing about parenthood. It was flat-out work. To be any good at it, stasis wasn't okay. Sonny was always changing and growing, becoming better than she was. And it could be exhausting.

But she wouldn't trade it for anything, because it was the best thing in the world too. And who wanted to settle for a life without growth anyway? That'd be colossally boring.

So long as that growth was limited to her and Charlie, she was good. That thought made her think back on JP again as she threw on her barn boots and went to grab the stainless steel supplies that she kept in her workspace. She stepped out into the early morning and shoved a ball cap over her sloppy bun. Sonny rarely worried about dressing for the girls since she didn't think they gave a rip about what she wore. They were just too happy she was showing up to empty their udders to care that she was wearing a thin cotton tank top and kitten print flannel pants tucked into her rubber boots.

Crossing over the large expanse of June grass, Sonny deeply inhaled the scent of rich earth and smiled. She didn't know how JP put up with the constant attention. It contented her soul to be out in the morning freshness with no people crammed in next to her. Here, those few precious miles to civilization made a world of difference. Sonny could breathe and have privacy. Nobody was right there looking from behind their fence to see what she was doing.

As much as society claimed to be in the modern age, single mothers still faced a peculiar type of scrutiny. But here, five miles away, Sonny had a beautiful kind of freedom. Nobody was looking to see how she measured up. She could just be. Whatever curiosity she felt for JP was going to have to remain just that—curiosity. Because she wouldn't trade her anonymity for anything in the world.

Sonny passed the fenced-in vegetable garden and noted with satisfaction that everything was growing well. She and Charlie had planned out this year's crop with extra care. He was thrilled that they'd found a novel variety of yellow heirloom watermelons and couldn't wait until the day he got to sink his teeth into a juicy bite.

Vader ran past her, his long blue-merle-and-white coat bobbing in the air. He was an average gregarious and smart Aussie shepherd. When he caught her eye, he grinned a huge doggy grin and took off toward the pasture beyond the barn. No doubt he was hoping a field mouse had taken up residence and would give him a good time.

Sonny reached the barn and shoved the creaking, buckled wooden door open. Inside her ladies waited, eager to barter their milk for a tasty treat. She heard shuffling around as she began to set up.

When she'd first started the research on goat farming, Sonny had fallen in love with Nubian goats and their long, rabbit-like ears and generous milking capabilities. The ears gave them such a sweet appearance that their juvenile pranks didn't bug her. Giving them a designated pasture with toys and shelter kept most of the shenanigans at bay. The kids loved to play King of the Mountain on the old picnic table she'd tossed out there, and they head butted and bleated to their little hearts' content.

One of the goats bleated for attention and Sonny recognized which one of them it was instantly. Donna was her lead goat and had a big personality. When she heard Sonny in the mornings, she made a ruckus until it was time to milk.

"Morning, Donna. You have to give me a few minutes, but I'm almost ready for ya."

It'd been a steep learning curve, but Sonny had the milking system down now and could finish all the goats in about thirty minutes. When she was done she had around six gallons of rich milk that would soon turn into Gouda with her help. Her business, Sonnyside Farms, had been quoted as "having the tastiest goat Gouda this side of the Atlantic" in last month's *5280* magazine. It was the Front Range's go-to mag for the lowdown on LoDo and the surrounding areas. Their local food and business section had done a profile on her cheese and touted it as the best new thing in the growing alternative dairy world.

Lost in her thoughts, Sonny was just finishing with the cleanup after letting the goats out to pasture and didn't hear the barn door protest its opening. She started when Charlie poked his disheveled head in and said excitedly, "Hey, Mom. Someone's here to see you, but I'm not supposed to say who. It's a surprise." Then he disappeared. No doubt back to whatever early morning cartoon was on the TV.

Odd. She wasn't expecting anybody. Brushing her palms against her flannels, Sonny took a step toward the door to see who the visitor was, when it squeaked open and JP stepped over the threshold. Stunned, her hands frozen in midair, she cringed as JP gave her a thorough once-over. In the dim light of the barn it was hard to read the expression in his eyes. But it looked like a smile was tugging at the corners of his mouth.

"That's a real nice outfit there, Sonny."

Oh crap! Sonny snuck a panicked look at her pink pajama pants haphazardly shoved into her rubber waders and felt the bottom drop out of her stomach. Why was he here? What did he want?

Ugh. Was he really there now, staring at her in her pajamas? Sonny blinked twice, halfway convinced it had to be a dream. But, nope. JP was still there. She reached up and straightened her ball cap, searching for composure.

He took a step closer, looking good in worn jeans and a grey T-shirt that hugged his body and showed off his hard, sculpted muscles. His short light brown hair was a little messy, like brushing it was too much effort so he'd given it no more than a quick finger-comb on his way out the door. And he'd skipped shaving.

The day's growth made her forget that JP Trudeau was only twenty-six.

He looked all man, standing there in her ramshackle barn with his aviator sunglasses hooked on the front collar of his shirt and his eyes full of shadow and mystery. The air surrounding them seemed to spark to life, the charged vibration putting her on feminine alert. The whole scenario was so unexpected that the only thing she could do was react.

She was alone with a strong, agile, athletic man who dripped sex appeal, who made her knees go soft against all judgment with that crooked, all-knowing grin of his. He had it on her now and she could feel her legs turning to Jell-O. Awesome.

Sonny found her voice. "What are you doing here?" Extremely off balance at his sudden presence, she took a step forward and promptly tripped over a bucket, spilling fresh milk everywhere. Pitching off center, she flung her arms out in front of her, going down so fast she barely had time to register the fall. The ball cap she wore dislodged and slipped down, covering her eyes.

Bracing for impact, Sonny was surprised when a pair of hard, large hands grabbed her by the waist and righted her. Holding still, she tried to regain her bearings. Her whole body became acutely aware of the man holding her in his strong arms. They cradled her gently.

The warmth of his breath fanned across her neck, giving her goosebumps. "Are you all right?"

Her vision was still compromised by the ball cap. Forced to look down, Sonny's eyes went wide when she realized she was staring directly at his package. The bulge was anything but humble. Dear God. Try as she might, she couldn't take her eyes off it. It was like standing in front of Michelangelo's David and trying not to take a peek at his goods. It just wasn't happening. Problem was, once you got started, it was nearly impossible to stop.

It was hypnotic.

JP shifted and the brim of her hat bumped his chest. Her eyes still glued to the fly of his jeans, Sonny swallowed hard as she felt him begin to move, walking her backward until she came up against a wall. Her heart slammed to life and thoughts scattered like ashes when she felt a hard hand slide slowly up her side. When it reached her face, long fingers briefly caressed her chin before tenderly putting pressure on it, forcing her to look up. His other hand gently removed her ball cap and her hair spilled free from its confines, tumbling over her shoulders.

Sonny braced and reluctantly made eye contact. Heat

flooded her cheeks at what she saw and self-preservation kicked in. She pushed back and broke contact, pure female awareness making her scared.

She knew that look and rejected it. "I'm not interested, Trudeau."

JP REACHED OUT an arm to snag her, but she slipped just out of reach—for the moment. Did she really think she could get away from him?

There was a reason he played shortstop in the Major Leagues. He was damn fast. And now that he'd decided to make Sonny his woman she was about to find out just how quick he could be. All night he'd tossed and turned for her, his curiosity rampant. When he'd finally rolled out of bed, he'd had one clear goal: to see Sonny. Nothing else had existed outside that.

Her leaving her cell phone at the restaurant last night had been the perfect excuse. All he'd had to do was an Internet search for her business to get her address. And now here he was, unexpectedly very up close and personal with her. So close he could smell the scent of her shampoo, and it was doing funny things to him. Things like making him want to bury his nose in her hair and inhale.

No way was he going to miss this golden opportunity.

With a devil's grin, he moved and had her back against the aging barn wall before she'd finished gasping. "Look me in the eyes right now and tell me I don't affect you, that you're not interested." He traced a lazy path down the side of her neck with his fingertips and felt her shiver. "Because I don't believe that line for an instant, sunshine."

Close enough to feel the heat she was throwing from her deliciously curved body, JP laughed softly when she tried to sidestep and squeeze free. Her shyness was so damn cute. He raised an arm and blocked her in, his palm flush against the rough, splintering wood. Leaning in close, he grinned when she blushed and her gaze flickered to his lips. Her mouth opened on a soft rush of breath and for a suspended moment something sparked and held between them.

But then Sonny shook back her rose-gold curls and tipped her chin with defiance. "Believe what you want, JP. I don't have to prove anything to you." Her denim-blue eyes flashed with emotion. "This might come as a surprise, but I'm not interested in playing with a celebrity like you. I have a business to run and a son to raise. I don't need the headache."

There was an underlying nervousness to her tone that didn't quite jive with the tough-as-nails attitude she was trying to project. Either she was scared or he affected her more than she wanted to admit. She didn't look scared.

JP dropped his gaze to her mouth, wanting to kiss those juicy lips bad, and felt her body brush against his. He could feel her pulse, fast and frantic, under his fingertips.

It made his pulse kick up a notch in anticipation. "There's a surefire way to end this little disagreement right now, because I say you're lying. I say you *are* interested in a celebrity like me." He cupped her chin with his hand and watched her thick lashes flutter as she broke eye contact. But she didn't pull away. "In fact, I say you're interested in *me*."

JP knew he had her.

Her voice came soft and a little shaky. "How do I prove I'm not?" The way she was staring at his mouth contradicted her words. So did the way her body was leaning into him.

Lowering his head until he was a whisper away, he issued the challenge. "Kiss me."

Her gaze flew to his, her eyes wide with shock. "You want me to do *what*?"

What he knew they both wanted.

"Kiss me. Prove to me you're not interested and I'll leave here. You can go back to your business and your son and never see my celebrity ass again."

Contemplating for a minute, she bit her plump bottom lip and stared at him. It was too much temptation for him to ignore. He'd wanted to do this ever since he'd laid eyes on her.

But before he could flatten her against the wall and take her mouth in a searing kiss like he wanted to, she rose on tiptoes and placed a perfunctory one on his lips. "There."

"That's not a kiss, Sonny. Not a real one anyway." Her lips had barely brushed his.

Her gaze was on his mouth again and she whispered, shifting a little closer. "Oh, well. I suppose I should try another one?"

JP murmured as her lips touched his, "Yes, you should." She whimpered against him and he felt her hands flutter before they smoothed over his shoulders. Her body went soft and pliant as a marshmallow.

He let her keep up the seductive assault on his mouth until she sagged against him and her hands fisted in the back of his shirt. When she moaned and slid her tongue over his bottom lip he knew he had her right where he wanted her.

Pulling back, he took in her glazed, passion-drunk expression and tasted the victory. Damn straight she was interested.

"See you next week, sunshine."

He'd actually only stopped by to bring back the cell phone she'd dropped while climbing into her minivan last night and he reached into his pocket for it. She'd peeled out of the parking lot in such a hurry he'd been left waving it in the air and hollering like a dumbass. He figured seeing her in her current state was payback enough. Satisfaction radiated through him at her thoroughly bemused expression.

Sonny obviously hadn't been properly kissed in far too long.

Feeling smug, JP tossed her cell phone on a nearby hay bale and turned to leave. He was stopped by Sonny's words.

"So that's what you came for? To give me back my phone?" She seemed to be building up bluster and it made her voice sharp. "Then why did you want me to kiss you?"

JP took a good look at Sonny. He had four sisters and

recognized a woman working herself into a lather when he saw it. And because he had four sisters, he also knew that there was something more going on than what appeared on the surface.

It took some of the smugness out of his step. Her eyes had gone round as saucers and dark as a summer thunderstorm. A frown pulled at his brows. "The two of us kissing isn't the worst thing in the world, Sonny."

"I didn't ask for it." She pushed at her hair and stared him down.

Her attitude got his back up. But he wanted her to let her guard down. And that meant that he needed her to trust him.

So even though he wanted nothing more than to push her down into the hay and kiss her everywhere, he reached out and tapped her cell phone instead. "Yeah, you dropped this in the parking lot last night." Pushing it in her direction, he added, "Also, I forgot to mention at the restaurant that one of our batboys is out for the next few weeks. His family is heading to Taos last minute and I thought Charlie might be interested in filling in this week during the games against Milwaukee. He's technically too young, but I already got the go-ahead on it since it's only temporary."

Some air seemed to go out of her and Sonny deflated. Her shoulders relaxed and she gave him a look full of chagrin. "Oh." She wiped her palms against her thighs and smiled tentatively. "Charlie would love that, thanks."

"Anytime." Because he couldn't resist, JP put his sunglasses on and grinned, quick and hot as lightning. "Thanks for the kiss, sweetness. It was damn sexy."

Chapter Five

CHARLIE HAD BEEN beyond thrilled when she'd told him about playing batboy for the week. On the morning of the first game, he'd popped out of bed at sunrise and had his chores done in record time, a big silly grin on his face the whole time.

Sonny had been watching him for the past hour from her seat along the first base line and it hadn't waned. In fact, as fans trickled into Coors Field and the teams warmed up, Charlie's tireless smile seemed as fully charged as ever. JP had taken him under his wing when they'd first arrived and when Charlie had emerged from the locker room he was sporting an authentic Denver Rush jersey. Honestly, she wasn't sure she'd ever seen him so happy and it made her heart do little flops of joy.

And it gave her warm fuzzies for the guy who'd made it possible.

JP had an angle, no doubt about it. Even though Sonny

hadn't been on the market for ages, she could still recognize the signs. Especially when they weren't subtle. And he was anything but. In fact, JP seemed to be a straight shooter. Most of the time she'd appreciate that kind of quality in a person, but not today.

Not after he'd kissed her senseless and left her feeling things she was better off not feeling.

Charlie caught her eye and waved, bobbling a few baseball bats. The Rush's ace pitcher strode by and gave him a quick hand reorganizing and a reassuring pat on the back. Pride swelled inside Sonny for her boy. Just look at him out there, she thought. He was growing up so fast.

For now he was still her boy and she was so excited for him to have this experience with the pro team. It really was great of JP to facilitate this opportunity for Charlie. Whether or not he'd done it to soften her up didn't matter. The result was that her son was having the time of his life and she had him to thank.

She would too. In a public place. Where he couldn't kiss her again.

Sonny propped her feet on the seat in front of her and sighed. She was such a liar. JP kissing her was exactly what she wanted to happen again. In those moments he'd made her feel things she hadn't experienced in years— maybe ever. Charlie's dad sure had never kissed her like that. He'd never left her light-headed and floaty and intensely aroused.

With JP she'd felt all those things. And all her instincts told her to shut it down now. Kissing JP was like standing on a precipice. One wrong move and she could tumble a long, long way down. The last thing she needed was to fall for a sports star who lived a life in the public eye. Even if she could somehow get around that—which she couldn't—dating a celebrity would only put her and Charlie in the spotlight too. God, what if they went after her son and decided to make him a poster child for something? He already dealt with enough scrutiny just from being the kid of a single parent. And yes, it did happen, even in this modern age of same sex marriage and legalized pot. School functions were the worst—all the parents and staff gave him vaguely pitying looks. *Poor Charlie Miller. He doesn't have a daddy.*

They never said anything, but she felt it just the same. She knew he did too. And she hated it. Hated that he had to grow up with that kind of cloud over his head.

She knew all too well what it felt like.

Becoming involved with JP would only escalate that judgment to a national scale and have strangers prying into their personal business. And she couldn't deal with that. She'd already spent most of her life feeling like the world was watching, waiting for her to fail. She didn't want Charlie to feel that way too. That was Grace's delightful legacy—giving Sonny a deep-rooted paranoia that what she was doing wasn't good enough. Dating JP and opening herself to public scrutiny would only provide a platform for complete strangers to say as much.

No frigging way. She and JP just couldn't be.

Ever.

She knew that. Sonny's rational brain preached caution. Told her to turn around now because it was nothing but a dead end packed full of trouble. And she heard it, really she did.

But then the memory of his hard-muscled body pressed up against her would flash in her mind and she forgot all about caution. All she could think of was how good it felt to be held by a man.

Even now, just the sight of JP in his baseball uniform warming up on the grass had her blood pressure up. Now that she knew what his body felt like under the clothes, she couldn't help the butterflies that leapt in her belly when he began stretching, his highly toned body flexing deliciously with the movement.

What was she supposed to make of him? Reluctantly she admitted that it was flattering to have a man like JP interested in her. Beyond that, it was disconcerting and frightening. For starters, Sonny was thirty-one-year-old single mother. JP was a twenty-six-year-old hotshot baseball star. She knitted scarves and he dated super-models.

Sonny blew out a frustrated breath and waved back at Charlie. Really she was just making a big deal out of nothing. All she was doing was wasting energy speculating and driving herself nuts in the process. It was one stupid kiss. There was no way that JP Trudeau could possibly be serious about her anyway. Real life didn't work that way.

Sonny had learned at an early age that fairy-tale endings were only things a person read about in books.

As it always did when she thought such things, her optimism dropped and she frowned. Today was too good a day to let anything get her down. And it never did her any good to wallow.

With effort, Sonny shook off the vaguely sad feeling and forced a smile for the young couple who needed to get by. Muttering an apology, she lowered her feet to the floor. They scooted through and sat half a dozen seats down.

While she'd been lost in thought, Coors Field had filled with eager baseball fans. The sun had shifted position in the sky and the game was about to get under way. Glancing around for Charlie, she spotted him standing near JP by the dugout. The two were deep in conversation and she couldn't help noticing how easy the shortstop seemed with her boy.

Men were one of those things in short supply in Charlie's life. Most of the time Sonny was okay with it—she had to be. It was only times like this, when Charlie was so obviously eating up the male attention, that she had any misgivings about her decisions. But those misgivings were outweighed by the potential consequences of inviting someone into their life.

Whatever Charlie was missing now would just have to be because she wasn't willing to risk the consequences. She wasn't willing to risk screwing it up for him.

Heavy from the thoughts, Sonny inhaled and looked up at the sky. Beautiful blue and cloudless, it steadied her nerves and calmed her. It lifted the weight. Taking a moment to soak it in, palms against the sun-warmed denim of her jeans, Sonny let herself just feel thankful for what she had.

It smoothed the emotional waters and lowered the stress. Over the years she'd learned some effective ways to keep calm and in control. She'd had to, otherwise there was no way she'd have made it this far.

What she needed to do now was so simple: she just needed to utilize said coping skills. This thing with JP was nothing she couldn't handle.

With one last look at the shortstop, Sonny settled in and prepared to watch the game.

JP ENTERED THE locker room, riding high on the win against the Brewers and feeling buzzy. He and the boys had played a helluva good game. Peter Kowalskin had pitched right up to the ninth inning, throwing heat until the end. The team's catcher, Mark Cutter, caught a pop fly and executed a triple play. And he'd nabbed his share of doubles for the night.

Crossing over the thick rug depicting the Rush's mascot, Goldpan Sam, and his pickax, JP headed toward his locker. He only had a few minutes before the media barged in. If luck was on his side, he'd be changed and out the door quick enough to find Sonny before she left with Charlie

"Hey, Trudeau." Mark hailed him.

Scanning the room, he found Cutter undressing in front of his locker. "What's up?"

The blond catcher eyed him as he unwrapped a bandage around his ankle. "Word is you got a woman thing going, bro."

Drake walked by just then in nothing but a towel and slapped JP's back, laughing. "It's true. Our boy's got a bad case of the hot and horny."

JP raked a hand through his hair, leaving the soft brown tresses spiked and sweaty. He ignored Drake's comment and replied to Mark, "I'm working on it, man."

Mark tossed the bandage into the locker behind him and rolled his shoulders. "She's got a kid, right?"

JP nodded.

"Are you up for that?"

Slicing a look at Mark, JP determined the question was one of genuine concern, not judgment. "He's a good kid."

Peter piped up from nearby. "Is the dad in the picture?" Apparently JP's love life was an open topic of discussion in the locker room.

Thinking back to their conversation at the restaurant, he shook his head. "Don't think so. Charlie said it'd always been just the two of them, so I get the feeling the dude punted when he was really young."

Drake called from the shower, "A kid without a dad is a sad thing."

JP frowned at the veteran first baseman. He sounded like a fortune cookie. "You got a problem with me seeing a single mom, hoss?"

Drake poked his head out from behind the shower wall, shampoo dripping down his neck. "Nah. Just stating facts, is all. We're all different, brother. If this is your tale, then tell it."

That's right. It was his tale. "Who I date is my business." JP looked at his teammates, irked at being poked about his personal life. "Anybody have something else to say about it?"

They all shook their heads.

For a bunch of raunchy baseball players they sure acted like a group of gossiping old busybodies. JP shook his head and headed to the showers as the doors opened and reporters filled the locker room. He made quick work of it and was dressed in no time. After answering a few questions, he grabbed his duffel and hit the corridor in search of Sonny.

He caught sight of Charlie and headed over. Sonny was standing next to the kid in jeans and a tight-fitting Rush T-shirt. JP had never seen his team's logo look so good as it did splayed across her chest. The *R* and *H* pushed out real nice.

Charlie waved and JP wondered how he could finagle some time alone with Sonny. He figured that this was one of the issues with dating a woman with a kid—getting her alone. Some guys would be able to manage the inconvenience. Some guys couldn't.

Sonny caught sight of him and seemed to stiffen some before giving him a smile. Something about the way she moved had him thinking that she was still pretty off from their kiss. And it fascinated him. She was turning out to be much more complex than he'd originally guessed. One moment she was ballsy as a bull with three gonads; the next she was blushing and unsure. It was like who Sonny thought she was and who she really was didn't quite line up.

The discrepancy turned him on and had him curious

as all hell. Who was the real Sonny? He was drawn by the challenge. But could he deal with some serious inconvenience on the way to finding out?

Sonny smiled as he drew close and said, "Congrats on the win. This puts you guys in good position heading into the All-Star break, doesn't it?"

Glad that she seemed to have enjoyed the game, JP adjusted the duffle on his shoulder and nodded. He liked it a whole lot that she was into baseball. "Yeah it does. Especially if we sweep next week's series against St. Louis."

Her smile spread and her shoulders relaxed. "Thanks again for getting Charlie the gig. He had the best time, as you can see."

The kid did look extra happy, now that she mentioned it. He was kind of hopping from one foot to the other with a huge grin, a bundle of youthful energy.

JP slid a look at Sonny out of the corner of his eye and smiled playfully. "Ten bucks says he's passed out before you even hit the interstate."

Her eyes warmed and she shook her head. "Nuh-uh. I'm not taking a losing bet."

The way her eyes sparkled with humor lured him in and he found himself getting sucked into her. Ducking his head, JP leaned in close and whispered against her ear, "Coward."

Though he felt her tense at his nearness, she didn't shy away. Instead, Sonny gave a sexy little hum and murmured a reply. "Realist."

Arousal pooled low in his belly. Her full lips were centimeters way, teasing him, calling him. He felt the energy charge between them—the awareness almost electric. The way her breath fanned across his collar bone set the skin on fire, every nerve alive and jittery.

Kissing her again had just become the most important mission he'd ever undertaken. Because he remembered the way her lips had felt against his—so ripe and luscious, like a juicy mango. And her tongue gliding hotly over his bottom lip had to be about the sexiest thing he'd experienced. It was the way she'd done it, with so much shy passion.

Sonny undone would be the stuff of fantasy.

JP grew instantly hard. Sonny was so close he could smell the clean scent of her skin and the underlying muskiness of sexual arousal. She wanted him.

Forgetting where he was, JP was about to kiss her when Peter walked on scene and said rather loudly, "Hey, Charlie. Why don't you come with me for a second? We'll find a ball and I'll autograph it for ya."

Tossing JP a knowing look, the pitcher hooked an arm around the kid's shoulders, turning his attention away. They were out of sight in moments. That left him all alone with Sonny. Knowing that he owed Pete big-time, JP decided not to waste the opportunity.

On a low growl, JP captured Sonny's lips in a hungry kiss. Pent-up arousal burst forth and he fisted his hands in her hair, holding her captive to his growing desire. Even when she moaned and gave into the kiss readily, he didn't let up. All he'd wanted to do since the last time he'd kissed her was kiss her again. Now that he was doing it, lust slammed into him like a freight train.

Slender arms wrapped around his neck and she was kissing him back, her body pressing against him with awakened need. When her tongue rubbed seductively against his, he groaned and took the kiss deeper, darker.

All he knew was the scent and feel of Sonny. His erection began to throb for her.

Dimly the echo of Peter's voice penetrated the sexual haze and JP stiffened. "And that is how Babe Ruth got his name, champ."

Sonny melted against him, eyes closed, a dreamy smile on her kiss-swollen lips. He wanted to sink into them again, but the voices were getting closer. Louder.

Opportunity had knocked and now it was slamming the door.

Damn.

Chapter Six

SONNY CLOSED THE trunk on her minivan and sighed. Gathering the wicker basket and linens, she made her way to the small outbuilding that housed her cheese-making equipment. Once a bunkhouse for hired help when the place had been a dairy farm, now the building held two extra-large refrigerators, a gas stove, a long counter for working, and various stainless steel pots and pans. Rennet, salt, and other ingredients were stored on rustic wooden shelves in attractive containers.

She loved her workspace. The scarred oak floor needed refinishing, but had a ton of character. And she'd painted the walls a cheerful citrus hue. Prints dotted the room, the scenes mostly bucolic to keep in theme with her business.

Although the giant hand-painted wooden giraffe in the corner didn't fit the theme, it'd spoken to her at a flea market last summer and she'd had to bring it home.

Now it had the lofty position of coat rack and currently sported a purple chenille scarf around its neck and a charcoal grey fedora.

Her work space was basically an oversized kitchen. Much of the business loan had gone toward renovating the space and decking it out with the needed equipment and curing rooms—otherwise known as her pantries. Always aware of the budget, she'd shopped refurb and thrift stores looking for what she needed.

That's why her fridges were an awesome retro avocado color—they'd been made in the heyday of CFCs and extreme energy inefficiency. But instead of being dumped in a landfill, some environmentally conscientious business in Boulder had taken to stripping them down and rebuilding them to modern-day standards. The result was a new fridge at about half the cost.

It never failed to amaze her—all the cool, resourceful things people came up with.

Slipping off her pink flip-flops, Sonny strode to the long Formica counter and sat the basket down. With her weekly deliveries done and Charlie at a play date with Sam for the day, she had the chance to get ahead on work.

A warm breeze came through the open windows, bringing with it the scent of summer flowers and recently mowed grass. Busying herself with straightening, Sonny hummed a tune and pretended that the kiss with JP yesterday had never happened.

Life was normal. It was predictable. Nothing had changed.

She bobbled a mason jar and swore as it crashed to the floor. Why was she lying?

Everything had changed.

Two weeks ago JP Trudeau was nothing more than a name on a roster to her. He was the hot ballplayer with the badass moves on the field. That's all.

Now he was the guy who'd kissed her stupid. Twice.

Janie, when she'd been a single mom, had been Frenched out of the blue by some college-bound eighteen-year-old who'd shown up at her door selling magazine subscriptions. She had called Sonny completely flabbergasted and out-of-sorts, convinced the world had gone topsy because some barely legal hormone factory had shoved his tongue down her throat after signing her up for *National Geographic Kids*—and she'd *liked* it. Sonny had laughed then, thinking that it was about time somebody rattled Janie's cage.

She wasn't laughing now.

It was a whole different kettle of fish being on the receiving end of things. And JP wasn't a hormone-crazed teenager. Oh no. He was all man, and that made it so much worse. Saying no to him was getting harder, especially since her interest annoyingly seemed to grow after every kiss, regardless of how she felt about everything.

Plus, she was a barrelful of screwed-up when it came to men. She knew that. Her feelings about his fame aside, any relationship with JP was bound to become a mess. Once her fears got a hold of her it was all downhill.

Sonny shook her head and pushed a loose strand of hair back into her low bun, lost deep in the ocean of her thoughts. Self-denial had worked so well for her. Happiness and satisfaction hadn't been hard to find with blinders on. All she'd seen was Charlie and her work. And it had contented her, that life of simplicity and minimalism.

So why did it all seem so constricting after two lusty kisses from a hot guy?

The cell phone in her shorts pocket went off, the theme song to *The Office* filling the room. Reaching into the khaki fabric, she pulled out the old flip phone and scanned the number.

"You got Sonny."

"Hey, sunshine. I snagged your number from Charlie yesterday. Hope you don't mind."

Speak of the devil.

Of course she minded. She didn't need this distraction. She didn't need *him*. "I'm busy right now, JP."

Her curt tone didn't even faze him. "No doubt. But hey, I have a favor to ask. You're going to be around in about an hour, right?"

"Yes. Why?" Suspicion crept up her spine.

If he knew how she felt, he didn't sound like it. Or he didn't care. The guy was totally nonchalant. "Because I thought I'd stop over and buy some milk, if you have it."

Maybe he didn't have an ulterior motive. "I have some, yeah."

She was about to ask why he needed it when he cut her off. "Great. See you then."

With that he hung up and Sonny was left with dead air. Frowning, she closed the phone and looked out the windows without really seeing. Her brain was fuzzy with speculation and she barely registered the expanse of grass and old maples and aspens dotting the landscape.

What was JP up to?

Shaking her head to clear her brain, Sonny said out loud with frustration, "What the hell happened to my life? Two weeks ago it was normal. Now I've got a baseball player stealing kisses and refusing to leave me alone."

Being left alone was the only way she knew how to keep a handle on things. JP's persistence was screwing it up. And it didn't seem like he was going to be giving up any time soon. So it was up to her to figure out what to do about it.

Someone called her name from outside and Sonny poked her head out the door to find Janie looking for her. Glad to see a friendly face, she stepped out into the sunshine. "Hey, lady. What are you doing here?"

Janie rushed forward, her arms full of active toddler. "I'm so glad you're here."

She set her daughter down and the two-year-old took off over the grass, bent on running as far and fast as she could in no particular direction. "I just found out last minute that Ben has a business get-together for us to go to tonight. He swears he mentioned it to me weeks ago, but that man has a faulty memory. We're supposed to bring something and I don't have time to make anything. Hillary has horse riding lessons up near Berthoud and Michael has to be at a birthday party at four."

Her friend gave Sonny a bedraggled look. "I'm swamped and I thought I could persuade you to toss together a fancy cheese platter for me."

She looked overworked. Poor thing. "Of course I'll put something together." Sonny glanced at Janie's growing belly and added, "How's the morning sickness?"

Janie waved a hand and grimaced. "The universe has not been kind the fourth time around. I'm in my second trimester and still sick as a dog."

Sympathy flooded her. God, she remembered the days of early pregnancy sickness. For months she'd walked a tight line between nausea and straight-up vomiting. How any woman could withstand it more than once was beyond her. And here now Janie was remarried and going on her fourth. Her friend was Wonder Woman.

Beckoning with a wave, Sonny slipped back into her workshop and headed for one of the custom-built pantries. Inside were round after round of goat cheeses in various stages of drying. Selecting two and pulling them out, she set them on the counter and went in search of a tray.

"Hey, Sonny? Do you mind if I let Kelly play with Vader? He's trying to get her to play with him and keeps dropping a flat soccer ball at her feet." Janie's voice came from just outside the door.

"Of course." Sonny called back over her shoulder. "He's bored with Charlie gone. If she kicks it for him, he'll chase it down and dribble it between his paws."

Janie sounded impressed. "Really? Since when did he get so trick-savvy?"

"Since Charlie taught him to do it about a month ago." It was pretty impressive, actually. Vader looked just like one of those super well-trained dogs in the movies. No one would guess by looking at him that last week he'd eaten an entire apple pie off the counter.

Sonny found the tray she'd been looking for and pulled it down. She turned as the brunette head of her friend came into view. "I'm assuming silver is good enough for this thing, right?"

Gratitude made Janie's aqua-blue eyes bright and watery. Or maybe it was the hormones. "That's perfect, hon. Thanks again for doing this. I was so mad at Ben this morning when he dropped this bomb on me."

Sonny was all sympathy. "I bet."

Taking a knife in hand, she made quick work of the cheese and arranged pieces artfully on the tray. After she was finished and the rest of the cheese was back in the fridge, Sonny handed the tray to her girlfriend and gave her a quick hug.

Janie sniffled against her shoulder. "I hate being pregnant. I get so moody and hormonal. I mean, I love Ben with everything I have. But some days I want to wring his neck, you know?"

She couldn't imagine why. It wasn't like Janie had a lot going on or anything. Deciding that work could wait, Sonny patted Janie's back and said, "I know, sweetie." Stepping outside just as Vader dashed past after a ball and Kelly's laughter split the air, Sonny continued, "I was just thinking this morning about the time when that college kid shoved his tongue down your throat. Do you remember that?"

Her friend snorted and grinned, the memory effectively soothing the hormonal tide. "God, I haven't thought about that in years."

Sonny snagged the ball from Vader and tossed it in Kelly's direction. The chubby toddler squealed with delight and clapped her hands. "That was only a few weeks before you met Ben, wasn't it?"

Janie placed her hands on her hips and nodded, her eyes on her daughter. "Yeah. I'd just finished my degree at CU and was doing data entry from home so I could be with the kids for the summer. That kid shocked me back into the world of the living, that's for sure. It was like being awakened from a sexual coma."

She could relate.

A goat bleated in the distance and the breeze picked up, stirring the aspen leaves into a delicate dance. Janie speared a look at her, her eyes narrowed. "Why were you thinking about that?"

Suddenly uncomfortable, Sonny hedged, "No particular reason."

Janie's eyes narrowed further. *"Really."*

Well, hell. She should have known better than to hide anything from Janie. The woman was like a bloodhound once she caught scent of something. Still, she gave it another try anyway. "It just popped into my head is all."

Her friend was silent for a moment and then gasped. "Somebody kissed you!"

Denial was instantaneous. "Nuh-uh."

"Don't you lie to me, Sonny Luanne Miller."

God, she sounded like a mother. It was effective, too. "All right, fine. Somebody did kiss me."

Triumph lit Janie's face. "I knew it! Was it good?"

Sonny looked at her friend and caved. She needed to tell someone. "It was *so* good."

Janie called out to her daughter, "Kelly sweetie, don't do that. I don't think Vader wants to wear your headband right now, darling." Then she looked back at Sonny. "When did this happen?"

She thought back and replied, "The first time was about two weeks ago."

"There was more than one?" Janie's eyes were round as snow globes. "Why have you been holding out on me?"

Why had she been keeping it secret? Good question. "It's happened twice, and I didn't tell you about it because I've been busy."

Her friend jabbed her in the shoulder. "That's for not telling me. I'm an old married woman with a herd of kids, you know. I need to live vicariously through you."

That made her laugh. "You're not old. But you do have a herd of kids, that's true."

And Sonny knew for a fact that Janie was ridiculously happy about it. Even if she was always running around crazy. Married life suited her.

Janie turned the topic back to the kisses. "So, tell me about them already. They were from the UPS guy, weren't they? I know you have it bad for those brown shorts."

"Please. It's the FedEx uniforms."

Janie chuckled, but prodded her. "Seriously, who was it? I'm dying to know."

Because it'd been playing at the back of her mind for days, Sonny asked instead, "When you met Ben, were you ready?"

"Heck no. Not in a million years."

"What made you change your mind?"

Janie placed a hand on her gently rounded belly and looked at Sonny. "I didn't. Ben changed it for me."

See now, that didn't compute. "But you had two kids, J. How did you get past the fear of screwing everything up?"

Understanding softened Janie's eyes and they got all watery again. "I fell in love, Sonny. I didn't plan it or look for it."

"Weren't you scared?"

Kelly ran over to Janie and she scooped her up and planted a kiss on her cheek. "I was terrified. I had one wrecked marriage behind me and a tenuous hold on the present. But Ben pushed through my fears. He made me see that the only thing to be terrified of was never being loved at all."

Sonny lifted her gaze to the sky and inhaled deep, her own eyes feeling a little watery. "What if it had been a mistake? What if it hadn't ended in marriage and happy ever after?"

"I had to take that chance. Being without Ben wasn't an option." She cuddled her daughter and continued, "Besides, nobody has a bead on the future. We can't see how it's all going to unfold and we can't predict the bruises."

"I don't want bruises."

Janie gave her a level look. "Well then don't go around kissing anybody."

Good advice, that.

The sound of gravel crunching caught their attention and they turned just in time to see a shiny red Toyota truck pull into the drive. Crap. She'd forgotten all about his arrival and now her stomach took a nosedive.

Kelly pointed over her mom's shoulder and exclaimed, "Car!"

Janie squinted against the sun and asked, "Who's that?"

The nobody she's not supposed to be kissing. "That's JP Trudeau. Shortstop for the Rush."

"What's he doing here and how do you know him?" It took Janie a minute and then she whispered fiercely, "Is he the one you've been sampling?"

Both of them watched—one in avid fascination, the other equal parts nerves and uncertainty—as the truck door swung open. It seemed like a small eternity before JP rounded the hood of his Toyota and came into full view. When he did, he stopped and surveyed the property, eyes shielded behind a pair of old-school aviators.

Something besides nerves came to life in her stomach, too, as she took in the sight of his fit, toned body in a white T-shirt and faded jeans. He stood like a man completely and utterly confident in himself.

That man knew his place in the world.

Sonny wasn't the only one left speechless at the sight of him. Janie stood next to her with her mouth open, eyes glued on the sexy ballplayer. Then she swallowed hard and tapped Sonny's shoulder.

"I lied earlier, Sonny."

Her eyes were glued on him too. "Yeah? About what?"

"About the kissing. You should be doing a whole lotta kissing."

Chapter Seven

JP SCANNED THE yard and found Sonny standing next to a brunette woman with a toddler. All of them, including the baby, were staring at him. Though he'd been in the big leagues for a while now, that kind of reaction still surprised him. In his mind he was just Jason Patrick Trudeau: Iowa-born farm kid from the sticks who was good at playing ball and had a thing for pretty ladies.

Right now he was looking at one very pretty lady. Standing barefoot in the grass, her creamy legs went clear to her chin in those khaki shorts and her figure was outlined mighty fine in her dark pink tank top. She'd pulled her hair back at the nape of her neck and loose strands of red-gold waffled in the breeze. The long line of her neck was elegant and graceful, and he wanted his lips on it bad.

Mostly he just wanted her bad. Period.

Yesterday after the game, he and the guys had grabbed a few beers at a club in LoDo that Mark owned. While the talk had revolved mostly around the game, there'd come a point when the conversation had turned to women. More specifically, Sonny. The guys had been full of suggestions on how to win her over. Most of them he'd ruled out as plain dumb, but there'd been one that he'd taken to heart.

It'd come from Mark's sister, Leslie. She ran the club and had taken a break, sitting at the long table with the players. Although she was dating fielder John Crispin, JP had started to suspect that she had an interest somewhere else. It was hard not to notice how often she stole glances at Peter when she was sitting directly across from him. That's probably the only reason he noticed though, because Leslie was a cool one. Not much showed on her surface.

But she had a razor-sharp intelligence that he respected. So when she'd told him that Sonny was most likely feeling overwhelmed and needed time to get used to him being around, he'd listened. Women like Sonny, who'd been burned and left with a bagful of responsibility, were cautious and needed to be coaxed gently. They needed time to trust and see that it wasn't misplaced.

He figured he could do that. But that didn't mean he wasn't going to push through her resistance. And it sure didn't mean he wasn't going to be kissing her again. It simply meant that he'd have to let her think it was her idea.

Which shouldn't be too hard, considering the way she'd gone boneless on him yesterday. It'd taken no coaxing at all to get her to kiss him back, so it shouldn't be too hard to get her to do it first.

And there was no time like the present to get the ball rolling.

As he strode across the grass toward her, he saw her friend elbow her in the side and whisper, making him smile. The little girl on her hip hadn't stopped staring at him since he'd arrived. Since he had a bunch of nieces and nephews and was used to it, her open curiosity didn't bug him. Besides, he liked kids. They had an honesty about them that was refreshing.

He liked Sonny too. Not just in a sexual way, either. But in a friendship, enjoyed-talking-to-her-and-making-her-laugh sort of way. His parents were still the best of friends, so he figured maybe he was on the right track to finding what they had by the way he was feeling.

Before Sonny, there hadn't been many women that he'd really clicked with. And that had led him to be picky, which wasn't a bad thing. It did mean, though, that he dated less than people thought he did. He'd rather be alone than waste time in a relationship that didn't satisfy on all the levels.

Sonny now, she satisfied.

As he approached, an image of his parents flashed across his brain. In the warm months they spent the evenings together on the front porch, sipping tea and talking through the day's events as the sun went down. There was such an easy intimacy between them. Some day he wanted that for himself—and he wasn't ashamed to admit it.

JP was probably the only twenty-six-year-old guy on earth who didn't just think with the junk in his pants.

But he thought of his parents, his siblings and their partners, and he understood that relationships were more than sex. Oh, it was a big part of them and he wanted it with Sonny in the worst way. No doubt about that.

But he also wanted something real.

That's probably part of the reason why he was so attracted to Sonny. Everything about her was real.

And that's why he was there at her place, planning on buying milk that he didn't need so that she'd get used to him being around. He'd even contemplated a dairy allergy as his excuse, but decided against it. Lying to her didn't seem right.

Instead, he was going to stick with the premise that her milk might be better on his body, and since he was a jock, his body being in peak performance was essential. All of that was true. But it didn't mean he was actually going to drink the stuff. Goat milk had a funky taste.

That was the part he was going to omit.

He reached the women and stopped, giving them a grin. "Hey." Taking off his shades, he stretched out a hand toward Sonny's friend. "I'm JP."

She fumbled a little with the toddler until a hand was free and smiled wide. "Nice to meet you. I'm Janie, and this is Kelly."

JP saw the girl stare shyly at him while her head rested on her mom's shoulder. "Cute kid."

"Thanks."

He watched as Janie turned to Sonny and said, "I've got to run, lady. Thanks again for the tray. I'll call you tomorrow and give you the rundown on how things went."

With that she grabbed a silver tray from Sonny and she and the toddler hustled off, leaving JP all alone with his dream woman.

He thought of something. "Where's Charlie?"

Sonny stared at Janie's retreating back over his shoulder, her expression a little desperate. "He's at a play date with his best friend Sam."

Meaning: they were completely and utterly alone.

A big part of him—the part with a case of the hot and horny, according to Drake—wanted to take advantage of the alone time to press her. But he wasn't ruled by his dick, and he had a few brain cells, so he threw that idea out the window real quick.

Hoping to put her at ease, he hooked his thumbs in the front pocket of his jeans and said, "How's that work with his diabetes?" He actually did want to know.

She probably didn't even realize it, but her eyes dropped to where his thumbs were—right smack on the front of his pants. On second thought, the way color rushed to her face, he'd have to guess that she did know it. And he liked that she knew it. It meant that Sonny wasn't immune to him.

Quickly averting her gaze, she cleared her throat and replied, "It's not a big deal. Cheryl, Sam's mom, knows how to handle his shots and how to check his blood sugar. But really, Charlie's super responsible with it. I think the fear of what could happen to him if he doesn't take care of himself scares the pee out of him. Because of that he's incredibly vigilant. It's been months since I've even had to nag him to check his glucose before it was time to eat."

JP was impressed. "That's sounds awful grown-up for a ten year old."

Talking about her son put a smile on her face and softened her features. Sonny really was a beautiful woman. "Tell me about it. Now if I can only get him to empty his pockets before he throws his pants in the wash."

Half the time JP forgot to do that too. "Good luck with that one, sunshine. Us guys love to forget that we shoved a ton of crap in them."

"I'm sure. He's going to be bummed he missed you, by the way. But he'll see you tomorrow at the game." She gestured over her shoulder at the small brick building behind her. "The milk is in my workspace here."

Her workspace had some sort of dark purple flower growing all over it. If he was a chick he'd have thought it was beautiful and gone on about the aesthetics of it. Since he was a guy he settled for "nice."

His mom, the gardening guru, would be sadly disappointed at his lack of botanical knowledge. She'd tried to teach him, but it hadn't stuck. He could, however, tell the difference between a zucchini and a squash, so that was something.

JP followed her inside and let out a soft whistle. It was a pretty slick setup she had, and the décor was fun and simple. He knocked into an oversized wooden giraffe by the door and a grey hat fell to the floor. While bending down to pick it up he scoped a look at Sonny's ass and felt the warmth of arousal start to heat his blood. The woman had about the shapeliest butt he'd ever had the pleasure of seeing.

Straightening, he placed the mobster-style hat back on the giraffe and tilted it over one eye for effect. Give the thing a zoot suit and Thompson machine gun and it had a real chance at showbiz. He said as much to Sonny and she laughed.

Her laughter was infectious and he was so damn proud of himself for making her do it that he found himself grinning back at her like a fool. He would prostrate himself on the altar of her dignity anytime if it made her do that again. Hell, he'd dress up in a zoot suit himself, because when she laughed the whole world seemed lighter.

JP LOOKED AWFULLY proud of himself, Sonny thought as she pulled some fresh milk from the fridge. Still grinning over his comment, she handed him the old-fashioned glass jug. "This is from early this morning. I'm actually not supposed to sell raw unpasteurized goat milk for human consumption per FDA regulations, and my license doesn't include it, so you can just have it."

He reached out and took the jug, his fingertips brushing against her hand and leaving a trail of tingling nerves in their wake. His brows pulled low and he seemed uncertain. "Are you sure?"

Absolutely. Some rules she just didn't break. "Yep. It's all yours."

"Thanks."

His eyes locked on hers, the gorgeous warm honey of them making her knees weak. That single-minded focus of his was as disconcerting as it was intoxicating. And it made her wonder what it would be like to have that focus on her in another way. A naked way. He had the kind of bedroom eyes that promised heaven could be found with him, should she be tempted. It ought to be illegal for a man to possess eyes like his.

Against her better judgment, Sonny discovered she *was* tempted. Heat pooled low in her belly and she could feel herself getting wet. It'd been so long for her that she'd almost been swept away by the sensation before she'd recognized it. And when her gaze dropped to his mouth, she heard his deep intake of breath and quickly looked away.

What was she doing being tempted by JP? She blamed Janie for this. Her best friend's words echoed in her head. *Kissing. You should be doing a whole lotta kissing.* The not-so-subliminal message was playing in her head like a song stuck on repeat.

Suddenly the room closed in and his large, toned frame took up the entire space. All she could see were broad shoulders, sculpted arms, hard pecs, and flat abs. She was afraid to look any lower. The way she was feeling right now, if she saw that he had an erection she might be inclined to do something with it.

And that would be about as stupid as dirt, because he was off limits. Besides, everybody and their dog knew that she was an idiot when it came to men. As soon as she'd been naked with one, all her issues and insecurities rose to the surface and she became all kinds of dysfunctional crazy—pushing them away and creating roadblock after roadblock.

Which was why she hadn't been with a man in over five years. Charlie had been just a preschooler the one and only time she'd ventured into relationship territory. She'd thought it was love and he'd proved different. The end result had been so bad that she'd swore it would never happen again.

Because truth was she couldn't be trusted.

All the therapy in Colorado wouldn't change that fact. Some things were just in people's natures. Being relationship-challenged was in hers.

Good thing for her that JP was a famous celebrity. Just the thought was sobering.

With that reminder, Sonny released a slow breath and took a step back. The air had gone hot and stuffy, and she suddenly needed to be outside in the fresh breeze. She needed some space, period. Being around JP made her brain stop functioning and her hormones take over.

Leaving him standing in the middle of her work kitchen, Sonny strode outside and inhaled deep. Damn her libido. Why did it have to crop up at this moment? The first time she'd noticed it had been at the charity event when she'd caught sight of JP. Before that, it'd been mostly nonexistent. What was it about the shortstop that brought it roaring to life?

And why now?

Lost in her thoughts, she didn't notice he'd joined her outside until he spoke quietly, startling her. "Everything okay, Sonny?"

Not at all. "Yep. Just peachy. Why do you ask?"

He seemed to settle in comfortably next to her, his

arms crossed casually and his feet spread. She was tall, but he had a full head on her. He'd put his glasses back on and had taken a page from her book, staring out over her property.

"You hightailed it out of there like your ass was on fire, that's why."

Oh. "It was hot in there."

Humor warmed his deep voice. "True that."

He didn't push her and they stood together companionably in silence. And it felt surprisingly good and comfortable. Like maybe they were becoming friends.

And if they were becoming friends then JP deserved some honesty. "I'm shit at relationships."

He just kept on staring at her yard. "Is that a fact?"

Why didn't her admission bug him? He acted like she'd said the sky was blue. "I mean it, JP. Charlie is the only relationship in my life that I haven't fucked up in some way or another." And it pained her to admit it.

She'd half expected him to cut bait and run at that—maybe even half hoped he would—so she was taken aback by what he did next. He leaned down until his mouth was level with her ear. Sonny stilled, her breath caught in her chest as she waited for his move, anticipation racing under her skin.

It didn't take long.

Light and sweet as whipped frosting, he kissed the hair above her ear and whispered, "Lucky for us, I don't scare easily."

Chapter Eight

FOR THE NEXT week, JP made excuse after excuse to drop by Sonny's place to see her. And after he'd returned from an away trip to St. Louis and swung by again, his fridge was so full of cheese rounds and milk that there was barely any room left in it for a six-pack of beer.

His strategy was working though. Each time he was around her he kept everything easy and low-key, and Sonny was loosening up degree by degree. The last time she'd even nearly kissed him. Charlie walking into the room with a friend had stopped her though.

It was about time, too, because he was running out of excuses. There were only so many scenarios he could come up with that sounded plausible for why he'd needed to buy goat cheese. And he still had to figure out what to do with all the milk before it went bad. Probably Drake would take it if he offered. That dude drank more milk than anybody he'd ever seen. Said it was for his growing bones.

Or his neighbor's cat probably wouldn't protest over being given it, either. It might be a way to actually get the feline to shut up. His condo shared a bedroom wall with the neighbor's place and for hours on end that damn cat yowled like it was being tortured. He'd knocked once to talk to the owner about keeping it down, but had been told by a woman watching the place that the neighbor and the feline who owned her were off at a cat show.

Which just figured, right? Crazy *Best in Show* people. Apparently the cat yowled so much because she was a pedigree Siamese and hadn't been fixed for show purposes. JP had pleaded with the owner the next time he'd run into her to just let the frigging cat get knocked up so that he could have some peace and quiet. Nobody liked a cranky pussy.

He got the door slammed in his face for saying that one. And now it was time for JP to find a new place to live. Because if he had to listen to a sexually frustrated Siamese caterwaul for much longer in the middle of the night he was going to hurt somebody.

"Hey, Trudeau. Get your head out of the clouds. We've got a game about to start."

The bark of the team manager's voice snapped him out of his musings and he blinked, trying to tune back into the world around him. See? No sleep made him slow and unfocused.

Fucking cat.

Grabbing his baseball mitt from the dugout bench, JP wrenched his hat down tight and took to the field. On his way he saw Charlie decked out in his Rush jersey. The kid was collecting balls along the third base line and had the biggest smile on his face. Pulling strings to get the kid the job had been the right thing to do. He acted like every game was Christmas.

As JP passed, he cuffed the kid's shoulder good-naturedly and said, "Keep up the good work, slugger."

Charlie beamed up at him. "Being a batboy rocks!"

Yeah, he'd made the right call alright.

Taking position between second and third, JP shoved his head in the game with effort. They were about to take on the Padres, and he needed his wits about him. San Diego had a hitter who was famous for line drives to left field, and he was third to bat on the roster. JP'd been up against him before and knew he had to get focused; otherwise he should just hand the guy a bunch of RBIs and call it a day.

A clear head for split decisions was a shortstop's necessity. It was one of those positions that required complete confidence and instant decision-making ability. JP had to be able to read and play the field in an instant.

Thinking about pussies of any kind would only get him screwed—and not the fun kind, either.

With even more effort, he forced any extraneous thoughts from his mind. Music pumped from the speakers and the fans revved up as Kowalskin took to the pitcher's mound. It shouldn't surprise anyone that Pete had chosen "I'm Sexy and I Know It" by LMFAO for his walkout song. For a while it'd been that song by Notorious B.I.G., "Big Papa." Before that it had been AC/DC's "Back in Black." It was like he had musical ADHD.

JP liked his own walkout song: "The Way You Move" by Outkast. He'd used it since the minors and it had served him well. So well, in fact, that he'd become superstitious about changing it, afraid if he did he'd get jinxed.

Some things were better off being left alone.

As he dug his cleats into the dirt a Padre stepped into the batter's box and readied for the first pitch. It came in a blur of rocket speed and the crowd cheered the strike with barely contained enthusiasm. Pete's arm was on fire this season.

Gaining an easy first out, the Rush got set for the next hitter. After a foul ball, the San Diego player connected and sent the ball toward short. JP shuffled and read the ball, knowing it would drop and fall without a bounce just past the infield green. Anticipating it, JP darted forward and flipped out his glove. He snagged the ball by the tip of his mitt and was already reaching for it with his throwing hand.

Seeing the player dash toward first base at top speed, JP zeroed in on the front of Drake's jersey and sent the ball flying. Stretching out, one foot still on base, the veteran first baseman caught the ball and earned the Rush their second out of the first inning.

The roar of the crowd helped pump adrenaline through him. Playing ball in the majors was a dream come true. And having so many fans turn out to support the Rush was incredible. Sometimes the noise was so loud he couldn't hear the umps making calls.

It was the greatest game on earth and he got to be a part of it.

By the time the bottom of the ninth had come around, the Padres and Rush were tied and his team had home field advantage. Knowing that they had one last chance to score, JP headed out to bat, intent on bringing outfielder Carl Brexler home for the win.

Swinging the bat in a circle to loosen his shoulder, JP resettled his helmet and stepped up to the plate. Reconsidering, he stepped out of the box with a hand held up, halting play. Charlie was standing in the dugout by the steps, eyes locked on the game. When he saw JP looking at him, the kid grinned and gave him two excited thumbs up. For some reason the boy's sign of encouragement made his chest feel a little warm and tight.

Shaking it off, JP pointed at the kid and tipped his head to him. Then he stepped back into the box and pulled the bat, cocked and ready for action. The Padres pitcher wound up and sent it flying. Following the ball with eagle eyes, JP held until the last minute and then he swung, connecting hard with the white leather.

As soon as he felt the bat vibrate he dropped it and took off at full speed toward first. The ball cleared second base and dropped dead in the outfield, barely rolling once it hit the ground. San Diego's center fielder scooped it up, but it was too late. JP had made it to first and Brexler had crossed home safely for the win.

The Rush won 5-4.

Back in the locker room the boys were in high spirits. They were having one of those seasons where everything was clicking, and they were well on their way to the playoffs. Arriving at his designated space, JP reached into his locker and stiffened when he received a hard smack on the ass.

Looking over his shoulder to find Peter there, he relaxed and joked, "Please sir, may I have another?" *Animal House,* with John Belushi, was one of his dad's favorite films.

Laughing, Pete retorted, "Only if you're good, pretty boy."

Before he could respond to that, Mark garnered his attention. He tossed a sweat-soaked towel at JP and said, "The fiancé wants to have pizza and beer at our place and watch the recap on ESPN. You in?"

JP hooked his thumb at Pete. "Only if he's gonna be there to do that again." He winked at the pitcher. "I liked it."

Drake snorted nearby and stated, "You need to get laid, boy."

Amen to that. "I'm working on it, hoss."

The player scratched the thick patch of curly, brown chest hair and shook his head. "How's a guy as pretty as you have such a hard time getting a woman in the sack?"

Because he chose women with standards. "I don't see any problem."

Drake made a *tsk-tsk* sound and shot him a look full of mock pity. "Do I need to sit you down and give you a tutorial, brother?"

"You got any pop-up books?"

"Nah, but I got a shit ton of movies."

Wasn't that the truth. Drake's porn collection was legendary.

Cutter interjected while he took off his shin guards, "Bring your lady friend and her kid. This thing's a family event."

Pete dropped his pants and wrapped a towel around his waist. "Man, I'm still amazed you landed somebody as awesome as Lorelei. You let her know that I'm available when she gets tired of you, all right?"

"She gets tired out every night, bro," Mark said, and he looked damn happy about it.

Out of the corner of his eye, JP saw Charlie enter the locker room, his hands full of equipment. The kid was in the wrong place, but JP thought it was a good opportunity to talk to him about going to Mark's. "Hey, slugger."

Charlie looked over the pile in his arms. "Where's this stuff go?"

Drake answered, "In the equipment room down the hall, little big man. Want me to take you?"

The veteran stepped toward Charlie and JP cut him off. "I'll take him."

Leading the way, they dropped the stuff in the room. Charlie kept up a monologue the whole way, eager to share his version of the day's game. All the chattering kind of made his eyes cross, but JP hung in there, knowing that the boy would run out of steam eventually.

When Charlie finally stopped for air, JP spoke up. "So hey, some of the guys are heading to Cutter's place for pizza and to watch the recap on the sports channel. I don't suppose you'd want to tag along, would you?"

Charlie stopped dead in his cleats. "Are you serious? That'd be awesome!"

JP looked down at the kid. "Yeah?"

"Totally!" The boy pumped his fist.

Sweet. "You think your mom will be up for it?"

Charlie wrinkled his nose as he considered. "I think so. I mean, it's not Saturday or anything."

That's right. He'd forgotten about her weird Saturday phobia. "Cool. I need to shower and change. Why don't you find your mom and ask her while I'm cleaning up?" He had dirt smeared across his face and the front of his jersey from a slide into second. He'd dug hard and still had some sandy grains in his mouth.

The kid's blue eyes were full of earnestness. "Okay." He took a step and stopped, turning back to JP. Suddenly looking shy, Charlie asked, "If she says yes, do you think I could ride with you?"

That same warm and tight feeling from earlier settled in his chest again as he took in the boy's hopeful expression. How could he turn that down? "Of course. But your mom's got to say you can, all right?"

Charlie nodded vigorously. "Okay."

JP tapped the brim of the boy's ball cap, lowering it over his eyes. "Go find your mom and I'll meet you two outside the locker room in fifteen minutes."

Pushing the bill back up, Charlie grinned big, already inching down the hall. "You got it!"

Watching his back for a minute before it disappeared, JP thought about the boy. He really was a good kid. Eager and bright and curious. To be honest, he kind of reminded JP of himself as a kid. There was a lot there he could relate to.

Because of that it made him think about how much he'd needed his dad when he was Charlie's age. How he'd looked to his dad for guidance, direction, and encouragement. Though John Trudeau wasn't perfect by any means, he was hands down the greatest man he knew. He'd taught JP what it meant to be a man.

Who was going to teach Charlie?

Sonny was a terrific mom. That much was clearly evident. But there were some things a boy needed to know that only a man could show him. Things about how to be in the world and how to relate to those around him.

The boy should know these things, JP thought as he re-entered the locker room. Pushing his musings aside, he made quick work of a shower and dressed in near record time. He was clean and ready in under ten minutes. He ran into Pete at the door. The pitcher had his duffle, too, and was carrying a motorcycle helmet. A few months back he'd bought a Ducati and now he rode the thing everywhere. Said it was the next best thing to flying.

"You heading over to Cutter's place too?" JP asked as they passed through the door into the hall.

The pitcher nodded, his pale blue eyes full of humor. "You know it. I wouldn't miss an opportunity to see our boy pussyfoot around his sweet little fiancée."

Yeah, that was going to be fun.

Catching sight of Sonny down the hall, Pete whistled softly. "Damn, dude. That's one fine looking woman you're after."

JP glanced down to where she was standing, looking gorgeous and casual in a little yellow tank top, ripped jeans and flip-flops. She had a few hemp bracelets on her wrists and her hair was down. He knew how soft it felt and his fingertips tingled at the memory.

When she waved at them, his chest started to get all tight again. He was starting to think that maybe he had an affliction or something, and wondered briefly if he should have it checked out.

Charlie came running up to him. "Mom says I can go with you."

Pete shot JP a look. "You're giving the kid a ride?"

He shot one right back. "Got an issue with that?"

Kowalskin shook his head. "None. It just surprised me is all, taking it up a notch like that."

Charlie looked from JP to Peter and back. "What are you guys talking about?"

JP placed a hand on the boy's shoulder and squeezed gently. "Responsibility. Chauffeuring you around town is a big deal." He gave Charlie an easy smile.

"Oh. Well, before you can do that you gots to give my mom directions."

Peter chuckled and slapped JP on the back. "See you there, Mr. Belvedere."

Charlie wrinkled his nose, confused. "Who's Mr. Belvedere?"

JP glanced at Pete's retreating form. "Beats me, kid."

But whoever it was, he was sure it wasn't a compliment.

Chapter Nine

SONNY ACCEPTED THE beer JP held out to her and watched the commotion behind him. When they had arrived at Mark Cutter's place they'd found some of the players deep in a card game. Apparently there had been some kind of bet and the player with the worst hand was saddled with the consequence of breakdancing on the hardwood floor for everyone's amusement.

Pitcher Peter Kowalskin had lost and was currently shoving furniture out of the way to clear a spot. The catcher's condo was huge, but she guessed that Peter needed more space to properly execute his moves. She watched the dark-haired player push a leather couch flush against the wall while Drake Paulson egged him on.

Taking a pull of the yeasty New Belgium microbrew, Sonny pointed the bottle at the pitcher and asked JP, "Is this sort of thing normal for you guys?"

He stood next to her, his butt leaning against a table

and his long, hard legs crossed at the ankles. "Yeah. The guys do stuff like this all the time."

And here she'd thought ballplayers were sophisticated and refined.

Stealing a peek at him, she replied, "What about you?"

He grinned down at her, his brown eyes dancing. "Nah. I'm more composed and mature than that."

Right. "Uh-huh." She wasn't buying that for a minute.

JP rubbed his chin, the other hand holding the beer bottle loosely on his thigh. "Well, there was that time a few weeks back after we won the Phillies game."

"And . . .? What happened?"

A drop of beer shimmered on his bottom lip and he wiped it with a thumb, making her breath catch in her throat. The guy had a terrific pair of lips—firm and full and well-sculpted. And he knew how to use them. Boy did he ever.

No wonder the media adored him.

Forcing herself to look away, Sonny waited for his response. Hormones awakened from their slumber, causing her blood to warm, and she tried hard to push them aside. JP did all kinds of crazy things to her libido, and after it being on hiatus for half a decade she was a little afraid she might blow a fuse or something.

"The guys wanted to celebrate the win and I'd made clutch plays that game, so they decided I was the guest of honor. I downed way too many pitchers of beer and busted my nuts on the mechanical bull at the bar. Jacobs over there got me back to the hotel and I passed out with a giant bag of ice on my balls. The next morning I woke up with a mild case of frostbite and couldn't walk right for over a week. Wearing a cup was torture."

Her eyes went huge and she choked on her beer. "Are you serious?"

The look he gave her was almost comical in its embarrassment. "Sadly, yes."

"And here I was thinking that you were impressively mature for your age." Myth successfully dispelled.

JP slid a look at her and she got sidetracked by his thick black lashes. "You know the truth just makes you want me more."

A laugh rose in her chest and let loose. "Oh, for sure."

They grinned at each other. Then JP's gaze dropped to her mouth and his head began to lower, causing her heart beat to speed up. The spark of amusement in his eyes melted as the heat turned up, and they went dark like burnt whiskey.

Charlie chose that moment to appear and Sonny jerked away from the shortstop. Funny, but she felt out of breath. "What's up, kiddo?"

Her son waggled his thumb at another boy standing next to him. They looked about the same age. "Me and Ryan want to play his 3DS. He's got a Pokemon game and Mark said we could use the guest room. Is that okay?"

She didn't see why not. "Of course. Just make sure if you two create a mess, you clean it up."

Charlie nodded and waved up at JP. "See ya." And the boys took off, already the best of friends.

"What the hell are Pokemon?" JP asked. "I've been meaning to ask him."

Sonny shook her head. "Don't. I did once and Charlie went on so long about them that my brain cramped."

The shortstop smirked. "I noticed he likes to talk."

That was an understatement. "I love my son, but he can make your ears numb from yapping so much."

Another drop of beer clung to his lip and this time he licked it off, his expression suddenly serious. "Charlie mentioned on the ride over that you're thirty-one. Does my age bother you?"

That gave her pause. "Honestly? It does some, yes. I know it's only five years, but it feels bigger than that. Maybe it's because we're at such different places in our lives."

JP seemed to consider that and his eyelids lowered, shielding his eyes. "Not so different, Sonny."

Her gaze lifted to his face, surprised. "You don't think?" From where she was standing there was a whole world between them.

"Sometimes things look different on the outside that aren't. But you have to peel back the layers to see the similarities."

"Why aren't you like the typical twenty-something guy, JP?" she demanded to know with equal parts exasperation and frustration. It'd been a question she'd chewed on for a few weeks now.

"Because I'm special." He answered through a crooked grin.

She couldn't help smiling back. "For real, though. Sometimes I worry that you're just too young and naïve to know better than to go sniffing around a single mom my age."

The look he was giving her went instantly dark and hot. "Do I look naïve, Sonny?"

Not in the least. "I just can't wrap my head around why you're interested in me." She gestured with a hand at the other ballplayers. "You're a young, hot, professional athlete."

JP stared hard at her for a few moments. Instead of answering, he said, "I have a terrific family. I'm one of six kids. Did you know that?" She shook her head and he continued. "We're all really close, even though I live here and they're all still in Iowa. My youngest sister Sadie is sixteen and after she was born the doctors discovered my mom had cervical cancer. I was about Charlie's age when she went through surgery and chemo. She almost died and it was scary as hell. But we stuck together with support and love and a lot of sacrifice to get her through."

Compassion filled her. "That must have been tough."

He nodded. "It was. But I saw the way my dad held steady like a rock for her and us kids. He did it because there was nothing more important or better out there than his family."

"I get what you're saying." At least she thought she did. "But you don't have a wife and kids. You're good looking, smart, and you've got a whole career ahead of you. You can have whatever you want."

JP straightened from the table and gave her a look full of unreadable emotions. "Peel the layers, Sonny." And then he walked away, leaving her standing there in stunned silence.

Though she hadn't meant to, she could tell that she'd

upset him. What was it with the shortstop? Try as she might, she just couldn't get a handle on him. She'd thought he would be glad that she was letting him off the hook so easily. A little flirting, a few kisses—but it didn't have to be anything more. If she were a young single guy like him she wouldn't choose somebody like her. It was too much work. Too much baggage and preexisting conditions.

Or maybe that's what she was telling herself to keep a wall between them.

Thinking that she should apologize, Sonny set her beer bottle down and was about to set off in search of JP when she was stopped by her hostess, Lorelei Littleton. They'd met when she'd first arrived, but there'd been so much going on that there hadn't been much opportunity to chat. It seemed that the pretty brunette had found some time.

The catcher's fiancée settled beside her and gave her a friendly smile. "Sorry it's taken so long to get a chance to talk. Team get-togethers like this can get hectic." She pointed to where the pitcher had taken center stage in the living room. "As evidenced by what we are about to see here."

Following Lorelei's gaze, she bit back a laugh as Peter held his hands out at his sides and prepared to bust a move. He'd turned his ball cap backward and rolled up the sleeves of his plain white T-shirt. A tattoo showed briefly on the inside of his right bicep and he had on Vans or Skechers or something. They were some kind of skater shoe.

Sonny thought of something. "Is Peter from Philadelphia?"

Lorelei looked at her with curiosity, "What makes you ask that?"

She tilted her head to the side and studied the pitcher. "He kind of has that G. Love-East Coast-Philly vibe."

Lorelei tipped her head to the side, too, and considered. "You know, I think you're right." Straightening, she called out to the player, "Hey, Kowalskin! Are you from Philly?"

Peter tossed her a lopsided grin full of a whole lot of naughty and broke out a breakdance move. "You know it, sweetness."

At that moment a gorgeous woman stepped up beside Lorelei and gave her an air kiss on the cheek. The blonde was absolutely stunning with her sleek shoulder-length bob, floral-print halter sundress, and heeled espadrilles. Her nails were poppy red and her makeup was flawless. "Hey, y'all. Sorry I'm late." Belatedly she noticed the rearranged furniture. "What do we have going on here?"

Lorelei made introductions. "Sonny, this is Mark's sister, Leslie." She turned to the other woman. "Sonny's boy Charlie is filling in for one of the regular batboys."

Leslie's smile was all Southern charm and hospitality. "Nice to meet you. *Love* your hair."

Happy for the compliment, Sonny replied, "I was just thinking the same about yours." It was the perfect shade of cool blonde. Probably cost a small fortune to maintain, too.

Music cut through the noise and someone let out an ear-piercing whistle. That brought Leslie back around, asking, "What are the guys up to?"

Lorelei leaned toward Sonny to give Leslie a better view through the crowd. "Peter's about to entertain us all with some breakdancing."

Leslie gave them a slightly exasperated look. "Did he lose a bet, y'all?"

Both Sonny and Lorelei nodded and said simultaneously, "Yep."

The toned and curvy blonde sighed and rolled her eyes. "It never ends with that man, does it?"

Lorelei laughed and put her hand on the table for support. "Nope, and that's what makes him fun."

"Y'all know that he probably lost the bet on purpose just so that he could show off, right?" Though Mark's sister shook her head disapprovingly, there was something in the way her eyes watched the pitcher that didn't square with the verbalized annoyance. It was noticeable enough to catch Sonny's attention, but then Peter started dancing and it streaked right out of her head like it'd never been there in the first place.

She couldn't believe what she was seeing.

Instead of being some sort of comedy routine like she'd expected, the lean and lanky ballplayer was good. Really, really good. He moved like he was born doing it.

The crowd cheered him on and when he dropped to the floor and curled into a spin, the noise level rose even louder. It was like *Dance Party USA* up in there.

Peter ended the routine by kicking his feet out and flipping up onto them. The guy barely seemed out of breath by the vigorous dancing. It brought home to Sonny just how incredibly fit professional ballplayers had to be. And by the nimble way that the pitcher moved, she wondered if he wasn't one of those players who'd taken ballet lessons for balance too.

Everyone clapped and shouted their approval as Peter melted back into the masses, straightening his hat as he went. Some player's kid held out a hand and he high-fived him on his way to the balcony.

Lorelei spoke up, and Sonny tuned back in to the women next to her. "Am I the only one who noticed Peter's shirt rode up a lot while he did that?"

Leslie shook her head. "No. We all saw it too."

Lorelei looked from Sonny to Leslie and back. Then she grinned like she was sharing a deliciously wicked secret. "His abs weren't bad."

Not bad at all. If one liked them ripped and tight and flat as a pancake with a jet-black happy trail.

The blonde made a noncommittal sound in her throat. "They're all right."

Obviously she had eyesight problems.

Mark appeared in front of them, his hands loaded with plates of food. While Peter had been giving them a show, the pizza had arrived. The catcher had made up a plate for his fiancée and offered it to her. "Is this enough, baby?"

Sonny watched Lorelei place a hand on his cheek as she greeted him with a kiss, her huge diamond ring sparkling under the lights. "Thanks, hon. If I want more I know where to find it."

Cutter grinned at her, his gray eyes full of love for his woman. "Anything for you." He stole another kiss and then headed off to join the rest of his boys.

Watching the interplay between the two of them made Sonny intensely aware that she'd never had that before. That kind of love and adoration and caring. And she didn't mean just in the past ten years. She meant *ever*.

It made her more than just a bit uncomfortable to realize that not once in her whole life had she been loved like that by anyone. Other than Charlie. But no one else. Not her mother or her father or her grandmother. Most especially not Charlie's dad.

How sad was that?

Catching sight of JP across the room, Sonny let her gaze roam over the shortstop. What was he doing with her? Did he really want to see if they had that connection between them? The way he'd talked earlier made it sound like he wasn't just after her for sex or some casual fling.

Just the opposite, in fact. He had sounded like he wanted something more along the lines of what Mark and Lorelei had. If that was so, how did she feel about it? Maybe more importantly, was she willing to do anything about it? Even knowing that it most probably—well, most definitely, given her history—would end in the worst kind of train wreck? Should she risk it just on the tiniest, slightest fraction of a chance that maybe it actually wouldn't end in disaster? Because even if it did there was still her need for privacy.

Three weeks ago she would have said, "No way." One week ago she would have said, "Fat chance."

But now? Now she wasn't completely certain.

Chapter Ten

JP LEANED AGAINST the wall and crossed his arms over his chest. Across the room he could see Sonny. She was talking to Mark's lady and laughing easily, the slender line of her throat exposed when she tilted her head back. He had a big urge to kiss the milky skin and took another swig of beer.

It wasn't going to happen, though, because the next move was up to her. He'd said his part. It had to be her that took the next step. That way she knew she was in control of her own decision.

It might just kill him waiting, but his gut told him that Sonny was worth it.

After he'd walked away from her, he'd watched her from a distance to gauge how she felt around his crew. Ball teams were tight knit and he wanted to see her reaction to it. By the way she was laughing and had her head together with Lorelei it seemed a fair guess to say that she liked it fine.

Cutter showed up beside him, a pile of pizza and beer in hand. "The fiancée seems smitten with your new lady."

Yeah, he'd noticed. "I see that."

The catcher set his plate on the bookcase beside him. "It can only mean that she's all right, brother, if Lorelei likes her. So, well done. You thinking about keeping her?"

"I was planning on it." He just had to convince her first. Lucky for her he was a patient guy, because with Sonny it might take a while. He settled his mind around the realization that he was in for a game of long ball and took another pull from the bottle. It might not be so bad, he tried to convince himself.

Sonny burst out laughing and the sound carried across the large room to JP. His body reacted and he grew hard and achy for her. Casually as he could, he shifted to give more play at the front of his jeans and took a long drink of chilled brew to cool his ardor.

Yeah, waiting might just kill him, all right.

But when he looked at Sonny and her smile lit the night sky and warmed his chest, he didn't mind so much. All that mattered was that they got there eventually.

And when they finally got there, he was going to take his slow, sweet time with her.

At that moment she looked up and their gazes connected, the distance across the room vanishing in an instant. Energy traveled down his body and set his nerves tingling awake. With his eyes locked on hers JP lifted his beer bottle and took a slow, deliberate drink, his gaze never straying.

He could see clearly the ways the two of them would fit

together. Sonny was the first woman he'd been interested in that he could say that about. And he figured that was a good thing. Because at the end of the day he wanted a partner he could sit on the porch with while the sun went down. The fact that she had Charlie didn't make him hesitate. He knew what it meant to date a single mom—what his role could end up being. He figured he had his dad to thank for that, for being such a great father that JP saw it as a positive thing. Not something to shit bricks over. Besides, having helped raise his younger siblings gave him a leg up. It meant he wasn't completely inexperienced.

It never occurred to JP to stop and consider what was happening. Everything was unfolding mostly the way he expected it to, *because* he expected it to. So what if Sonny was scared and overcautious? So what if he let her call the shots about the timing? He knew where it was all going to end up, so what did it matter when? Besides, he felt confident that he was figuring her out, which should only speed the process, right?

JP realized he was still staring and broke eye contact, the front of his jeans still uncomfortably tight. Mark nudged him in the shoulder. "What are your plans for the break?"

By break, he figured Mark meant All-Star week. JP shrugged his shoulders and stole a peek back at Sonny. She was talking to Mark's sister now. "Not sure. But I'm sure something will come up."

The catcher had been voted in to the All-Star Game that the Rush were hosting at Coors Field in just over a week. So had Peter and Drake. His ego wanted to be offended that he hadn't been invited, but his brain triumphed with logic. Those guys had earned their place in the game from years of play. JP, though making big waves in the sport, was still newer to the pros. These sorts of things took a while.

JP raked a hand over his hair and pointed his bottle at Drake. "How much you want to bet that he takes first in the Home Run Derby?" The dude knew how to hit 'em.

The catcher grinned. "Let's make it a bennie, 'cause I think that slugger from the Giants will beat him out."

JP looked at Mark, an eyebrow raised in surprise. "You think Ramirez has the bounce on Paulson?"

The player nodded. "Yeah. I hear he's juicing."

Steroid abuse was a dark cloud over Major League Baseball. Some years back there'd been a huge industry-wide shake-up over it when a few prominent players in the league had been discovered. Barry Bonds was the least of it—though he may have been one of the most outspoken.

So far as JP knew, his team was clean. And he thought he'd know if it were different. But the boys, well, all of them were on the up-and-up. "I still say Drake can take him."

Mark smiled, his gray eyes lit with humor. "You're on, then."

The two of them clinked their beer bottles together to seal the bet. Out of the corner of his eye he saw Sonny look at her phone and then straighten from the table. She excused herself and walked away, and JP assumed she was off in search of Charlie. Checking his own phone for the time, he noted it was getting late. The recap was about to finish. If he was going to catch her before she left he'd better get a move on, though he hoped she wouldn't leave without saying goodbye.

Movement on the big screen caught his eye, and he glanced over. When he saw what was on, he chuckled. Sonny was going to love this.

Catching her eye before she disappeared down the hall, JP tilted his head toward the flat screen and smiled, trying to turn her attention to the TV. She got the message, so he gave the screen his attention and missed her reaction. The news was showing footage of an interview he'd given before the game. Charlie had gotten screen time, too, as he and JP had some fun hamming it up for the camera. The clip ended with his arm slung over the kid's shoulder, his hip cocked, while he relaxed and the reporter interviewed a super excited Charlie.

He glanced back at Sonny just quick enough to glimpse what looked like a frown disappearing from her face before she turned away and said something over her shoulder to Lorelei. It had happened so fast he couldn't be sure. But he couldn't figure why she'd be upset over a little air time for Charlie, and he dismissed it. She'd no doubt enjoyed seeing him on the news. The kid had been thrilled about it.

He left Mark and followed Sonny. He saw her head down a hall and disappear into one of the rooms. Charlie had said he'd be playing Pokemon in one, so he assumed she'd gone to find him. Maybe if he got lucky she'd be all alone when he walked in and they'd get a few minutes together.

On his way he passed Peter and Drake talking shop and cuffed the pitcher on the shoulder. He grinned when the player rolled his shoulder and flipped him the bird. Razzing Pete was always a good time.

Crossing the threshold at the first door, JP found the office space empty. Smirking at a framed poster of Mark on the wall, he turned and headed back out. Sonny must be in the other room. Not that he wouldn't enjoy looking through all of the catcher's trophies and awards, but the woman was what he was most interested in. All of Mark's baseball glory would have to wait.

The door to the second room was closed. JP turned the knob, opening it. Sonny spun around like she'd been caught stealing, surprise plastered across her face.

Her hand flew to her chest and she declared, "You scared the crap out of me!"

A quick scan revealed that they were alone. Charlie and his friend must have vacated the room already. Closing the door gently behind him, JP stepped into the room, his attention centered on the beautiful woman in the middle of the room. "Where's Charlie?"

Sonny waved her hand. "He went with his little friend to snag another slice of pizza." Her eyes narrowed slightly on him. "What are you doing in here?"

JP hooked his thumbs in the front pockets of his jeans and leaned back against the closed door, relaxing. "Looking for you." She kind of floundered at that and he added, amused, "Did you catch the interview?"

He watched her nod and break eye contact. "Charlie looked like he was having a blast."

The tone of her voice had his instincts buzzing and he cocked his head, studying her. "Are you not okay with him being on TV with me? You know we were just having fun, right?"

"I know that." With a hand she brushed her hair over her shoulder, sent him a look full of uncertainty, and changed the subject. "I thought you were mad at me." She sounded kind of put out about the idea of it.

He had been mad. But he'd gotten over it real quick. Although it still grated that she didn't see all the things they shared in common—like their country kid roots, enjoyment of baseball, and loyalty to family. More than that, it irked the hell out of him that she didn't think she was worth him pursuing. Like she had absolutely no concept of her own desirability.

Maybe there were men out there who were too shallow and self-involved to be interested in a woman with a kid. JP wasn't denying that fact. But he wasn't one of them. And he didn't know who Sonny had insulted more with her off-base assumption—him or her.

Only time was going to convince her otherwise, though. And that was okay with him. He was a patient guy. There was a confidence in having her figured out. It gave JP the advantage because he knew what she was going to do. And since he figured he knew what she would do then, he could predict it some and lead her down the road to where he wanted her.

Relaxing against the door, JP replied, "I was mad, but I got over it."

Sadness streaked across her sweet face and then was gone, and she straightened her shoulders. "I didn't mean to upset you earlier. I'm sorry."

He could tell that she was sorry. Her blue eyes got all big and soft, and her hands were held out in supplication. "You made a lot of assumptions, Sonny. In doing so you took away my right to make my own decisions, to see what I see."

She blew out a breath. "I know I did. I apologize."

Without realizing it she'd stepped all over one of his biggest pet peeves: people telling him what he should be thinking or wanting. JP didn't work like most people. He cut his own path, had his own thoughts. He'd never been part of the herd. Didn't Sonny see that about him yet?

Patience, he reminded himself. "No need, sunshine." Her fears were just clouding her vision was all. She'd get the right of it in time. "Once you get to know me better, you'll see that you've been laboring under a misconception."

Staying quiet, she bit her bottom lip and gave him big doe eyes, making his gut tighten. Feeling his muscles tense, JP forced them to relax. He wasn't there to scare her. Sonny had enough fears floating around in that head of hers.

Besides, the next move was hers.

So even though he wanted nothing more than to kiss that bottom lip she loved to chew on so much, he turned his attention to the room they were standing in. It had the added benefit of diffusing the arousal some.

They were in a spare room with a low bed and Asian styling. In the far corner was a pile of empty boxes. Lorelei must already be starting to pack. Which reminded JP that he should talk to Mark about the condo. The catcher had been making noises about finding a new place as soon as possible. Although there was room, Lorelei wasn't much of a city girl and Mark wanted to find her something with some land. And that meant that the condo would be available. No more horny, yowling Siamese.

Tuning back in to Sonny, JP tipped his head to the side and studied her. She seemed agitated about something. Her brow was wrinkled and she was fidgeting. The woman clearly had a bee in her bonnet.

With his gaze on her, JP rolled his shoulders back and waited. It didn't take long. Sonny muttered under her breath and swore. Then she marched right up to him and planted a kiss on his cheek, surprising him. "I don't like that I upset you and I'm sorry."

JP held perfectly still. "You mentioned that already."

She was so close he could smell the scent of her hair. "I know, but I mean it." She cocked her head and looked up at him. "We're becoming friends, right?"

Among other things. "You can say that."

She grimaced and patted his chest absentmindedly with a slender hand. "Friends shouldn't tick friends off."

The way she kept stroking his chest was driving him crazy. "I suppose we could kiss and make up."

Sonny seemed to realize what she was doing and yanked her hand away, blushing. "Then we wouldn't be friends, JP."

"Sure we would." He wanted her hand on him again. "We'd just be the kissing kind."

SONNY COULDN'T BELIEVE that she'd been petting his chest like he was some plush-coated feline. Embarrassed, she glanced up at him through her lashes and found him looking down at her, a small half smile on his lips. His eyes held warmth and an invitation that she was finding exceedingly difficult to refuse. More to the point, she was beginning to have a hard time recalling why she'd needed to refuse him in the first place.

JP made her want to do very naughty, very unwise things. Things like kissing. A whole lotta kissing.

Damn that Janie.

Trying to come up with a witty response, Sonny dropped her gaze to his chest. The palm of her hand still held traces of his body heat and the shape of his pectoral muscle was imprinted in her memory for life. It was hard and hot and just the right amount of built. And for the life of her she couldn't stop her hands from wanting to slide all over him. Seeing the muscular shape of his chest beneath the thin black cotton of his T-shirt scrambled her reasoning skills and pushed her hesitation right on out the window.

It was just a kiss, right?

Just one little, innocent kiss. It didn't have to mean that she'd abandoned all of her convictions about him and his lifestyle or her ideas about staying single and keeping her life complication-free. It simply meant that she was alone in a room with a man who made her want—and she hadn't wanted in such a long time.

JP was a good guy, and kissing was probably just an entertaining way for him to pass the time. Right?

A small voice at the back of her mind told her it was so much more than that, and she knew it. Knew it, but refused to acknowledge it because she really, *really* wanted to kiss the daylights out of the gorgeous shortstop. He tugged at strings that had been laying unused and collecting cobwebs. So why the hell not?

It was just a kiss.

They were standing so close that she could feel his body heat radiating off him. It feathered across her skin and pulled her in, intoxicating her with the feel. It was heady and magnetic, and she wanted to dip her feet in the pool of his sexuality. To dangle her toes in the waters of his arousal and let the slow-moving current caress her, wrap around her, and drown her with sensuality.

Caught in the tide of desire, she reached out and placed her hands on the flat of his stomach, her palms flush against the corrugated muscle. She heard the sharp intake of his breath and it fueled her. Enticed her. Made her forget who she was.

For the moment she wasn't Sonny, single mother haunted by the dismal wreckage of relationships past. She was just a woman standing in front of man who made her feel the rush of sexual awareness.

And she was going to let herself taste it, just this once.

Watching her hands, she slid them over the soft cotton, feeling his body through the fabric. Downward they roamed, lazily exploring the area of his abdomen where his jeans rested low on his waist. His shirt had ridden up and a small strip of golden skin was exposed and she ran a fingertip over it, hypnotized by the velvety hot feel of it.

A gap between the denim and his hip called to her,

and her finger dipped inside. JP made a hissing sound as she explored the ridge of taught muscle that formed a V down to his groin. As her finger dipped lower, she became aware of the heavy ache between her legs. She felt slick and swollen and needy there.

With her head slightly down she couldn't see his expression, but his breath fanned over her ear in short, thready bursts. It was thrilling, this silent and erotic exploration of his body. Though he held perfectly still, Sonny could feel the tension swirling and coiling inside him. Knowing that at any minute he could strike, like a riled viper, only made the moment more delicious.

It was like having a hungry tiger on a breakaway leash.

Sonny had never imagined that it would feel so good— so dangerous—and yet she felt so incredibly powerful. It went straight to her head.

She glided both hands under the hem of his shirt and felt his stomach quiver at her touch. Emboldened, her fingers dipped into the waistband of his jeans again and he jerked, hissing once more yet staying quiet. Sonny smiled over the heady feeling of power and let her fingers slip down a fraction more.

Her eyes went wide at what she encountered. Burning hot and slick with his arousal, the plump head of his penis pushed against her, escaping from the barrier of his briefs. Lost in the moment, Sonny traced the soft, steely ridge of his erection and heard him groan against her ear.

Until that second JP had kept his hands from her. But now they gripped her hips, the restrained strength in them arousing her further. What would it be like to feel those hard hands on her skin? His long, strong fingers inside her?

Lifting her gaze, it slid over his chest, up the length of his throat and over his square chin to his mouth. Going further she came to his eyes and felt a shiver at the emotion she found there. Dark as molasses, JP's eyes were hungry and locked on her mouth.

The moment had come. "Kiss me."

He shook his head, the movements short and jerky. "No."

A frown pulled at her brow. "Why not?" She knew he wanted it. Her fingers stroked the evidence.

His hands tightened on her hips almost painfully. "You're in control of this, Sonny." His voice sounded rough and edgy. "I need you to know that you call the shots."

She slid her fingers down the hard length of him and curled them around the base. "You want me to stop?"

Those hands of his flexed and his fingers curled into her hard enough to bruise. It turned her on. "Hell no. Woman, I want you."

She stroked back up, feeling bold. "Then what's the problem?"

His head fell back against the door and he growled, "You have to know that you did this—that you decided this."

She did know it. The consequences she'd think about later. "Then I've decided you should kiss me."

His dark, stormy gaze searched hers. "Remember you brought this on yourself. I'm not responsible for what's about to happen."

That sounded like a threat. And she liked it. Made her feel wanton and reckless. "Shut up, JP."

"Just trying to be a good guy and do the right thing." His voice sounded strained and tight.

Oh, he was such a great guy. Sonny rose on her tiptoes and whispered against his mouth. "I want this."

He snapped like a wishbone and his mouth was on her before she'd taken another breath. He devoured her with teeth and tongue, feeding her a kiss of unbridled male lust. It made her knees buckle and removed any lingering doubt about JP being a grown man. He pushed against her hands and she whimpered. Everything about him was uncompromisingly adult man.

In one dizzying motion, he spun until her back was against the door and he'd gripped the back of her thighs, pulling them up and around his waist. When her legs were wrapped around his waist he thrust into her, his erection rubbing against the seam of her jeans, creating friction hot enough to start a fire.

She felt like she was on fire.

Streaking her hands over his rock-hard body, Sonny moaned against his lips and dug her nails into his back. JP ripped his mouth from hers and swore. Then he was kissing her neck, teeth nipping at her throat.

When a hand covered her breast and squeezed, she nearly came undone. And when he rolled her nipple between his thumb and finger and pinched, she cried out softly, totally gone with need.

She wanted to be naked. Now.

Sonny was yanking at his shirt when the knock at

the door registered. JP heard it too and growled, "Fuck. Ignore it."

Then he was kissing her again, his tongue rubbing against hers in a way that made her forget everything but him. All she knew was JP and the way he made her feel.

The doorknob rattled. "Mom?" Through the sexual haze Charlie's voice registered. *"Mom?"*

Sonny tore her mouth free and froze. Shit.

JP dropped his head to her shoulder, panting. Then he raised it and stared at her, his expression unreadable. Sonny stared at him helplessly, her body bombarded with sexual need.

The knock sounded again. *"Mom."*

For a few tense moments they stared at each other as reality came crashing back. JP muttered, "Kid's got timing."

No kidding. She could still feel his erection against her crotch. "True that."

JP smiled at her use of his phrase and the tension melted from him. A laugh bubbled in her chest and Sonny let it loose. Then they were both laughing, the awkwardness of the situation diffusing, and something lifted inside Sonny. She felt a lightness that was absolutely freeing.

And it was all because of JP.

Chapter Eleven

THREE DAYS LATER Sonny was hit hard with a cold. It came out of the blue, like summer colds often do. She woke up feeling like hell and looking worse. Such terrible timing too. It was Charlie's last day as batboy, and it was the last game before the All-Star break. Sonny knew that it would crush him to miss out on it.

Rolling out of bed, she promptly flopped back when her head began pounding and her eyes filled up with tears after she sneezed. She began shivering and pulled the comforter over her, even though she was already wearing flannel pants and wool socks. Great, a fever.

Just. Frigging. Lovely.

Scraping together every ounce of energy she hand, Sonny crawled back out of bed and stumbled to the kitchen in search of Echinacea, herbal tea, and ibuprofen. Charlie was in the living room watching some Disney show. He took one look at her and stated, "You look awful, Mom."

Duh.

With a handful of tissue, Sonny waved him off and continued on her way as she blew her nose loudly. Summer colds always put her in a bad mood. Though she shouldn't be surprised that she had come down with one. They always seemed to follow on the heels of allergy season. And for her June was the worst time of the year for allergies, what with everything blooming.

Her head was throbbing and her eyes were watering profusely by the time the tea was ready and she'd downed some ibuprofen. On the upside, her brain hurt too bad to think about what had happened the other night with JP and all the implications that went with it. She'd been avoiding having that conversation with herself for days. Silence might be golden, but denial was even better.

For the moment. Sonny wasn't foolish enough to think she could get away with it for too much longer. But why not relish in the bliss of intentional ignorance while she could?

The day was perfect and cloudless outside the kitchen windows, taunting her. A slight breeze came in through the screen door that led to the porch, flirting shamelessly with the rich, ripe scents of earth and summer. Even through the stuffy—yet paradoxically runny—nose, she could smell all the wonderful scents. Some farmer nearby must have cut their first crop of hay, because the fresh green scent of it made her sneeze. Such a bummer, too, because she normally loved the smell of a recently cut hay field.

Sonny snuggled further into the chenille throw blanket she'd pulled around her shoulders and took a sip of chamomile tea. The honey and lemon she'd added to it pumped up the mild flavor. Grabbing a seat at the kitchen table, she'd just settled in when her phone began to ring.

With a great big sigh she heaved herself back out of the chair and went in search of her cell. Finding it on the counter under a stack of mail, she blew her nose again and picked it up without checking the number.

"This is Sonny."

"You sound like shit."

Of course it would be JP. "Thanks."

She heard rustling and then, "What's wrong with you? You sick?" Genuine concern colored his voice.

No, she was talking that way for the fun of it. "I hab a cold." Sniffle, sniffle.

"That's too bad. Can I do anything?"

How about make it go away? "No."

"Ok. Well, let me know if I can, all right?"

"Yeah."

She thought he was going to hang up, but then he said, "We haven't talked since the other night when things got heated. I wanted to touch base and make sure everything was okay. I'm sorry it's taken me this long to call, but it's been pretty hectic here."

Well, it's not like she'd hurried to contact him. "It's okay." Just the opposite, actually. She'd been hoping they wouldn't have to have this discussion for a long, long time. Like, maybe never.

"Should we talk about it?"

Since when did a guy want to "talk"? "I'b good. We

don't neeb to talk." No way was she opening that can of worms right now.

His quiet laugh was warm and deep. "All right, sunshine. You're off the hook for now. Get some rest. I'll catch up with you later."

"Okay."

She was about to hang up when he hastily added, "Wait. What about the game this afternoon?"

Sonny bit back a sneeze, making her eyes sting and replied, "What do you mean? What about it?"

"I mean, you don't sound like you're going to make it. So will Charlie need a ride?"

She'd been thinking about that situation. "I'b not sure what I'b going to do yet." The sneeze couldn't be held back any longer and it let loose hard enough to make her teeth rattle.

Sonny didn't have to see JP to know he flinched; she could hear it in his voice and was mildly horrified. "Did you hurt yourself with that?"

She was so not in the mood right now for smartass comments. "Shut it."

Again he laughed quietly and the sound smoothed the ruffles. "Sure."

That was better, Sonny thought. "Thank you."

"Yeah. Hey, I can swing up and give Charlie a ride to the game this afternoon if you want."

God no. JP couldn't see her like this! She'd rather poke herself in the eye with a burning twig than have him see her in this state. "That's nice ob you, but I'b good. He'll be there."

He didn't sound convinced, but replied, "All right. If you change your mind just give me a shout."

"Will do."

"Take care of yourself. I'll check in with you later, okay?"

Nobody had worried about her when she was sick since she was a kid. Part of her wanted to protest that she didn't need anyone fussing over her. The other part thought it was incredibly sweet that JP seemed to care. "Okay."

After saying goodbye Sonny hung up and immediately dialed Janie's number. There was no way she was going to make it through a whole game with the way she was feeling, and there was an even bigger no way that JP was going to pick up Charlie and catch sight of her like this. So she needed a plan, and the one she'd come up with involved begging or bribing Ben to take him.

Fortunately it didn't take either. After a short phone call to her best friend things were all set. Ben had been happy to take Charlie and enjoy an afternoon at the ballpark. Grateful for the help, Sonny gave her thanks and hung up.

Her head felt heavy, like it was filled with lead, so she leaned forward and lowered her forehead to the counter. Minutes passed while she stood with the blanket around her shoulders and her head on the countertop. The cool, yellow tile felt wonderful against her overheated skin.

Vader scratched at the door to be let out, and Sonny's head shot up, nearly pitching her backward. The dog's whimpering reminded her that she'd overslept and hadn't milked the goats yet. They were long overdue. Now she had another thing to feel terrible about. Great.

Dragging her butt to the mudroom, she grabbed her hat and shoved her feet into her boots before she headed to the shop for her supplies. It took longer than normal, but she got the girls milked out and settled in the field for the day. When she was done she crawled back in bed and pulled the covers over her head.

Charlie was still gone the second time she rolled out of bed for the day. Trying to feel human, Sonny showered and got dressed—if one wanted to call fleece pajama pants and an old grungy oversized grey CU sweatshirt "dressed." Either way, she felt marginally better and went in search of more tea.

When Charlie got home just after dark, he did his shot routine, ate, and then headed straight to bed. The poor kid was worked.

She had just settled down in front of the TV and started an episode of *Hart of Dixie* on Netflix when a knock sounded at the door. Vader growled and she signaled for him to be quiet, even though she was startled. Who could possibly be knocking on her door this late at night?

Padding to the door, Vader at her side, Sonny blew her nose with a tissue and turned the knob. She opened the door, saw JP on the other side, and promptly slammed it shut again on a flash of panic. *Oh holy shit*, was all she could think.

JP stood on the other side looking impossibly gorgeous in jeans, a charcoal T-shirt, and a Rush ball cap. He had a paper bag in his hand.

And he'd just seen her looking like death warmed over.

His voice was muffled through the door. "Damn it, Sonny. Open the door."

Nuh-uh. No way. No how.

A knock sounded again. "I brought you something."

A bribe. Well now, that changed things. Sort of. "I'm not fit for company, JP." At least she sounded mostly normal this evening.

"I don't care. Let me in." His voice was rife with frustration.

Wasn't it bad enough that she'd temporarily lost her sanity with him the other night and indulged in the dark side? Now he had seen her sick and looking pasty and terrible too.

Life was so unfair.

"Sonny, if you don't let me in I'm just going to camp out on your porch all night long. You wouldn't leave me out here in the cold now, would you?"

Well . . . "I don't want you to catch this thing. So why don't you leave the bag by the door and get on home?" Maybe making it about him would do the trick and he'd leave.

She could hear him sigh through the door. "I never get sick. I have the immune system of Superman. Let. Me. In."

Fine. It's not like she had much dignity left after the way she'd jumped him and shoved her hands down his pants anyway. Stupid latent hormones.

Though it was pointless, Sonny patted her messy bun

and smoothed her hands down the front of her sweat-shirt. A few crumbs of toast and a couple pieces of egg fell to the floor. Vader was on them instantly and hoovered them up, delighted to find the unexpected treat.

God, she was just all kinds of classy, wasn't she? Egg? Come on. Really?

Cursing karma, Sonny sucked it up and opened the door. JP was leaning against the door frame, arms and legs crossed and an annoyed expression on his face. And he looked so good that her hormones started firing even though she felt like sludge. Just once she'd appreciate it if they would do what she wanted when it came to JP. And that would be nothing—absolutely nothing. Just like how they used to be before the shortstop had swaggered into her predictable life.

He gave her a thorough once-over, from her sloppily piled hair to her monkey slippers. "I thought you could use this, so here." He held the bag out to her and kind of grimaced. "You look about as good as you sounded, sunshine."

Feeling at a loss, Sonny blindly took the outstretched paper bag. "What is this?"

"If you invite me inside I'll show you," JP said around a crooked half grin.

He probably *would* camp out on her porch if she didn't let him in, so she stepped to the side. "After you."

Vader promptly shoved his nose in JP's crotch and sniffed. Unfazed, the player gave the dog a good pet and kept walking. "Good boy." He glanced over at Sonny. "This has to be Vader. Am I right?"

She nodded and turned toward the kitchen. "Yep," she answered, surprised that he remembered the dog's name. "I'm going to put this bag in the kitchen."

JP must have noted the small mountain of Charlie's shoes by the door because he kicked his off before following her. "Nice place you have here." He pointed to the Maori mask hanging over the mantle as they passed the floor-to-ceiling stone fireplace. "That's a very cool mask. Is it African?"

Sonny shook her head and continued to the eat-in kitchen. "No, it's from an indigenous tribe down in New Zealand."

"You mean the Maori?"

Surprise had her glancing back at him over her shoulder and momentarily forgetting her self-consciousness at her appearance. "How did you know that?"

JP shrugged his wide shoulders. "I was in New Zealand last year."

Sonny stopped in her tracks and pegged him with a look. "Shut up. Seriously?" It was her number one place to travel. Someday.

They entered the kitchen and he glanced around the large, open space. "Seriously. A rock climbing buddy of mine and I went down there on vacation during the off-season. He wanted to check out the topography. There's some rock faces that he'd heard were pretty challenging, but they ended up being too crumbly for good climbing."

Setting the bag on the counter, Sonny pulled a tissue from the pouch of her sweatshirt and discretely dabbed at her nose before shoving it away again and looking at JP. "You climb?"

He didn't really seem the type. She'd lived in Boulder County most of her life and had seen her fair share of climbers over the years. Her last boyfriend, The Jerk, had been one. He was the one who'd hung around just long enough to get her naked a few times and stir up her big pot of crazy. Then he'd decided her having a kid was a real drag and broke it off with a text he sent her from Argentina, breaking her heart and trust in one abbreviated message. Nothing JP was wearing came from North Face or REI and he looked like he'd showered at least once in the past week. And he didn't smell like weed.

JP was holding her vintage Garfield and Arlene ceramic salt and pepper shakers, playing with them. They had little magnets that pulled them together in a kiss. "I climb occasionally, yeah. But I'm more of a mountain biker if I get to choose."

That she could believe. Because she was dying to know, Sonny blurted out, "Why are you really here, JP?"

"Because I was worried about you." He pointed to the paper bag. "There's chicken noodle soup from Panera in there. I doubt it's still hot, so it'll probably have to be reheated."

Flummoxed and touched at his thoughtfulness, Sonny pulled the large to-go container from the bag. Nobody had ever brought her soup before. Now she felt bad for slamming the door in his face. "That was very nice of you. Thank you."

Straightening, he placed the shakers back on the

counter and walked over to her. Coming up behind her, he reached over her shoulder and grabbed the soup. Then he dropped a casual kiss on the top of her head and made for the microwave. "No worries. Why don't you go relax on the couch while I heat this up?"

Sonny stared at him with wide, watery, googley eyes. She didn't know what to make of him. Or the way he moved about her kitchen so comfortably. The protest came automatically. "I can do it."

He waved her off, not even sparing her a glance. "Go. You need to sit. I'll be there in a few."

A cough decided to wrack her bones at that moment, punctuating his point. He raised a brow at her and said, "See?" He jerked his head toward the living room. "Go."

She didn't really have the energy to be stubborn. "Let me know if you need anything."

JP merely grunted, too busy fiddling in *her* kitchen to bother with a reply. So she left him there and plodded out to the couch. Once there she flopped onto the deep cushions and curled her feet under her. *Hart of Dixie* was paused on the small flat screen in front of her. Rachel Bilson looked gorgeous and composed, even in near one hundred percent Alabama humidity.

She was contemplating starting the show when JP came out of the kitchen. He'd transferred the soup to one of her white ceramic bowls and was carrying a tall glass of water. It did funny things to her, seeing him in her home at night all relaxed in his socks. The only other guy to ever do that was Charlie. It was a new and not entirely comfortable energy.

At least for her. Vader, on the other hand, was more than happy to have a man in the house. He'd been stuck like Velcro to JP's side since he'd strode in all manly and full of testosterone. It's like the dog had finally found his soul mate. Even now he was heeling like a champ at JP's side, all happy doggie grins.

She wanted to cry *Traitor!,* but she couldn't actually blame him. If she were a dog she'd probably act like that around JP too. *Oh pet me! Pet me!*

When JP passed the television he looked at the scene paused on the screen and asked, "What are you watching?"

Her guilty pleasure. "It's a show called *Hart of Dixie* about a New York woman who inherits a medical practice in small-town Alabama."

He handed her the water and soup, then sat down next to her. "Yeah? Is it good?"

Sonny took a sip of the cool water and nodded. "It has numerous love triangles, an ex-NHL player as the mayor, and a pet alligator."

JP grinned and curled an arm around her shoulders, tucking her into his side. "Sweet."

A peek at him out of the corner of her eye had her insides shaking. The man was so darned comfortable in her home. He'd even propped his feet up on her coffee table, and Vader had taken up residence by his side. It was all highly disconcerting.

But it turned out to be very relaxed and easy. Sonny ate her soup while they watched an episode and JP absentmindedly petted her dog. It did occur to her at one point how domestic it all was. But before she could wrap her cold-hampered brain around that fact, the chicken soup kicked in and she became groggy.

Catching herself dozing with her head on JP's shoulder, Sonny sat up straight, but her eyes betrayed her and drifted closed again. On the verge of deep sleep, she felt JP reposition until her head was against his chest and his arms were wrapped loosely around her, snuggling her close.

She mumbled something incoherent and he kissed her hair. "*Shhhh*, sunshine. Just sleep."

He started up another episode and her last thought before she fell sound asleep against him was that she could get used to this.

Chapter Twelve

JP WAS UP bright and early the next morning and headed for Moab before the sun had broken the horizon. It was the first day of the midseason break and he was bailing out of town, heading out to Utah to fight the desert heat with his friend, Garrett Lawson. They'd packed his Tacoma full of the gear they needed for a few days of camping, climbing, and mountain biking. Garrett's yellow lab, Yeti, had hopped in the back seat and was sprawled out, already snoring. A veteran traveler, the lab knew how to pass the time in style.

He and Garrett went way back, having met at summer camp when JP was twelve. Older by a handful of years, Garrett had been his cabin counselor the first year. And through the luck of the draw, for the next six, JP had always gotten lodged with the professional climber. Over time Garrett had become like a big brother, and now that they both lived in the same place they hung out often.

It was Garrett who'd first introduced him to the fun of Moab. And it was Garrett who'd taught him how to rock climb and repel to begin with.

Now that he was a well-known figure in the climbing world, Garrett travelled all over the globe taking on the hardest routes and most notorious climbs. Then he wrote about them for magazines. He'd even produced a critically acclaimed documentary when he'd taken on the Himalayas in Nepal a few years back.

They finally arrived outside Moab and JP had just turned off onto the dirt road that led to the Onion Creek campground where they were going to pitch tents when Garrett asked, "So, bra, what's up with you on the lady front?"

The memory of last night's visit to Sonny's popped into his head and he couldn't quite hide the smile that tugged at his lips. "I've got something cooking with a sweet thing who lives outside Longmont."

Garrett shifted his gaze from the steep red clay cliffs and looked at JP from behind a pair of Oakleys. "No shit?"

JP nodded and drove through some creek overflow, surprised that the water was still that high in July. Usually it was drier than a hundred-year-old bone. "Her name's Sonny and she's got a kid—a ten-year-old boy who's terrific."

The climber scratched his scruffy chin and rolled down the window, letting in the fresh air. Yeti promptly popped up from the back seat and shoved his head out the window. "That's great, dude. Things are going well?"

Garrett knew him as well as anyone could and JP didn't have to monitor anything. He guessed the lanky rock-head was his best friend, outside of his brother Ray. "They are. She's got some hang-ups from old relationships and it's obvious she dislikes that I'm a public figure, but nothing that's a deal breaker. I know I can get her to come around about the fame thing."

Garrett flashed a grin. "How's the sex?"

What sex? "We're taking it slow."

The blond climber laughed. "In other words, you've got no game."

"She's special, G."

They came to an empty camp site and JP pulled his truck in and stopped. As soon as the engine turned off, Yeti leapt over the backseat and out the window, clipping Garrett's shoulder on the way. He began sniffing the ground, and when he found a spot worthy enough, the dog hiked a leg and peed on a sun-bleached shrub.

JP unfolded from the truck and stretched. It wasn't even noon yet and they were in the shadow of the canyon wall, but it was already damn hot. Sweat beaded almost immediately on his forehead and he used the hem of his T-shirt to swipe at it. Thinking better of it, JP stripped off the white cotton and tied it over his head like a do-rag.

By the time they'd set up camp, the sun was at full blaze and both of them were bare-chested in shorts and flip-flops. Stopping for a cold drink, JP popped the lid on a cooler and grabbed a bottle of Arizona iced tea. He hollered over to Garrett, who was busy oiling the gears on his bike by a pile of boulders. "You got any reception on your cell? I can't get any." Coverage in Onion Creek was always spotty for him.

The climber was crouched in front of his bike and pulled his phone from a back pocket. He checked the status and tossed the cell to JP. "I have one bar."

Snagging the phone in midair, JP dialed Sonny's number from memory and got voicemail. He was debating whether or not to leave a message, but when he heard the beep, he automatically started talking. "Hey, sunshine. How are you this morning? I thought I'd check in on you and see how you were faring. You were out cold when I put you to bed last night." He glanced over at Garrett, who was busy pretending not to listen. "I'm out of town for a few days, but will be back soon. A buddy and I are hanging out in Moab."

JP ran out of things to say. He hated leaving messages. "Okay, well, I'll talk to you soon." He was about to hang up, and then he added quietly, "I'll be thinking about you, Sonny."

Ending the call, JP tossed the phone back to Garrett and blew out a breath. Being away from Sonny was a lot tougher than he'd expected it to be. He couldn't keep from thinking about her, wondering how she was feeling, and wishing he could hold her again like he had last night.

Garrett strode over to the truck and said as he reached inside for some climbing gear. "You've got it bad, bra. Your 'sweet thing' has a hold on you."

JP thought back to how Sonny had looked last night when he'd tucked her into her bed, all frizzy-haired and sleep-flushed, and couldn't stop his smile. "True that. And I am more than okay with it."

"WHAT ARE WE going to do today, Mom?" Charlie asked over breakfast. It had been two days since JP had showed up at her door with chicken soup, and she was feeling much better. Her coloring was back to normal and her energy was restored.

And over those two days she'd thought about JP only about a hundred million times.

A big part of her wanted to be like an ostrich and stick her head in the sand. Wanted to pretend that she didn't know what was going on with him. She wanted to act like she didn't know what to make of him and his behavior.

But she wasn't a kid anymore.

She was a grown woman with a kid of her own, and she prided herself on her ability to be honest with the facts. And it was time to shed some light on those facts and what they all meant. Then Sonny had to decide how she felt about *what* it all meant.

Because the honest truth was that JP was completely, totally for real. Even if he was a famous celebrity.

The other night solidified that fact. Sonny still couldn't believe that they'd cuddled on the couch watching television. And then he'd carried her to *bed*. Which, by the way, was more proof of just how frigging fit pro athletes were because she was not a lightweight by any shot.

But he'd done it anyway. She had vague memories of him pulling the covers snug around her and kissing her cheek softly. So even though they'd been hot and heavy recently, that's not what he'd come over for. No, the guy had been sweet and nice and, *pffft*, well, just absolutely wonderful.

What kind of man brought a sick woman soup and cuddled on the couch with her while she watched chick shows? JP Trudeau, that's who.

Charlie's voice pierced her mental ramblings. "Earth to Mom." He waved a hand in front of her face. "I asked what we're gonna do today."

Sonny gave him a quick one-arm squeeze on her way to rinse her plate in the sink. "Sorry, kiddo. Spaced out for a while." The plate went in the dishwasher and she turned back to Charlie. "I was thinking we could break out from the norm and I'd do this thing called 'work,' and then we'd really go crazy after and do this fun activity known as 'grocery shopping.'"

Charlie tossed back his blond head and exclaimed, *"Noooooo!"* Then he gave her a playful grin, his blue eyes dancing.

"Sorry, Charlie."

"But, Mom, we *always* do that." A pout transformed his happy face. "You're not sick any more. Let's go do something fun."

Fun. What was that? She barely remembered. "I need to work, honey. I have curds that I just put into the cheese presses and I need to rotate the Gouda I have aging."

Her son sulked on his barstool. "How long is *that* gonna take?"

Sonny couldn't really blame Charlie for being bored

and cooped up. It was summer break—a time for fun and frolick. A time to play.

But she had work. Being responsible sucked the big one sometimes.

Her boy's cabin fever was infectious, and by the time Sonny had worked for a few hours in her shop she was antsy and ready to break free. It was just past eleven in the morning and the rest of the day stretched before her, beckoning her out to play.

On her way back to the house she passed Charlie and Vader playing tug-of-war with a half-eaten volleyball. He'd gotten over his pout and was having a good time with the dog. When she walked by, he glanced up and said amiably, "What's for lunch?"

It was one of those questions that she heard every single day. Along with "What's for breakfast?" and "What's for dinner?" It really was true that growing boys were nothing but bottomless stomachs and too-big feet. Sometimes she felt like a feeding factory.

The sound of gravel crunching signaled a vehicle approaching. Leaving Charlie with Vader, she walked to the side of the house. When she rounded the corner Sonny looked up the long road and felt butterflies take flight in her belly. A red Double Cab Toyota Tacoma was making its way down her drive, with a deeply tanned elbow resting out the open driver-side window. Through the front glass she could make out aviator sunglasses, broad shoulders, and messy hair.

JP had come calling.

It was the first time they'd seen each other since she'd

fallen asleep on his chest, and she felt incredibly self-conscious. Something had changed between them and she wasn't sure of herself anymore. She wasn't sure where things stood, period.

One thing she did know, though, was that when JP climbed out of his truck and she caught a good look of him in cargo shorts and flip-flops, looking like a bronzed Adonis, her heart tripped in her chest. It perched precariously on the edge of a very tall cliff. A stiff wind would blow it over, sending it into free fall.

When had it even become in the *vicinity* of a cliff?

And where had she been while this had all gone down? Because she could swear that she'd been aware and adamant against this very thing the whole time. Sonny Miller didn't want a man—especially one loved and adored by millions—and she was perfectly single and happy, remember?

JP caught sight of her and grinned, devastating her.

Crap.

Sonny glanced in partial panic around the yard, thinking that there had to be something out there that she could use to get rid of these feelings swirling around inside her, unwanted and unwelcome. Maybe a hand trowel could dig them out?

God, she wasn't ready for this.

Her heart racing, Sonny watched JP stride right on up to her, and she absently patted her hair. With every step he took, the butterflies kicked up a notch. The last words from the message he'd left her echoed in her head. *I'll be thinking about you, Sonny.*

When he reached her side, he slid an arm around her waist and pulled her in for a positively delicious kiss. Forgetting that Charlie was just around the house in the backyard, Sonny had no resistance and kissed him back passionately, her body and heart betraying her mind.

JP drew back and rested his forehead against hers, his sunglasses bumping against her nose. "I missed you."

That right there. There it was. The reason that she hadn't been able to stay immune to him. He was so damn good and sweet and honest. *I mean*, she thought, *who just up and says exactly what they're feeling and thinking?*

And how was she supposed to stay away?

Before she could think about it, she heard Charlie call out, "Who's here, Mom? Is it Sam?"

Pushing out of JP's embrace, Sonny smoothed her hands down her shirt and cleared her throat. Would he stop looking at her like that? She could see his eyes through the amber-colored lenses, and they were focused intently on her. It was making her squirm.

Sonny tucked a strand of hair behind an ear and broke eye contact. "Why don't you come over here and find out?" she hollered back at her son.

JP spoke, forcing her to look at him again. "You look good, Sonny. Are you feeling recovered?"

She nodded. "I am." Though she was still embarrassed about it, she added, "Thank you for taking care of me the other night. You didn't have to."

"I know I didn't. I wanted to."

See? There it was again. He was acting like the sweetest man on earth and making a wreck of the barriers she'd so meticulously erected around herself years ago. The way that things were going she wouldn't have any left before the day was through.

A voice at the back of her mind asked if she even wanted them there anymore. Sonny automatically rejected the thought. Of course she wanted them there. Didn't she?

Charlie chose that moment to come barreling around the corner, Vader hot on his heels. When he spotted JP, her son pumped a fist and skidded to a halt. "All right!"

JP held out a hand and they bumped fists in a complicated handshake that only members of the male persuasion could replicate. When they were done the shortstop hooked his thumb over his shoulder at his truck and said, "How do you feel about a day of tubing the river with me, slugger?"

Charlie's eyes went huge. "Yeah? No way. Seriously?"

JP nodded and glanced at Sonny. "Think we could convince your mom to go with us?"

Sonny looked at the bed of the Toyota and saw three large tubes strapped down. They were the kind that had handles built into them and loops for rope to thread through. A small blue cooler sat in the back next to them.

Longing flooded Sonny. How wonderful it would be to play hooky for the day and go splash in the river, to feel the cold water swirl around her. It'd been a couple years since she'd had a day of tubing. Last summer had been so hectic with starting the business that she hadn't been able to get away. Charlie, on the other hand, had gone with Sam's family a few times. It was one of his favorite activities.

Shading her eyes with a hand, she took in the deep, cloudless blue of the sky. A light breeze played with the loose strands of her hair and birds chirped joyfully in the trees nearby. It was a perfect summer day. One meant to be enjoyed.

But she had to work.

Both males were looking at her with hopeful, expectant expressions. Her protest was halfhearted. "I would love to, but I have to work, guys. Cheese doesn't make itself." Well, it did, sort of. But that wasn't the point.

Charlie batted his eyelashes at her and pressed his palms together. "*Pleeeeease?* Come on, Mom."

JP taunted playfully, "Yeah, c'mon, Mom."

They stared at her, waiting. The ballplayer waggled his eyebrows and jerked his head in the direction of his truck. "You know you wanna."

You know what? She did want to. Screw it. "Okay. Let's do it. Let's go tubing." Why not? It was just one day, right? It didn't mean anything.

Charlie did a little victory dance. "*Yes!*"

JP seemed awful smug, his grin totally naughty as he watched her. He held out his fist and bumped knuckles with her boy. "*Woop.*"

Too excited by the prospect of an afternoon of fun to take offense, Sonny grinned. "Let me throw a bag together."

Leaving the guys talking, she headed toward the house and marveled at the jitters in her stomach. God, she felt like a teenager, chucking it all for an afternoon of fun and sun with the hot boy. She couldn't remember the last time she'd felt this way.

In the kitchen, rummaging through the cupboards by the time the guys came in, Sonny reached for a water bottle on the top shelf in the back. Not quite tall enough in bare feet, she rose to her tiptoes and tried again.

Suddenly she felt a rock-hard chest press up against her back, pushing her gently forward into the countertop. An arm pinned her in on each side—one of her hands flush against the cabinet, the other stretched out toward the water bottle. The heat radiating from his body flirted with her, enticing her closer.

Because she really wanted to, she leaned back into JP a tiny bit and felt his breath hot on her ear. "Here. Let me help you with that."

Awareness sparked like a brush fire between them and Sonny inhaled sharply. Her nipples puckered tightly when she felt him move behind her, his penis growing hard against her butt. It would feel so good to push back into him a little and rub slowly.

The thought sent heat straight to her groin and she went instantly wet.

"Hey, Mom. I need to get my insulin kit." Charlie strode into the kitchen, oblivious, and JP jerked away from Sonny. "Can we eat at a restaurant later?"

Sonny let out a shaky breath, her body on overload from all the hormones.

JP did that to her. Wow.

Hoping she sounded normal, she replied, "We'll have to see, hon. If we do, it's your last food splurge for a while, okay? We've been having a lot of treats lately. It's fine once in a while, but not all the time." Going into Mom-mode helped her get a grip. Man, sexual frustration could be brutal.

Who knew?

Sonny stole a glance at JP and bit her lip to hide a grin. Though he tried to hide it, she could tell he was suffering too. His face kind of had a pinched quality to it, and he was standing awfully stiff.

For some reason it all suddenly made her want to laugh. Having a kid kept things interesting for sure.

Charlie grabbed an ice pack from the freezer and stuffed it into his diabetes kit to keep everything cool. "Deal. Can we make it pizza then?"

JP raked a hand through his hair and shot her a look that was hot and dark. "Anything you want, Charlie."

Oh, he was feeling it bad.

Sonny couldn't keep the laugh inside anymore and it bubbled up and out. JP tipped his head to the side and looked at her questioningly. Feeling spontaneous and playful, she blocked Charlie from seeing with her body, snuck out a hand, and rubbed the top of JP's thigh suggestively. His eyebrows shot up in surprise. She tossed him a sassy grin in return.

His gaze narrowed on her, honing in with serious intensity.

Her smiled melted in the sudden heat and she let her hand fall away. Playing with JP really was like baiting a tiger. Yowza.

An image flashed in her mind of what it would be like to have that focused intensity on her while she was naked. She nearly whimpered. And it wasn't from fear.

Being the center of attention in bed with JP would be amazing.

Sonny stole another glance at him, arousal still an echo inside her.

Today was going to be mighty interesting.

Chapter Thirteen

THE POUDRE RIVER was wide, cool, and crystal clear when they arrived: perfect conditions for an afternoon of tubing. JP had found a place to park near the river on the outskirts of Fort Collins where huge cottonwoods shaded the slow moving water. An assortment of SUVs and compact cars were crowded into the small pullout.

Excitement made Sonny jittery as she climbed out of the truck. She could barely contain the thrill of playing hooky for a day to spend it with JP. It felt youthful and eager and silly. And, well, just plain *fun*.

The midday sun beat down on her bare shoulders and kissed her cheeks. A few hours out in this and she'd acquire a few new freckles across her nose if she didn't put on a hat. That she didn't mind. It was the whole cancer thing that she wasn't keen on. Reaching back into the Toyota, she grabbed her hat and put it on.

Charlie threw open the back door and jumped out,

eager to get in the water. His bright orange swim trunks were on the big side and hung down past his knees. A pair of strappy water sandals in bold blue made him look like a Broncos fan.

The sound of water moving over rocks raised her spirits even higher, and Sonny lifted her gaze to the sky. Above her a hawk flew effortlessly, its wings outspread as it glided on the gently moving air. It didn't matter how many times she saw one of the great birds, it awed her every single time. They were beautiful.

The hawk stopped gliding and dove into the cover of the trees just as JP pulled an inner tube from the truck bed. He called over to Charlie, "Hey, kid. This one's yours."

Her son darted over to the far side of the truck and grabbed the fancy tube. Most of the time when they went tubing all they had to use were black rubber ones. They didn't have handles to hold on to, and the air valve stuck out and would poke you in some very private and unhappy places.

Suddenly the hair on the nape of her neck got tangled in the knot of her bikini strings and pulled sharply. With a hand she extricated the fine hairs and adjusted the tie. She'd thrown on a pair of denim shorts with large front pockets and a white ribbed tank top over her flowered bikini. Her hair was tucked up under her wide-brimmed khaki hat.

In front of her was a path of flattened grass that led to a sandy bank. The water there was almost still and her toes itched to dip into the refreshing moisture. Baby-fine rocks shimmered as the current whispered over them.

Leaving the boys to grab the tubes, Sonny stepped the few feet to the river's edge and kicked off her flip-flops. Her toes dug into the sandy brink and she sighed. Oh, sweet heaven.

JP came up beside her and handed her a tube. "It looks like we weren't the only ones to think of this." He tipped his chin at the other cars.

Sonny shrugged good-naturedly. "Tubing in a cold river on a hot summer day was a genius collaboration of Mother Nature and Man."

JP grinned. "True that."

"How was your trip to Moab?" She'd been meaning to ask him. He was super tan from it. It was pretty hot.

He kicked off his shoes and shoved the flip-flops in one of the large cargo pockets built into his shorts. The black heels stuck out over the flap. "It was great. We climbed Fisher Towers and camped in Onion Creek. I clipped in on some challenging moves that I wasn't sure I was ready to take on, but Garret got me through it. I have the cuts and scrapes to prove it," he finished with a self-deprecating grin.

Charlie raced by, tell-tale streaks of unblended sunscreen drying across his thin bare chest. He was holding the tube in both hands and hit the water running. When he was in to his shins he dove forward onto the tube, his feet suspended behind him as it skidded off, carried away by the current.

Sonny called out, "Don't go anywhere yet, boy-o."

A group of college kids floated by just then and waved, the simple joy of floating on the river putting them in a jovial mood. One of them nearly collided with a fallen tree branch and overturned the tube just in time to avoid injury. The guy came up sputtering in the waist-deep water and got a ribbing from his friends as they continued downstream.

JP stepped into the shallow water with his tube and the small ice chest attached to it by a short rope. Sonny gave him a quizzical look. "What's in the chest?"

With the current swirling around his legs he adjusted the tube behind his thighs and sat back, smiling. "Beer, baby."

Nice.

Deciding it was time to get in, she ran back to the truck and tossed her shoes in the bed. The last time she'd worn flip-flops she lost them in the current within five minutes, and she didn't want a repeat performance. Glancing back at Charlie to double-check that he'd buckled his life jacket all the way, Sonny was satisfied to see he had and waded into the river. Not that she was worried. The kid was a stellar swimmer. But safety first and all that.

The water caressed her legs, cool and tantalizing. The guys had moved away from the bank and were chatting while they waited for her. Her boy shot JP a mischievous look and splashed him, water drenching the front of his T-shirt. Sonny stopped dead and gulped, taken totally off guard. JP was transformed into a wet T-shirted Mr. Darcy and he looked *good*. All biceps and sculpted shoulders and glistening, bronzed skin.

Charlie's shenanigans started an old-fashioned round of "splash," and the kid gave up using his hands and went straight to his feet, kicking with all his might. Their laughter filled the air and Sonny felt something inside her shift and get all gooey.

JP and her boy had a connection. She couldn't deny that. They genuinely liked spending time with each other. And it wasn't forced. If anything, Sonny had to say that there was just a chemistry between them. And it did funny things to her insides knowing that.

Just then JP called to her, water droplets dotting the lenses of his sunglasses. "Are you coming or not, slowpoke?"

Taking the plunge, Sonny jumped onto the tube and moved away from the sandbar. The tree cover faded behind her and she drifted into the open water, the sun reflecting off the glassy surface. "Keep your pants on, Trudeau."

"Hey, Mom," said Charlie, his hands treading against the current, holding him in place. "Do you think there's water snakes here?"

Jesus. Why did he have to go and say that? "I hope to heck not, dude." Now she wanted to pull her feet up. Maybe if she flexed her butt she could arch it out of the water too. She really, really hated snakes.

Charlie knew it too. He had this rubber snake that he scared the crap out of her with a few months back. He'd coiled the toy on her seat one day when they'd been running late for an appointment. All she'd seen when she whipped open the driver side door was a wound diamondback snake, and she'd screamed loud enough to be heard two counties over.

He'd laughed so hard about scaring her that he'd doubled over and got a stitch in his side. Which had served him right for pulling such a prank. For weeks he'd teased her, proud as could be at his own cleverness.

Obviously he wasn't done milking that one just yet.

Drifting on the gentle current, Sonny used her hands as rudders and maneuvered close to JP. Once she reached his side she said, "Can I get something from the cooler?"

JP reached behind him for the rope and pulled the bobbing cooler up beside him. "Sure thing, sweetness. What would you like?" Inside were a few different beverages, not just Fat Tire.

But that's what she wanted. "Beer me."

The shortstop reached inside and came out with two frosty cans. He handed one to her and popped the lid on his. Then he held it up in a toast. Sonny leaned toward him, pitched off balance, and was nearly dumped from the tube. Flailing, the beer can slipped out of her hand and fell into the water. It swept downstream and around the bend, out of sight.

She sighed. "Shit."

Charlie began paddling like mad after it. "I'll get it!"

JP handed her his can and called after her boy, "Beat you to it!" He looked back at Sonny real quick. "Meet you around the bend." With that he took off, racing to catch up to the renegade beer can and Charlie.

Who said chivalry was dead?

Feeling absolutely no need to join in the chase, Sonny relaxed into the donut hole and dropped her head back against the tube. She closed her eyes briefly and just drifted along the lazy current. The warmth from the sun lulled her into that dreamy place between awake and asleep. That place where all the weight lifted and everything was completely, utterly peaceful.

It felt oh so good.

JP WATCHED SONNY round the bend on her tube as it wandered aimlessly along the midsummer current. From the distance she looked fast asleep. He knew she wasn't, though, because every so often a hand would sift the water back and forth in a lazy pattern.

It felt good seeing her so relaxed like that. He imagined that she hadn't received many days like that since Charlie had come along. It had seemed like the right move when he'd thought of it on the drive back from Utah. He'd wanted to spend some time away from her place with the two of them, see how it went. Now he was glad he did.

And he had to admit that he was having a great time. The more time he spent with Sonny and her boy, the more he liked it. They had an easy way of being together that wasn't cliquish or exclusive. So it felt like there was room for him, contrary to what she'd claimed when they'd had their first date. Well, it hadn't really been a "date," but it had pretty much become so in his mind. It was easier to mentally file that way.

JP stood up in the water and moved off toward shore. Charlie was across and a little downstream from him at a picnic structure that the Parks Department had erected

under an enormous poplar tree. It gave tubers and kay-
akers a place to rest if they tired and wanted a break.
Another kid was up there that Charlie had said he knew
from school before he'd taken off to talk to him. The
kid's family was taking a breather in the grass and shade,
munching on Clif Bars.

They'd brought a portable stereo and Taylor Swift was
coming through the speakers quietly like irritating background noise to the much more enjoyable sound of birds
and moving water. Why that girl was so popular he just
couldn't figure.

Reaching the river bank, JP dug his toes into the sandy
shore, enjoying the way it squished beneath his feet.
When he hit mostly dry land he tossed the tube down
and planted his ass in the sandy dirt. A row of aging pop-
lars crowded the shoreline behind him, the branches of a
huge one arching far out over him, casting the rippling
water in dappling sun and shade.

It was a perfect day.

Still holding the beer, JP brought it to his lips and took
a slow pull. A pale yellow butterfly flittered in front of
him and a blue jay perched above him on an overhanging
branch. The heat was buffered by the lush leaves rustling
on the old trees, and a bee buzzed just off to his right.

And there was Sonny, peaceful as could be, drifting
slowly toward him. The current was directing her over to
shore and her body was printed with the sun dapples that
filtered through the branches. Her curves were displayed
deliciously as she lounged on the floating device.

She looked like a picture in the delicate light and his

throat seized up tight, emotion hitting him unexpectedly. Longing like he'd never known welled up inside of him as his gaze held steady on her.

He wanted that woman like he wanted to breathe.

It was a live ache inside him. He didn't care what she thought her hang-ups were. From where he was sitting she looked pretty much perfect. And, for those few moments that she floated toward him in slow motion, beautiful as a dream, he wanted so much to blurt out all of his feelings to her like a fool.

Light as a feather, Sonny glided onto the shore in front of him. Her hat had fallen back and strands of her hair curled around her face. Sunglasses hid her eyes from view and she had a satisfied half smile upturning her full lips. The woman looked like she'd found paradise in that inner tube.

He wanted to kiss her so bad his lips buzzed.

Sonny Miller had a hold on him like no one ever had before. And if he didn't get to make love to her soon he thought he might go crazy.

The water lapped quietly against the shore, her tube rocking back and forth with gentle motion. If he leaned forward a foot she'd be close enough to kiss. Going on instinct, JP bent toward her and pressed his lips lightly to hers.

He heard a little hum come from her and she melted against him, her skin sun-warmed and fragrant with the scent of summer. Lost in the experience, he moved closer still and deepened the kiss a degree. His tongue ran along the seam of her lips, seeking admittance, and when she opened for him and wrapped an arm around his neck his chest went so tight it was hard to breathe.

Taking his time, JP tasted her slowly. His tongue moved against hers in a leisurely, intoxicating rhythm. Sonny took over his senses and she was all he could see, feel, taste. All he wanted.

He felt her fingers dive into his hair as she moaned softly and arched into him. Her breasts pressed against his chest and her hard nipples branded him, made him burn. Needing to, JP slowly slid a hand up her waist, relishing the contours of her curves, until he came to the plump roundness of her breast. Her quick intake of breath aroused him further, had his erection straining against its confines.

With a finger he traced the underside of her breast back and forth until she arched against him, wordlessly asking for more. Teasing her, he slid his finger up the inside curve of her and then trailed lightly down to circle her nipple until it became a peak of sensitivity. When she groaned and kissed him more urgently he smiled against her lips before giving them a gentle nip.

"God, JP," she moaned as her head fell back.

The graceful line of her throat was exposed, and JP kissed a leisurely path down to her collarbone, exhilarating in the feel of her. Her skin tasted sweet like honey and hinted at something darker, smokier. And he wanted it. Wanted her.

Suddenly hungry, JP rolled her nipple between his fingers, pinching impatiently. Her gasp was like gasoline on his already burning fire and he growled low in his throat.

Feeling urgency beginning to claw at him, JP tore his lips from her and inhaled.

She made him burn. Her kiss-swollen lips had turned a deep pink and her skin was flushed when he looked at her. Her hat had fallen to the ground and her hair tumbled out, a tangled mess. Behind her sunglasses, she watched him silently. JP had never seen anything like her in his life.

Lowering his head, he kissed her lips softly and said against her mouth, "You are so beautiful."

At that moment it was the only thing he could think.

IN THE COVER of the trees behind them hid a slender, ambitious man who smirked as he lowered a camera with a giant zoom lens and whispered smugly, "Gotcha, Trudeau."

Chapter Fourteen

SONNY SNUCK A glance at JP out of the corner of her eye as he held the door to Beau Jo's pizza place open. Housed in an old sandstone building in downtown Fort Collins, the pizzeria was a town staple. The pedestrian-friendly area where it was located was known as "Old Town" and was comprised of narrow Victorian buildings painted bold colors. It was brimming with funky shops and an interesting assortment of bars. Every style, from trendy to mountain man, was represented within a few walkable square miles.

"Thanks," she said as she passed through the door. Ever since he'd kissed her on the river he'd been acting strange. Not like crazy-strange or anything, but just different. Thinking about what he'd said to her and how it had sounded still made her blush. He'd called her beautiful. And by the way he'd been looking at her so intensely and seriously, she knew he meant it. And now she was in very real danger of diving headlong into bed with JP. Because the truth was he'd snuck behind her defenses and gotten a hold of her heart even though she'd known they couldn't go anywhere.

It was everything he'd done, from getting Charlie the batboy gig to the wildflower he'd picked on the sandy river bank and placed behind her ear earlier. Two hours later it was still there, even though she was sure it was wilted, because she had refused to let it go. It was such a simple token of affection from a good man.

It's not like men such as him came along every day. Sonny was starting to suspect it was more like once in a lifetime.

Charlie bumped into her from behind and apologized. "Sorry, Mom."

Sometimes that kid had depth perception issues.

The heel of her foot stung from where he'd stomped on it, but Sonny ignored it. "No worries, hon."

Once they were seated outside on the patio and Charlie had checked his glucose levels, Sonny leaned back in her chair and people-watched. Every time she came to Fort Collins she did it. There were so many young families and college students that there was always something entertaining to see.

Like the young outdoorsy-hippie couple on the bicycles with their dogs in bike trailers that were passing by. Who does that?

Across the street in front of a narrow three-story shop painted a bold purple, a group of Asian tourists were busy taking turns snapping pictures of each other in front of some twisted metal sculpture. Down from them were a couple strolling who had to be in their eighties, both with cotton fluff hair, holding hands and drinking Starbucks.

A bunch of college boys stopped on the other side of the metal patio fence and stared hard at JP. The one in the green CSU T-shirt looked at his friends and then leaned forward and said, "Are you the shortstop for the Denver Rush?"

JP nodded. Not that you'd really know it was him by the way he looked right now. With his sandals, tan, and cargo shorts he could pass for just about any average Colorado guy. Except for the air of confidence that surrounded him. That was anything but average. He had a presence that made people sit up and take notice.

The boy turned to his friends. "Somebody gimme a pen." After a frantic search, someone held a pen out from the small crowd and the boy handed it to JP. "Will you sign my arm, dude? I don't have any paper."

Somehow Sonny was sure that wasn't the weirdest request he'd ever gotten. "There's a napkin here if you want." She held it up by a corner and let it dangle.

The brown-haired kids smiled gratefully. "Sweet. Thanks."

After she handed JP the napkin and he'd signed it, he passed it to the kid and shook hands with the others. And it brought the unwavering fact of his fame right back to the forefront.

While she looked on, JP made easy conversation with the college guys, chatting and grinning and talking shop. It was so blatantly obvious that he enjoyed the attention, the social interaction. For somebody like her, who was private to an almost ridiculous degree, it made her highly uncomfortable. Like she was under a magnifying glass and the whole world was staring down at her. She didn't think that she could ever get used to it—way too smothering. Even now her chest felt a little tight.

If she couldn't deal with it and he enjoyed his public life, then how could they ever really seriously consider being together?

Pondering that, Sonny watched the conversation and had a moment of awkwardness when she realized that JP wasn't that far removed, age-wise, from the group of boys.

But then she looked at him, the way he held himself, and the moment melted away. That was one issue she just didn't need to have about JP. Lord knew that if things headed where she was beginning to think they might, then she was going to have enough issues to contend with. Worrying that he was too young was a waste of time.

Surprisingly, it felt really good to put one issue to rest before it grabbed some traction. If only she could dismiss her issues over his fame and its consequences as easily. Or that suitcase full of baggage she'd been lugging around most of her life. One could always hope, right?

Charlie gained her attention. "Isn't it cool that we get to hang out with JP, Mom? Like, everybody knows him 'cause he's so awesome."

He said it was awesome now, but what about a year from now when he'd had to deal with these kinds of intrusions every day?

Sonny reached over, ruffled his hair and kept it light. "Sure it is, sweetheart. But you have to remember that JP is just a person like the rest of us." A really, really popular one. Still. She leaned toward him conspiratorially. "I bet he even farts just like the rest of us too."

That mental image sent the boy into a fit of laughter. JP must have overheard her whisper because he rejoined them at the table and said, "It's true, slugger. I'm the reigning fart king."

That, of course, made Charlie laugh even harder. It did her heart good to see him so happy, and it distracted her from the uncomfortable thoughts. Looking across the patio table to JP, Sonny's heart tripped in her chest when their gazes locked and they grinned. It was the first time she'd ever had one of those moments with a man over her boy.

And it flustered her to no end. What was she supposed to do about all of this? Two months ago this thing hadn't even been a blip on the radar. When they first met she'd been so resolved about it being just her and Charlie while he grew up. The last thing in the world she'd expected was something like this.

But now that she had it, what was she going to do with it?

Sonny replayed that question over and over in her mind while they ate Beau Jo's famous pizza on a sun-filled late afternoon. Even though Charlie had put on sunscreen, his cheeks were looking a little pink by the time the bill came. Even her shoulders were feeling on the hot side.

Before she could open her mouth to suggest splitting the bill, JP whipped it up off the table and had it paid for. Feeling the need to chip in, she reached into her purse and pulled out some cash and tossed it down on the table for a tip while he signed an autograph for the waiter.

Though the volume of Denver Rush fans that came out of the woodwork when he was around surprised her, what really got her was how incredibly friendly and humble he was about the whole thing even as he ate it up.

Yes, he clearly enjoyed being the center of attention. He enjoyed his perks. But he was so stinking *nice* about it.

Every single person was treated with full attention and appreciation. And it served to further drive the point home that JP was one hell of a catch. No pun intended.

And it really seemed like he wanted to be caught by her.

In fact, the ballplayer was pretty much jumping right into her glove. She didn't have to do much convincing. But the question that kept haunting her, that kept her from taking the next step was, why her?

She'd asked him that before and he'd made that cryptic speech about peeling layers, which she still wasn't entirely sure what that meant. Clarification would no doubt work wonders, but she was afraid to ask. Because then it would lead to a whole other conversation about her deep rooted insecurities. And she just wasn't really up for that.

Maybe if she summed it up with a simple, "Daddy issues," he'd buy it and leave it well enough alone. Probably not, though. JP had turned out to be eerily perceptive and he'd see right through that in record time. Because the truth was Sonny had more than mere issues with her father.

Mentally ticking her fingers, she added abandonment issues, commitment issues, mommy issues, and trust issues to the list. You know, the normal garden variety dysfunctions. Toss in a dash of fear of intimacy and it rounded out to be a pretty substantial fare. Although, intimacy issues could probably be put under the "commitment issues" heading, couldn't it?

Sonny shook her head, annoyed with where her thoughts had led her again. What would JP do when all that crap exploded all over him? Because, try as she might to keep it contained, it just came out. One minute she was mature, rational Sonny Miller. The next, she was a blubbering, confused, issue-ridden mess.

And that right there was the number one real reason she had avoided intimate relationships like the plague.

No way could she expect JP to accept that about her. God knows she wouldn't, if the roles were reversed.

Which pretty much left her back at square one with two choices:

First choice: Cut bait and run. Just end everything now with JP before the whole thing goes beyond a few hot kisses. Everybody gets out safe and in one piece.

Or, the second choice: Suck it up, be an adult, deal with his celebrity, and come clean with JP about everything. Let him choose what he wants to accept or not.

Hell, who knows? Maybe he's one of those guys who gets turned on by crazy.

Stealing a peek at him, Sonny dismissed the thought.

Nah. He just didn't seem the type. The guy was too grounded, too stable. If anything, he might find her amusing for a while until it all just became old.

Either way, she had a decision to make. She came to that realization with a sinking feeling as they prepared to pile in the cab of JP's Toyota. Why did it have to be so damn hard?

Charlie swooped under her arms and threw himself against the passenger side door with a triumphant grin. "I call shotgun!"

Forcing her thoughts to clear, Sonny replied, "Fat chance, kid. I get the front."

"Aww, Mom." He flung his arms out across the red door, palms flush against the glossy paint.

"Back seat, bucko, or we tie you to the roof." She was totally kidding.

He knew it too. "Only if I can wear goggles, Mom. I don't want bugs in my eyes."

"Oh, well, I think we can manage that." She looked over to JP. "Got any goggles he can borrow?"

The ballplayer rubbed his chin and pretended to think. "I'm sure I've got something that'll do."

Charlie realized the futility of his plan and gave up. "Man, adults are tough."

JP and Sonny locked gazes and said at the same time, "True that."

With a huff her boy climbed into the backseat. When everyone was settled inside he tapped JP on his shoulder. "Thanks for everything today. It rocked."

JP reached back over the seat and pulled her boy into a

pretend headlock. Charlie's body was halfway in the front and he was giggling against his bent elbow. "No problem, slugger. I'm glad I was able to make it happen."

The rest of the ride home was quiet in the fading afternoon light. By the time they'd pulled into the driveway it was almost full dark, and her son was fast asleep in the backseat. He may be growing up fast, but he was still her little boy. And he'd worn himself out.

Trying to decide whether to wake him up or not, JP took the decision out of her hands when he pulled her sleeping boy into his arms and headed toward the house. The way he cradled Charlie was so gentle that she felt tears sting the backs of her eyes.

She pointed to her son's room and as she watched JP carry her baby down the hall her heart took a long, slow roll. And when she reached the doorway and saw him tucking her boy in so carefully and tenderly, she realized she'd given up the fight to stay away from JP.

Sonny pulled away from the door frame and sighed, acceptance pouring through her. It was time to have that talk.

Backtracking to the kitchen, a welcome calm came over her that stemmed from the resolve she now felt. Charlie adored JP. That much was plain to see. Just as it was obvious even to a blind man that JP liked him right back.

Then there was her. Sonny didn't understand all of her feelings, but she knew that she had never felt this way about anyone ever before. And that meant something significant.

It meant she needed to try, even with all of her reservations.

Sonny was just about to grab the bottle of chardonnay that was chilling in the fridge when JP entered the room. "When that kid goes out, he really commits."

He looked so wonderful standing there in the harsh kitchen light. Sonny took a deep breath, preparing for what was to come. "Would you like some wine?"

JP's eye went dark and searching. "Are you asking me to stay?"

Yes, but she couldn't say it out loud quite yet so she evaded. "It's such a nice night that I thought we could sit on the front porch and talk and spend some time together."

He pinned her with a look that she couldn't read. "Do you really want that, Sonny?"

Did she? Though her insides were shaky, yes, yes she did. Swallowing hard, she answered, "I do." Wow. She couldn't believe she'd just said it. She, Sonny Miller, wanted JP Trudeau to stay. It was official.

With any luck, after he heard what she had to say he'd feel the same way.

Coming up behind her, JP wrapped his arms around her waist and kissed the spot on her neck just below her ear. "I'll take that wine."

Chapter Fifteen

THE MOON WAS bright and full when they settled on the front porch with their wine. Sonny tucked her bare feet underneath her on the padded chair and took a sip. Nerves danced along her skin as she contemplated how best to broach the topic. JP had settled next to her, his long muscular legs outstretched before him, wineglass in his hand.

Crickets sang in the grass nearby and a slight breeze stirred the warm evening air. In the distance the howl of a coyote could just be made out, the sound very faint. Under the light of the full moon her front yard looked magical, the old mature trees sentries to a mystical land beyond the veil.

The neighbor kid that pitched in with the farm once in a while when she was in a pinch had milked the goats and put them away for the night before dark. Every so often she heard noise coming from the barn as they settled down with their kids for some sleep.

It contented her, the sounds of the country. And it gave her courage to speak. "I've been wanting to talk to you about a few things, JP."

The shortstop cradled the glass in a large hand. "Is that so?"

He was so calm and nonthreatening that she was able to continue. "I like you. A lot."

He wiped his brow with his free hand. "*Phew*. That's good to know. I was sweating that big time."

Sonny batted a hand at him, smiling. "Oh shut up." She took another sip of wine. "Seriously, JP."

"I was being serious."

He so wasn't. "You're not making this easy."

JP leaned over and kissed her cheek. "Sorry. What's on your mind, sunshine?"

When he called her that her insides went all mushy, but there was something she had to get off her chest. Something she just had to say.

"I hate that you're a celebrity."

The words came out on a quiet rush. As soon as they were out a weight seemed to lift from her, and she peeked at him through her lashes to gauge his reaction.

For a moment he didn't speak. Instead he settled comfortably in his seat and took a sip of white wine. After what felt like a small eternity he lowered the glass to his knee. "I suspected so. It's not something I can change, Sonny."

She knew that, but as irrational as it was she still wished he could. "I'm not sure I'm up for it in the long run, JP. I need my privacy. I'm not okay with people poking around my or my son's personal business. I'm worried about what it could do to him in the long run." Maybe if she had a different past she wouldn't feel that way. "I'm not sure how to resolve it. I just know that it's there and it isn't budging."

"Give it time to see how it settles out, Sonny. Can you do that for me?"

Could she?

His amber eyes were filled with warmth and patience and her heart squeezed tight. Yeah, she could give it time. She smiled briefly. "Sure, JP. I can do that. But there're also some things about me that I need to tell you. Things you need to know so that you can choose what to do once you have the information."

He placed a reassuring hand on top of hers and squeezed. "Spill it, woman. Tell me what's so important."

Okay. *Humph*. Where did she start? "I think I've mentioned before that I'm terrible at relationships."

"I recall something of that sort, yeah."

"You grew up with both parents who loved you and guided you into adulthood, providing you with a healthy foundation to spring from, right?"

He nodded. "Yeah, pretty much."

This was the hard part. "I didn't have that. *At all*. My dad split when I was super young and then my mom did right after. She dumped me here, on this very porch in the middle of the day. Literally, she shoved me onto it, rang the doorbell, and left me with a letter for my grandmother to read."

JP squeezed her hand. "That sucks, Sonny. I'm sorry."

She waved him off. She needed to get it all out. "My grandmother didn't want me and I spent my childhood lost and troubled. I met Charlie's dad when I was nineteen and saw him as a way to escape. Only it turned out bad, real fast. With him, I thought I could compensate for all the love I'd needed growing up but never got." She gave him a look. "You can imagine how well that worked out."

JP's gaze was full of sympathy. "I can, yeah."

"The one time he hit me was the day I left." She had never said that out loud to anyone before besides her old therapist.

"Fucker."

Yeah.

Sonny inhaled and then blurt out the awful truth. "I've only been in a relationship with one other guy since him and that was a total wreck. Once I let a guy get close this thing happens to me, and I become super insecure and distrustful, and then I run away." Well, that wasn't the whole truth. "Or, I get so wrapped up in myself that I push the person away, before they can leave me."

"Why are you telling me this, Sonny?"

Didn't he get it? "Because I'm crazy!" she blurted out. "I'm falling for you and I want to be with you and I'm terrified that I'm going to do the same things to you that I've done in the past and I'm just going to wreck every goddamn thing." She ended with a slump of her shoulders, feeling dejected.

JP sat his glass on the concrete and grabbed her chin, forcing her to look at him. "Listen to me, Sonny. You got dealt a shitty hand and it gave you baggage. I accept that. Nobody is perfect."

She stared at him through wide, watery eyes. "But what if I ruin everything?"

His gaze was dark with swirling emotion. "Then I'm not who I think I am."

What was that supposed to mean? "Wouldn't you rather have a relationship that's simple and uncomplicated without all the messed up backstory? Somebody who doesn't care that you're famous and that everybody wants up in your grill?" She ended with a slight smile, trying to be funny.

He grinned back and shrugged his broad shoulders. "Simple is for wussies."

"But—" she started to protest and he cut her off by putting his hand over her mouth.

"Enough worrying. At some point you have to just let go and let yourself experience. You have to let life happen. It's not all bad."

He was right. Absolutely, one hundred percent right. But there was still this one tiny thing.

She broke eye contact. "I don't want to get hurt." Her heart still echoed with the pains of the past. When she kept herself closeted away and out of arm's reach it didn't hurt so bad. And nobody knew, because she didn't say anything.

Everybody thought that she had it together. The truth was that she kept it together because she didn't have a choice. And they all respected her resolve to keep single and put Charlie at the front of everything. She said it was for him—that she was protecting him.

The truth was she was trying to protect herself.

JP caressed her cheek. "Look at me." She looked. "I can't promise you that I'll never hurt you, Sonny. I'm a jackass sometimes. But I can promise you that I wouldn't have stepped into your life if I didn't intend to be here for a long time. I would never do that to you and Charlie."

It wasn't fair of her to ask for more than that. She knew there was no solid gold guarantee. And with him sitting there looking at her with eyes so honest and true she felt the need for one drop away. In her heart she knew that they were in good hands with JP. However things turned out.

Sonny also knew that if things turned sour it would be her doing, not his. And no, she didn't trust herself.

But she found that she trusted JP.

For now that was enough. "I think we should go inside."

Confusion clouded his eyes. "Am I leaving?"

Sonny stood and walked barefoot to the door. Pulling the screen open, she turned the knob on the heavy oak door and tossed him a smile full of suggestion over her shoulder. "Not any time soon."

"Then . . ." He shot out of his seat as the implication hit him. "Coming."

Sonny laughed. "That's the idea."

JP's mouth dropped open briefly and he said, his voice filled with appreciation, "Look at you, Sonny Miller, talking dirty."

She arched a brow at him, feeling saucy all of a sudden. "Want me to stop?"

He shook his head vehemently. "Hell no."

"Okay then." With that she left him standing on the porch in the moonlight.

She'd taken one step in the door when a strong arm wrapped tight around her waist and pulled her backward. Off balance, she fell against his hard sculpted chest.

"I have a better idea." JP whispered against her ear.

Better than what? Beds were for sleeping and for sex, weren't they? That's where she was headed.

But it wasn't where he was going. JP backed her off the porch into the grass where the moonlight spilled silver over them both.

SONNY HAD NEVER looked more beautiful to him than she did at that moment. Her skin was luminous in the pale light of the moon, her eyes deep pools swimming with emotion. Her body was rigid as she tried to keep it all under control.

Telling him about her past must have been hard. JP knew that he was lucky to have grown up in a stable, loving family. It seemed to become more and more of a rarity in the modern age. But he had, and because of it he had a good head on his shoulders, a solid sense of self-worth, and a profound love for family. To him, commitment wasn't a thing to fear. All he needed was to find the right woman.

And she was standing in front of him with big round eyes that were wells of mystery in the moonlight, biting her bottom lip.

As he raised his hand to place it on her neck just below her ear to pull her in for a kiss, he heard a loud rustling sound in the old maple tree next to them. Startled, Sonny whipped her head around as her body tensed.

JP looked into the branches and reached out, pulling her back snug against him. He pointed to a branch close to them and said, "It's an owl. Do you see it right there on the third branch up on this side?" The bird was big too.

She tipped her head back against his shoulder and looked up. The large night creature observed them silently. After a few minutes of watchfulness the owl spread its wings wide and took to the sky. All that could be heard was the soft *whoosh whoosh* of wings flapping, disturbing the quiet air.

After it was gone and the night was calm once again, Sonny rested her head against his shoulder and said, "Some Native American cultures believe that the owl represents wisdom and the mystical."

JP hugged her close. "Does that mean that what we're doing right now is wise and magical?"

A sexy little hum sounded in her throat. "Could be."

Running his hands over her hips, he kissed her temple and murmured against her hair, "I'll take that."

Since the moment he'd seen her at the charity event he'd thought about what it would be like to be right here with Sonny, to have her willing and open and ready for that next step. And now here they were, standing together on a balmy summer night under the stars about to make love. He knew it was a gamble with her feelings about him. But it was one that he was willing to make.

JP wanted to remember this always. To remember how she'd felt in his arms, her body warm and pliant for him.

Anticipation hummed along his veins, stirred his blood. While they stood there he grew almost painfully aware of her the shape of her body, the curves that pressed against him. The way her ass rounded and pushed back against him had him growing hard with need.

It was time.

JP let his hands roam her body, slowly exploring the sinuous shape of her. Her breathing became less steady, more erratic, punctuating the silence of night. The sound urged him on and he became bolder, his hands more demanding.

Stroking up her rib cage until he felt the plump weight of her breasts, he turned his hands over until they covered her, eliciting from her a soft gasp. Her nipples puckered tight against his palms. Rolling them gently, he reveled when she arched into him.

Her hands had moved to his thighs and were stroking him lightly, her ass pushing back against him. When he rocked his hard-on into her she moaned and turned her head into his neck, her breath hot on his skin. Her tongue slipped out, tasting him so tentatively, and his cock jerked, going rigid.

"You make me feel things, JP." Her voice had gone husky with arousal.

Good.

Desire permeated him and made his heart start pounding. *Her skin*, was all he could think. He needed to feel her skin against him. JP found the hem of her tank top and skimmed his hands underneath. Her skin was erotic silk against his fingertips, and he moaned softly.

He came to the barrier of her bikini top, and shoved the triangles of fabric to the side, impatient to have her breasts bare in his hands. They sprang free and he filled his palms with them, arousal nipping at him, urging him to simply take.

Sonny gasped and drew him down for a wet, open-mouthed kiss. Inhibition no longer a barrier holding her back, she thrust her breasts into his palms and dove her fingers into his hair. Wanting more, JP streaked a hand down her stomach and didn't stop until he was cupping her through her shorts. He found her hot and moist there and he thrust gently, teasingly against her until his cock was throbbing in time to the rhythm.

He kept up the sensual assault until she was so turned on her moans had taken on a desperate edge.

Needing to see her, all of her, naked in the moonlight, JP released her and slipped her tank top over her head. Then he removed the rest of her clothing and when she was wearing nothing but silver-tipped skin he turned her around to face him.

"You're beautiful," he breathed.

His lungs seized up tight as he took her in, his heart thundering in his chest. Sonny was perfection, and having her stand before him clothed in only moonlight made emotions slam into him hard. Unable to take it anymore, JP yanked his shirt over his head and pulled her in for a deep, drugging kiss.

The air around them changed and became charged

with sexual intensity. Like a live wire it sparked white hot between them and he groaned, his hands cupping the firm roundness of her bare cheeks. Her breasts against his chest nearly drove him mad with wanting her.

Tearing his mouth from hers, JP growled, "I thought I wanted slow with you, but I can't. I need to be inside you, Sonny." He squeezed her ass cheeks and pulled her even closer. "I need you."

"God." Her hands were on his shorts, fighting the zipper to free him. Victorious, she shoved fabric away until her hand was wrapped around him. Hunger ripped through him with violent force.

In an instant he had Sonny on her back in the sweet, fragrant grass. Her hair spilled over her shoulders like a goddess and he took her nipple into his mouth and flicked his tongue over the hard peak. Slender hands dove into his hair and held his head to her. "Yes," she moaned.

Teasing her with lips, teeth, and tongue, JP explored her body with a hand. When he came to the curls at the junction of her thighs, he slipped a finger along her slick folds and found her clit.

She cried out, "JP!"

But his finger wasn't enough. He wanted to taste her.

Moving down her quivering body, JP kissed a moist path to her center. The heavy scent of her arousal went straight to his head and he stroked his tongue boldly over her. Sonny cried out and arched against him, her thighs shaking with need.

Again and again he lapped at her, emotion and desire a heady concoction inside him. Her breathing grew labored and she went taught as a bowstring, her body straining for him. Knowing that she wanted release, JP slipped a finger inside her and curled it until he found her G-spot.

Her back arched and she threw her head back, her fingernails digging sharply into his shoulders. "Oh God."

JP kept up the erotic assault until she was panting and her body was trembling on the brink. He felt primal and raw, every instinct homed in on the woman writhing against his mouth. With every gasp and thrust of her hips, his need to make her come grew even stronger, and he didn't let up until she cried out in release.

Her body was still shaking with aftershocks when he grabbed a condom from his wallet and covered himself. Then he moved over her and in one thrust filled her completely. "Fuck," he groaned. Sonny was so damn hot and wet he almost came. But then she drew her legs up and wrapped them around him, taking him deeper.

Words, so many words were on the tip of his tongue for her. So much he wanted to say. But then she was kissing him and he stopped thinking. Every thrust drove him closer and closer to the brink until he felt her tighten around him and she cried out in ecstasy. He couldn't hold back any more, and he went over, his orgasm crashing through him like a tidal wave.

Nothing had ever felt better.

Chapter Sixteen

SONNY WOKE THE next morning alone in her bed. Sunlight streamed through the open windows in her room, signaling the beginning of a new day. Yawning, she rolled over and stretched luxuriously and immediately winced. Her body was tender in places that hadn't been used in a very long time and her inner thighs were sore.

A huge grin split her face. God, it felt good.

Giving in to the urge, Sonny grabbed a pillow and squealed into it, damn near giddy with delight. Last night had been beyond amazing.

And she, Sonny Miller, was an extremely satisfied woman.

JP had made love to her two more times last night, bringing her to mind-blowing orgasms each and every time. No wonder she was feeling tender this morning.

But she wouldn't trade it. Not for all the money in the

world. He had made her feel things that she'd never felt before.

It had been hard to send him home, but it was the right thing to do. It was way too early for a sleepover where she'd have to explain to Charlie what he was doing there first thing in the morning.

A bubble of happiness wrapped around her heart. But maybe sometime soon. Who knew? The whole world seemed so full of possibility all of a sudden. Just a few short months ago there had been no one in her life. Now there was JP and she felt so much hope for the future.

Never in her life had a man done the things that he did.

Throwing her arms out, Sonny raised her knees and kicked the bed with her heels. "*Whoo!*" she cried out. Then she started laughing so hard tears came to her eyes.

A knock sounded at the door, freezing the laugh in her throat. "What's going on in there, Mom?"

The laughter of a well-laid woman, Sonny thought. That's what was going on. "Nothing special, honey."

Liar. It was so, so special. But he shouldn't know that. Not yet at least.

"Okay." She thought he was leaving, but he added, "Janie called and left a message while you were sleeping in. Are you getting sick again?" he ended with worry coloring his tone.

"Nope." She hadn't felt this good in years.

Last night had been the most incredible experience of her life. She still couldn't believe she'd had sex outside under the stars. And not just once. But twice. The second time had been against a tree.

The third time they'd finally made it to the bed, where they'd dozed in each other's arms contentedly afterward until he'd had to go. They'd fit together like they were custom made.

Throwing the covers off, Sonny climbed out of bed and searched out some clothes. Pulling on a cami and jersey-knit yoga pants, she was about to open the door when something occurred to her.

She felt zero anxiety over what had happened between her and JP.

Standing in the center of her bedroom, Sonny paused and searched inside herself, marveling at what she found. For a woman who has spent most of her adult life avoiding intimate relationships, she had expected to feel some anxiousness or doubt over becoming involved. But she didn't. What did that say about her?

More to the point, what did it say about JP?

Pulled from her musings by the sound of her phone ringing, Sonny opened the door to her bedroom and went in search of it. Finding it on the fireplace mantel, she snatched it up and answered before it went to voice-mail.

"This is Sonny."

"Why didn't you pick up earlier?" It was Janie. "You weren't still asleep, were you?"

Like a baby. "As a matter of fact I was."

"Are you sick?" Janie instantly sounded concerned. Sonny was a notoriously early riser.

"I was just tired, that's all."

"You sound strange. Is everything okay?" She had

these mom instincts that were freakily perceptive, and they'd decided to kick in on her.

Sonny was better than okay. "Just peachy."

Some of the tension seemed to leave Janie's voice. "Well that's good. I'm relieved to hear it because I have plans for us today."

Like what? "Don't you have the kids?"

"Ben's taking the day off and spending it with the kids at the zoo." She sounded grateful for the break. It wasn't often she got an afternoon free of children. "Charlie is welcome to go, too."

"That sounds terrific. What are we up to, then?"

Janie paused for dramatic effect. "We're hitting the thrift stores in Boulder."

Ooh, good call. That was always a great time. Boulder's thrift stores were excellent and full of designer and one-of-a-kind items. It was like the Beverly Hills of consignment shopping. "Sounds good. Do you want to grab something to eat while we're out?"

"Of course."

Oh, right. She'd forgotten for a split second that she was talking to a pregnant woman. "There's that burger place on Pearl Street that you like so much. We can do that if you want."

Janie replied, "Let's play it by ear. We can talk about it more when you get here. How long do you think it'll take for you to get ready?"

Well, she was kind of sore and moving slowly. Go her. "Let's make it eleven. Will that work?" She wondered how long she'd be able to keep her mouth shut about last night when she saw Janie. Or maybe it was plastered all over her face and she wouldn't even have to say anything.

"That'll work. I'll see you then." They said their good-byes and hung up.

Sonny got busy with her chores and put in some time in her work space before hopping in the shower and getting ready to go.

And as it turned out, it *was* written all over her face. Janie took one look at her when she arrived and her eyes nearly popped out of her head. "In the car. Now. You have some explaining to do, Sonny Miller."

It wasn't really a hardship. She was dying to talk to her about it anyway. "Let me just say goodbye to Charlie and then we can head out."

Sonny found him in with the other kids and gave him a quick hug. Double-checking that his cell phone was charged, when she was satisfied she handed it back to him and gave him a kiss. "Be good for Ben, okay?" He nodded. "Have a great time, sweetheart. I'll see you later."

Taking her minivan, she made Janie wait until they'd arrived at their first destination in Boulder before she spilled the goods. She knew the suspense was killing her best friend, but couldn't resist the temptation to draw out the news. It's not as if she had stuff like this to share like, oh, ever.

They'd just exited the Honda when Janie stopped and demanded, "Well, are you going to tell me or not?"

Because she couldn't resist, Sonny gave her an innocent look. "What are you talking about?"

Aqua-blue eyes narrowed on her. "You know damn well what I'm talking about, and you're holding out on me."

Enjoying herself, she shrugged her shoulders delicately. "I'm not sure that I do."

The pregnant brunette looked about ready to throttle her. "You did something with that hot ballplayer."

Sonny locked the Honda and tossed the keys in her purse. "Maybe." There was no maybe about it. But it was so much fun to finally have a juicy carrot to dangle that she wasn't ready to give it up. For the better part of a decade her gossip basket had been virtually empty of any yummy tidbits. Now that there was a tasty morsel in there she wanted to milk it for all it was worth.

Janie waddled around the car and said, "Are you happy about it?"

An image flashed in her mind of JP last night, sweaty and intensely aroused. Her pulse kicked up a notch just thinking about it. "So, so happy."

Janie wrapped her up in a hug. "Then I'm happy for you." She pulled back and shot Sonny a pointed look. "But I want all the sordid details. Don't leave anything out."

Because it was her best friend she caved. "We were together last night and it blew my mind, Janie. Seriously."

The brunette gave her an extra tight squeeze. "It's about time somebody did, honey."

It surprised her to find that she agreed. Standing on this side of things—the side where she had sex with an incredibly gorgeous and good man—well, it brought a whole new perspective. One that was beginning to make her wonder what she'd been so afraid of in the first place.

A voice whispered in her mind, reminding her of his celebrity, and she mentally winced. Then she told it to back off because this was her moment for just plain happiness and she was going to have it.

Taking the lead, Sonny began walking toward the front entrance of the swanky Boulder consignment shop. Excitement over the impending treasure hunt had her walking a bit faster than normal. The last time she'd come to this place with Janie she'd discovered a set of Corning baking dishes from the seventies that she'd fallen in love with. They were white with blue chickens and orange flowers painted on them in that style so characteristic of the era.

She'd been after finding the mugs that went with the set, but to date hadn't had any luck. Maybe this time the universe would be in her favor. Just thinking about it had her pulse leaping into action.

The hunt for vintage fabulousness was on.

"Hey, Sonny. So, tell me something because I'm curious." Janie tucked a stray strand of her espresso-brown locks behind her ear. An unholy gleam was in her eyes. Whatever she was about to say was less than pure and innocent. "Did the ol' girl even remember how to work after all this time?"

Psssh. "Like a champ, sistah."

Janie placed a hand over her heart and faked sincerity. "Oh well, now that's a relief."

"Isn't it just?" She couldn't be in more agreement.

Sonny held the door open for Janie and the brunette said as she passed, "On a scale of one to ten, how good did he look naked?"

She didn't even blink. "Fifteen."

"I'M NOT TELLING you what her boobs look like, Drake, no matter how many times you ask. You gotta get over it, hoss."

JP watched out of the corner of his eye as Drake dropped down into the airplane seat beside him. The first baseman gave a long-suffering sigh. "Ain't fair, brother, dropping news of consensual relations with the foxy mom and not sharing crucial details."

"My bad."

"Ain't that the truth." He scratched his chest.

JP laughed because Drake was completely serious.

The team was on the flight home from an away series in Atlanta against the Braves. The Rush had come out on top of the series, and they were all feeling good about how things were starting to shape up for the playoffs. Now that the midseason break was over, the playoffs were starting to take center stage.

Stretching his legs out in front of him in the large first-class seat, JP laced his fingers behind his head and grinned. "I will say that it was worth the wait."

Drake's homely face fell and he looked sad as a basset hound. "Why you got to be cruel, man?"

Pete piped up from across the aisle. Eavesdropping was his specialty. "I think our boy is afraid we'll find out he's lame in the sack if he shares the deets."

Getting a ribbing from those two was par for the course. He still wasn't sharing more than he already had—and even that had been an accident. He'd made the mistake of sitting next to Drake in a confined space. That dude could detect the smallest change in behavior. It must have been the dip in his pheromones or something because the ballplayer had jumped all over him instantly.

Mark Cutter decided to make a break for the airplane bathroom and stood up from the seat in front of JP. Stepping into the aisle, he said, "Don't let these pansies harass you. They're just jealous that you got a woman."

He thought about that for a minute. He *did* have a woman. And he couldn't wait to touch down so he could go to her. Ever since he'd tasted her that night, JP had been dying to do it again. Sonny was under his skin and on his mind.

The watch on his wrist gave the time and he did a mental calculation. It would be pushing pretty late by the time he got to Sonny's place. Hopefully she would be in a good mood and not pissed that he had been gone for such a long time right after they'd finally got together.

It was the first time in his professional life that he'd even stopped to consider how much he was gone. He'd never felt self-conscious about it before, but he did now, thinking about her and how many days had passed. He and Sonny had just rounded a corner and gotten physical. Then he'd disappeared for the better part of a week.

Though he'd called her, it just wasn't the same.

Nothing could compare to the feel of her silky smooth legs wrapped around him, urging him to come.

Peter slapped his shoulder to get his attention. "What's the scoop with the kid?"

"What do you mean? In what way?"

The pitcher leaned his head back against the seat. "Does the kid know that you and his mom are in a relationship?"

JP shook his head. "I'm not sure, but I assume so."

Peter nailed him with a stare, his ice-blue eyes penetrating. "Why haven't you two told him? Or are you afraid to tell him?"

Why would he be afraid? He wanted this, remember? "I'm not afraid, Kowalskin. And I don't know. We haven't talked about it." But he was pretty sure Sonny had already told him. The boy knew what was going on between him and his mother. Didn't he?

Drake elbowed JP in the rib cage. "You worried about the kid approving?"

"Why wouldn't he?" He honestly wanted to know. If he was in Charlie's shoes, he'd be damn happy to have his mom date someone like him.

Drake gave him a peculiar look. "You may not be what he pictured in a step-dad, bro."

Why wouldn't he be? Shit. He'd be the best damn step-dad in the business.

Of course Charlie would want him.

Wouldn't he?

Chapter Seventeen

THE HOUSE WAS quiet—Charlie was at a sleepover—and Sonny couldn't stand it. Some days it was great. Other days, like now, when she was trying so hard to distract herself, the silence was just unnerving.

Deciding to take action, she put on Pandora Internet radio and cranked it loud. It was set on mixed-artist mode and automatically chose something random to play. Humming along to a song by nineties girl-wonder group En Vogue about men who were never gonna get it, Sonny grabbed the broom from the pantry and began sweeping.

It was late, and she should have been lounging happily in front of the flat screen or enjoying the luxury of a long uninterrupted bath. But she couldn't relax enough to do either. Nervous energy had her feeling antsy and restless. Well, no, that wasn't the whole truth.

She was jonesing for JP.

That's what was at the heart of it. A big part of her was nervous to see him again because she wasn't sure how he was going to act. But everything had been left on good terms. Really, she was just worrying for nothing. Wasn't she?

Ugh. The uncertainty that came after being with someone was such an awful feeling. Just the fact that she was already feeling it made her tense up with frustration. This was how it always started.

Rejecting the thought, Sonny cranked the music even louder and swept furiously. The house was long overdue for a deep clean. And having Charlie out of the house was the perfect time to do it. And if it was a handy excuse to not have to think about her new relationship with JP, then so be it. It's not like she was completely avoiding the issue.

Just mostly.

Catching sight of her profile in a hand-painted mirror on the wall, Sonny stopped in her tracks and blew a curl out of her face with a huff. Who was she kidding? She was totally avoiding everything.

For the first time in a very long time she wasn't sure of her next move. On one hand she wanted to dive headlong into this thing with JP. He pulled feelings out of her that were big and shiny and almost overwhelming.

As she swept around the fireplace she thought about who JP was and ticked off a mental list of his qualities. The man was smart and kind and totally smitten with her. In the privacy of her home all alone she could admit that truth. And it gave her butterflies in her stomach to the extreme.

Not to mention that the shortstop was good to Charlie.

If she were to think of any flaw (because the fame thing wasn't a flaw—it was a fact. A really irritating fact that wouldn't go away), it would be his sometimes overinflated ego. Sonny had never seen anyone more confident or secure in their choices. It must be nice to never second-guess oneself, to never worry over the best course of action.

No doubt it had its shortcomings, but in their case, JP's ego was a good thing. Because she was such a spaz it was nice that one of them had a handle on things. Surely JP wouldn't make a mistake. He was too sure of himself for that.

In fact, she was kind of relying on it. His self-assurance was her guide rope through the dark.

Speaking of JP, why hadn't he called her this evening?

Yesterday he'd left a message, but today there was nothing. And he was back in town. She'd watched some of the early game on the tube. Charlie had insisted on it.

Was it wrong to assume that, since they'd slept together and this was his first night back, he would have called her after the game? Because by looking at the time on the clock it suggested that she was. And she didn't like what that said. Not one little bit.

Michael Franti and Spearhead came on Pandora, singing "Say Hey (I Love You)," a song with a snappy Caribbean beat. Sonny leaned the broom against the fireplace and moved her hips to the rhythm, glad for the diversion.

Her whole body in motion, Sonny was rocking out hard and it felt so, so good. Tension melted away with every dip, spin, and shimmy. In the privacy of her home she let it all hang out, dancing and singing her heart out.

It was exhilarating.

Planting her feet, Sonny dipped and rotated her hips in a saucy grind, her arms flung up over her head in the air. Belting out about looking in their eyes and suddenly knowing, she did a big ol' booty shake and turned.

And came face to face with a wildly grinning JP.

"Jesus!" She froze, her heart racing frantically. How much had he seen?

The man made a twirling motion with a finger, his eyes lit with devilish humor. "Don't let me stop you, sweetheart. Keep going."

Sonny was going to die. Right there on her living room floor at the ripe old age of thirty-one. The cause of her demise was complete and utter embarrassment.

Please oh please oh please oh pleeease let me be dreaming, she thought desperately.

Blinking hard, she muttered a curse under her breath when she opened them again and he was still there. Taking a deep breath, though it did nothing to slow her racing heartbeat, Sonny rolled her eyes to the ceiling and let out her breath with a *whoosh*. Was there no end to the attacks on her dignity?

Belatedly realizing that she probably resembled a goldfish with her mouth open and floundering, she snapped it shut and attempted to be nonchalant. "I wasn't expecting you, JP."

"I knocked, but the music was so loud it was pointless. I just let myself in."

The embarrassment she felt over knowing that he saw her dancing like a stripper had her face flaming. She had never blushed so hard in her life. Not even the time her pants had fallen down in front of the entire eighth grade.

And if he didn't stop grinning at her like a mad man she was going to clobber him.

"That was some mighty fine dancing. If I asked real nice, could I get a repeat performance?" he finished with a straight face even though his amber eyes glittered with laughter.

Not in this lifetime. "I don't do encores." She tossed her haphazard braid over her shoulder and tried for calm and collected.

JP started to walk toward her, his long muscular legs stealthy as a leopard. "Seems if I recall right, the last time I was here you had plenty of encores."

Well that was different. "Why didn't you call earlier?" Maybe changing the topic would distract him. Besides, she really wanted to know.

"Because I wanted to surprise you." He shot her a pointed look. "Seems like I succeeded."

Ugh. Why was he teasing her like that? And why oh why did he have to look so damned gorgeous tonight? He wore low-slung jeans and a heather-grey T-shirt like they were tailor made for him. He'd skipped shaving and had a five o'clock shadow on his chiseled jaw. She didn't know whether to jump him or smack him for walking in on her and embarrassing her so badly.

His tongue wet his bottom lip, and suddenly all Sonny could think about was jumping his bones. She forgot all about being embarrassed. That edgy, restless feeling came running back with a vengeance. Only this time she had somewhere to put it: right smack on JP.

It didn't matter that she was already starting to have insecurities, that she still couldn't get around his fame. When he looked at her like he was doing now with his penetrating honey-colored eyes, all she could think about was getting him naked. Because the truth was that he scrambled her heart, not just her head.

Reaching for the remote, she turned the music down until it was a respectable decibel. Having him in her living room reminded her just how much she'd actually missed him while he was gone. And if she was missing him it was because he was special.

He got her emotions pumping. "How were the games against Atlanta?"

His gaze raked her from head to toe. "Hot." Sonny was pretty sure he didn't mean the weather.

Attempting small talk, she opened her mouth to speak, but he shut her up with a kiss worthy of a queen. A very, very naughty queen. And it felt amazing. Emotions swept through her and she opened immediately to him.

When JP broke the kiss he lowered his forehead to hers. "I missed you, Sonny."

His whispered words snuggled warm inside her chest. It felt good to be missed. "Charlie's at a sleepover."

JP arched a brow and hooked a hand into the front of her pants, pulling her flush against him. "Is that so?"

Uh-huh. "Yep."

The song changed again. This time a heavy, sensual

song came on. Sexy, crooning R&B. Sonny recognized the old song and felt the bass make her blood go thick and slow. Ginuwine's "Pony" filled the room, the singer going on about jumping on his saddle.

Suddenly that's exactly what Sonny wanted. And that was exactly what she was going to get. Everything else could wait.

It was time to give him that repeat performance.

Chapter Eighteen

JP SAW THE change in her the minute the song shifted, and his instincts went on high alert. Sonny placed a hand on his chest and backed him to the couch. When the back of his calves hit the sofa she shoved hard and he fell into the cushions off balance.

The woman had the kind of look in her eyes that made a man sit up and take notice. "What's on your mind there, Sonny?" If he was a gambling sort of guy he'd wager she was interested in some adult activities.

She placed a finger across his lips and said, "*Shhhh*."

For the better part of a week JP had thought about being with her again. And now that she was standing in front of him in a skimpy tank top that showed off her nipples to perfection, he went instantly achy and needy.

The song finally registered and JP swallowed. He was definitely horny. Then Sonny started moving her hips to the beat in front of him. Her hair tumbled in a loose braid over her shoulder, and on her face was the half smile of a siren. "Did you want that repeat?"

It hit him then. Sonny was going to do a strip tease.

God yeah. He swallowed again, his throat parched, and nodded.

Leaning back against the couch cushions, JP stretched his arms out along the back and waited, his gaze hot on her. He knew what she had going on underneath her clothes and it was killing him. It made him hard as stone for her.

The heavy beat of the song lulled him, and when she rocked her hips in time to it, the movement was hypnotizing. "You like watching me dance?" She stroked her hands over her body, briefly cupped her breasts, and his mouth went to sawdust.

All he could do was stare.

Though she'd been embarrassed before, she sure as hell wasn't now. Instead she was working it like a Pussycat Doll. With her back to him she circled her hips erotically and then arched her back, flipping her hair and shoving her ass toward him. All on its own one of his hands reached out to squeeze, but she slapped it away.

"Uh-uh."

God he wanted to take a bite out of that ass, it looked so damn juicy.

Straightening, her back still to him, Sonny pulled her tank top over her head and threw it on the floor a few feet away. Then with excruciating slowness she inched her pants off until she was gloriously naked before him—all he could see was shapely ass and the junction between her thighs.

His penis strained against the fly of his jeans. "Bring that sweet ass over here," he demanded. Before he leapt off the couch and took her right there on the cold hardwood floor.

Her eyes were dark and full of mystery as she glanced over her shoulder, seeming to consider. "I don't think I will." She was killing him. "I want to dance."

And she did. Naked and seductive as a gypsy. While he sat, aroused and ready, she moved sinuously in the dim light. Losing herself in the music, Sonny rocked and rotated and slid her hands over her curves until he was panting with restraint.

It was the most erotic thing he'd ever seen.

When he had reached the point where he couldn't take any more, she came to him and placed her hands on his thighs, leaning forward with her gorgeous breasts on full display. "Tell me you want me, JP."

"I want you." He had never been more serious. He wanted her like he wanted to breathe.

She traced a fingertip over his erection and smiled at him through her lashes, making him burn. "Well that's handy."

He heard the sound of his zipper opening and then he sprang free. She wrapped a hand around him lightly. "Jesus, Sonny." His head fell back against the cushion. *Whatever has gotten into her, please don't let it stop*, was all he could think.

He felt her move and the next thing he knew she was kneeling between his legs, gold-fire curls tumbling from a sloppy braid, her plump breasts begging to be kissed.

With the tips of her fingernails she traced matching paths up his inner thighs, his skin so sensitive to her touch that even through his jeans she branded him, claiming ownership with her butterfly-kiss touch.

Breath hissed between his bared teeth and he reached out to touch her, the desire to feel her silky skin overwhelming. Again she refused him and pushed his hand away. "Not yet." Giving in, JP let his hands drop to the cushions and watched the sexiest woman on earth look at him with desire in her eyes.

As he watched, Sonny ran the tip of her finger up the length of him. His cock leapt at her hot little caress, and she looked at him all coquettish. And when she rubbed her fingertip around the ridge with her bottom lip between her teeth, he almost lost control and came.

Her tongue replaced her fingertip and he bucked involuntarily. "Sweet Jesus."

She rose up and straddled him, one long gorgeous bare thigh on each side. "Condom," he panted and rolled, lifting his hip. She got one from his wallet and put it on him, stroking and teasing him along the way.

Finally she settled over him and he gritted his teeth. Then she was surrounding him, hot and wet and demanding, and he saw stars behind his eyes. Holy shit, the woman felt good. So goddamn good.

He had to touch her. Now. Grabbing a fistful of braid, JP pulled her in for a ravenous kiss, not relenting until she moaned helplessly against him. His other hand was on her breast, stroking her hip, grabbing her perfectly bare cheek. It roamed every inch of her body, desperate for the feel of her.

PLAYING THE FIELD 203

Peeling his lips from hers, JP gulped in air and went straight for a breast, sucking on her nipple hungrily as she rocked rhythmically on him. Her head fell back and she cried out, moving closer and closer to her release.

Gripping her hips hard, JP held her and thrust deep. Sonny moaned and cried out. Her orgasm swept through her and her muscles clamped down on him hard, milking him to his own completion. Feeling it build, he plunged into her again and let his release explode inside him. "Fuck!" he cried out, seeing stars again.

For long minutes they stayed like that. Then Sonny's head dropped limply on his shoulder. Their erratic breathing was the only sound in the house. When he started to slip from her, she rolled from him and tossed him a very satisfied smile.

Stretching her slender arms above her head she said, "That was *way* good."

JP rolled his head along the back of the couch and looked at her with one open eye. He was seriously relaxed. "True that." The woman had screwed him stupid.

Bless her heart for it.

While he watched her, she stood up and began gathering her clothes, which made him frown. "Stay naked."

She tossed him a look and shook her head. "No chance, JP."

God, he was relaxed. He could barely muster the strength to lift his head to frown at her directly. Sonny was potent as hell. "I like the way you look without any clothes on. Your body was made for it." He found the energy for a grin. "Especially that big freckle on your left ass cheek." That he had big plans for in the near future. The sexy mark was seriously hot.

Sonny laughed softly. "I'm glad, but I'm still getting dressed."

JP lowered his head back on the couch again. "Party pooper."

"That's part of my job description," she quipped and planted a cajoling kiss on his lips. "Sorry, baby."

Something inside him grew very still. The part that recognized that something profound had just taken place. It was the first time she'd called him "baby." Or any other pet name, come to think of it. Could it be that she was falling for him?

How fucking sweet would that be?

Lightning-fast, he snagged her around the waist and pulled her across him, tickling her ribcage. Sonny burst out laughing and thrashed against him, trying to get away. With her giggling in his arms the whole world felt right.

He pulled back and looked at her, her blue eyes bright like diamonds, and that's when he felt it, when it hit him. That's when he felt his heart step headlong into love and it rocked the hell out of him. It wasn't a gentle feeling. No, it felt like he'd been drilled in the chest with one of Pete's hundred-mile-an-hour fastballs.

It took his breath away.

The smile on her lips began to transform into a frown of worry and he shook himself, trying to shake it off, even though he was still reeling. Lowering his head, JP kissed her with trembling lips. Emotion threatened to overwhelm him so he pulled back and attempted an easy smile. He dug for control.

"Are you all right, JP?" Apparently it wasn't so easy.

He helped her sit up. "Yeah." Nope. Not even close.

A wary expression overcame her, and he tried to explain by lying. "I think I pulled something during the game today, that's all."

Anxiety eased from her expressive blue eyes and he breathed a sigh of relief. What just happened had taken him so by surprise that he needed some time to process it. Then he'd figure out how to tell her.

Sonny inclined her head toward the kitchen. "Do you need any ice to put on it?"

Twenty minutes ago he'd have said yes. It had been so hot in the room, he was mildly surprised the place was still standing. "I think I'll be fine. But thanks for the offer." He looked around and asked, "I could use the bathroom, though."

Attempting to re-braid the tangled mess of her hair, Sonny pointed an elbow down the far hall. "Second door on the right."

Once inside, he took care of business and washed his hands. But before leaving, he planted his palms on the blue tile and looked at himself in the mirror. On the outside he still looked the same. Same annoyingly long eyelashes. Same eyes, same nose, same chin. Same chest.

It was what was inside that had changed.

In such a huge way that it was going to take a long while before he got used to the new setup. Wanting Sonny and falling in love with Sonny were entirely different feelings, come to find out. There was so much to it, so many nuances that he needed time to sort it all through.

But one thing was clear. Sonny was his and he had to put some thought into how he wanted to move forward.

Still pondering it when he entered kitchen, he found Sonny heating a tea kettle with hot water. She was once again braided and dressed, and she looked so sweet and soft that he couldn't resist wrapping her up in his arms and breathing in the scent of her. "How did you know I'd want tea?"

Wrapping her arms over his, she squeezed gently and shrugged. "Good guess I suppose."

Dropping a kiss on her head, he disagreed. "Nah. It's more than that. You get me."

She was quiet for a minute, contemplating. "You'd be the first."

Deciding to keep it light because he could tell that statement was a loaded one, he said, "First is best, baby."

That got a small smile from her. He'd take it.

Sonny spun in his arms real quick, surprising him, and planted a kiss on his lips. "You're one of a kind."

He grinned cheekily, "Good of you to notice."

He *was* one of a kind. Maybe it gave him an ego that he believed that, but he didn't think so. He considered it healthy self-love.

As he took a mug out from the cupboard, he asked, "You going to tell me what inspired that back there? Not that I'm complaining," he added hastily.

Rifling through the boxes of tea, Sonny settled on one and shrugged. "I decided to be adventurous."

Hallelujah. "I'm all in favor of doing what I can to encourage this new trend." Anytime, anywhere.

She chuckled and held up two teas for him to choose
from. "That's real sweet of you."

He pointed to the chamomile and she grabbed a bag.
"Anything I can do to support a good cause."

The way the two of them moved together was like a
well-practiced dance. It was real nice just hanging out
with her at night when the world was quiet, talking
through the day. When he was with Sonny he was relaxed, and he found himself opening up about things he
most often kept inside. He knew they had some work to
do around her feelings, but he wasn't going to let his fame
be a deal breaker.

The tea kettle started whistling and she removed it
from the burner. Pouring hot water into the tea mugs,
Sonny then handed one to JP. "Random question for you."

He inhaled and smiled because he could smell the
chamomile under his nose and it made him happy.
"Random answer."

"What does JP stand for?"

"Just Perfect."

She made a face. "I'm serious. What's your full name?"

JP leaned his butt into the counter, crossed his legs
at the ankle, and took a tentative sip of his tea. It didn't
quite burn his tongue, which he considered the perfect
temperature, and he took another drink. "Jet Pack."

She leveled a look at him and he held out a hand.

"All right. Okay you got me, I'll confess. Are you
ready?" He took a pause for dramatic effect and then

said on a rushed exhale like what he was spilling was top secret, "It stands for Jumbo Penis."

Sonny laughed outright and added honey to her mug. "Now, we both know that's not true."

He feigned injury. "Ouch." She laughed again and he finally relented, "It stands for Jason Patrick."

Turning her head, she considered him. "Jason. *Hmmm.* It suits you."

"Yeah, my mom loves to use it when I'm home visiting. Makes her feel like I'm still twelve." Only with less dirt on his clothes. Most of the time.

"Well. What should we do now?"

JP glanced around. Everything was quiet and in relative order. Charlie was at a sleepover and the radio had stopped playing a while ago. He knew exactly what he wanted to do.

JP glanced around the house like he was making sure they were completely alone. What he was about to say was a little embarrassing, even for him.

The hell with it. "Got any more episodes of *Hart of Dixie*?"

Chapter Nineteen

JP HAD INVITED Sonny and Charlie to another ball game at Coors Field. She settled into her seat with a soda and popcorn and waited for her son, who was still out in the aisle. He was trailing behind her in the giant Rush jersey that JP had surprised him with. Though it swallowed him whole, her boy wore it proudly like he was the Prince of Wales and it carried his royal crest.

Sonny shielded her eyes with a hand and looked up at the sky. It was another absolutely gorgeous and sun-filled summer afternoon along the Front Range. The weather forecast was calling for rain overnight, but there was zero evidence of it now. The sky was totally cloud-free and there was very little humidity.

But that was one of the crazy things about living in Colorado. The weather was unpredictable. It blew hot and cold so fast that it could leave a person in trouble if they weren't prepared. And that's why she always kept a

survival kit and a few spare blankets in the trunk of her
minivan.

It had come in very handy last winter when she'd
been caught on one of the back roads during a big storm
after a work delivery. She had run into a pickup truck in
the ditch on the side of the road. The elderly woman had
been stuck in the cold for hours after her aging Datsun
had spun out of control on some ice. The blankets and
energy bars she'd provided the woman had been a life-
saver.

But for now the weather was perfect and Sonny had
taken advantage of it, wearing pink denim shorts and a
halter top. Though it wasn't exactly the most sporty of
outfits, it had fit her mood perfectly. She'd completed the
look with hemp bracelets and dangly earrings. And, of
course, flip-flops.

Charlie made his way over, calling out, "I can't wait to
watch JP play today."

Sonny assumed some of that enthusiasm had to do
with the fact that the kid was sporting the ballplayer's
jersey today. He was feeling all kinds of proud. And she
had to admit that she was too. It was interesting how different it felt watching JP play ball this time around versus
the first game she'd attended after they'd met.

There was this feeling of investment that wasn't there
last time. Her nerves jittered and danced. But it was more
than that. She'd slept with him. They had a relationship,
and that made it more personal.

It mattered how he played because she cared how
he was going to feel afterward. And if that wasn't a tell-

ing statement about her feelings, then she didn't know what was.

Holy cow.

Stunned by the implication of that statement, Sonny stared blankly at her son until he crinkled his nose and demanded, "What'd I do?"

Oh my, was all she could think. *When had that happened?*

When had she fallen in love with JP?

Reeling, Sonny stammered, "N-n-nothing, sweetie."

Concern filled his deep ocean eyes. "Are you okay?"

Not in the slightest. Shaking her head, she plastered a smile on and said, too cheerfully, "Absolutely!"

Charlie's eyes squinted like he didn't believe her. "You look like you saw a ghost, Mom." He put a hand on the front of his new jersey and added, "Please don't throw up on me. I don't wanna get it ruined 'cause it's brand new."

Ahh, the selflessness of youth.

Searching for composure, Sonny inhaled slowly while she counted to ten and let it out. "I'm not going to throw up on you, Charlie."

The kid actually looked relieved. The next time she had an earth-shattering epiphany and he told her not to barf, she was going to do it anyway, out of spite. God, what was she supposed to do now? This is usually the point where her train went straight off track to locoville. She *sooo* didn't want that to happen this time.

Tears stung her eyes and she blinked them back hard. There was no need to panic, she reassured herself. No need to freak out.

Charlie sat down next to her and pointed. "Look, JP's out on the field."

With her heart pounding Sonny looked across the field until she spotted him. He had his legs spread and was bent over, ready to snag some grounders. Her heart leapt at the sight of him all athletic and fit in his baseball uniform. The way his pants clung to his thighs was highly distracting. She knew just how hard they were and how much power was there. Rough, raw, thrusting power.

Sonny jerked her eyes from JP and glanced around. If she didn't control her thoughts she was going to embarrass herself. "He wants to have dinner with us after the game, if you're up for it."

Charlie nodded vigorously. "Totally."

Because she saw an opening, Sonny said casually, "Seems like you think he's pretty cool, sweetie."

Her kid glanced at her quickly before returning his attention to the ballplayers on the field. "I really like him. He's awesome."

And that right there pretty much summed it all up from the perspective of a ten-year-old boy. It didn't have to be any more complicated than that. Why was it so much damn harder for her?

"How would you feel if he hung out with us even after the baseball season was over?" Until she'd said it out loud she hadn't known she had even been considering it.

Feeling the panic begin to claw its way up her throat, Sonny shoved at it frantically. No need to think about commitment already. She hadn't even figured out how she felt about the other thing. "Never mind, buddy. Forget I said anything."

Charlie looked at her, confused. "What do you mean? Like you guys dating or something? Why would you do that?"

She shook her head, misreading the look in his eyes. "It's okay. Don't worry about it." He looked upset to her. Like he wasn't okay with her dating JP. And him not being okay with it made her feel sick inside.

Though his voice was soft, she still heard him say, "Why change things?"

What was wrong with her? How could she really date JP when her boy wasn't okay with it? Hadn't she sworn she'd never be like her mom? If she continued to date JP, even knowing it upset Charlie, wouldn't that make her just like Grace—choosing a man over her own child?

Just then Charlie started waving to somebody down the bleacher seats. It distracted Sonny and she leaned back and looked around him to find out who it was. Her eyebrows shot up in surprise when she saw that it was Lorelei and Leslie. The two women were making their way through the crowd toward them, their hands loaded down with sodas and hot dogs.

Charlie said over his shoulder, "We got company, Mom."

Goody. Just what she wanted after the revelations she'd just had. "Super, big C."

He loved it when she called him that. It made him giggle every single time. On cue he snorted, and she could see his slender shoulders shaking beneath the huge jersey.

She really loved her boy.

Sonny was feeling perfectly distracted from her problems by sentimentality, bubbles of love bursting all around her for her son. Whatever she'd done wrong in her life, Charlie was the one thing that she had done right.

Wrapping an arm around his shoulders from behind, she pulled him back for a quick hug and kissed him on the top of his ball cap. "I love you, Charlie."

He adjusted his hat as he straightened, trying hard not to look so pleased over her display of affection because he was a tween and all now. "Love you too," he returned quickly. It wouldn't do for him to be overheard. Mushy stuff was for girls.

Witnessing that blossoming independence was bittersweet.

Through the shaded lenses of her sunglasses, Sonny watched the women approach and gave them a friendly smile. "Hello, ladies," she said when they got within earshot.

Mark's fiancée plopped down in an empty seat and said to Charlie, "Whew. It's crowded here today."

Her boy nodded. "It's 'cause the Rush are doing so good this season."

Lorelei tucked her drink under her seat and smiled prettily. "You're spot on, Charlie. How you been, kid?"

He shrugged his shoulders and replied nonchalantly, "Can't complain."

Sonny nearly choked on her drink. That was such a manly thing he'd just said. It really was happening overnight.

Leslie maneuvered past the two of them and took the

empty seat next to Sonny. The blonde looked just as stunning as she had the last time they'd been together, even casual in jeans and a Ben Harper T-shirt. She had one of those bodies that was stacked in all the right places and toned, but not petite. The result was voluptuous pinup curves and a face that could break a man's heart with one glance.

Sonny would feel frumpy and plain sitting next to her if she wasn't so accepting of her own looks. Leslie was one of those women. "Hey y'all. Lorelei and I asked Mark to get us seats near you so we could chat during the game."

Lorelei brushed her dark hair over a shoulder. "We thought it would be fun, and we could get to know each other better."

Suspicion streaked across her brain, but she tried to ignore it. Still, why would they want to get to know her and Charlie better? He was done playing batboy.

Her eyes flew wide. Did they know about her and JP?

Leslie pointed down the field. "That's John Crispin out there. He and I have been dating for a little over a year. And y'all know about Lorelei and Mark." She turned to Sonny with an innocent smile that wasn't innocent at all. "What about you, darling? Who are you dating?"

Put on the spot at the absolute worst time, Sonny rolled her eyes to the sky and prayed for patience. How was she supposed to answer that when Charlie was sitting right next to her, without him knowing?

Her mouth opened to answer and closed with a snap. Then it promptly fell open again. What was there to say?

Lorelei took pity on her. "Hey, Charlie. Do you see

Mark over there?" Her son nodded. "Did you know that he started playing ball when he was in kindergarten?"

Charlie's face lit up. "Me too!"

The pretty brunette feigned surprise. "Really? Are you going to be a ballplayer when you grow up?"

That sent her son into a rambling monologue about the game, and Sonny tuned out even as Lorelei listened avidly. Returning her attention to Leslie, she evaded the question. "How long have you been in Colorado?"

Shrewd, tawny-colored eyes regarded her with humor. She must have decided to let it be because she answered, "Just a few years."

Peter Kowalskin was warming up on the pitcher's mound and the blonde's gaze lingered on him, making Sonny wonder, "How well do you know Peter?"

Leslie shrugged delicately, "As well as the next person, I suppose. Why do you ask?"

There was an edge to that question that had her backing off instinctively. "Just wondering, is all. He seems like a funny guy."

The man under discussion rocketed off a practice pitch that had the crowd cheering. "He has his moments," she said dismissively.

Just then JP crossed in front of them out on the diamond, his long legs eating up the ground. He looked so wonderfully male out there in his uniform that she couldn't stop the appreciative smile that crept up her lips.

Leslie craned her neck to make sure Charlie was still engaged with Lorelei. Satisfied, she speared Sonny with a look. "You and the shortstop."

That was all she said. Then she waited expectantly.

Fine. So much for privacy. "It's complicated."

Leslie's sharp gaze turned to one of sympathy. "It always is, sugar."

Amen to that.

The curvy blonde said breezily, "He's got some nice moves." Sonny's gaze flew to her face and she rushed to clarify, "On the field, y'all. He's got nice moves on the field. I wouldn't know anything about them off of it."

Suddenly all the players moved off the field and a local Denver band came out to sing the national anthem. After the band was done the Rush took to the grass, JP jogging to his spot between second and third.

"I'm Sexy and I Know It" blared through the speakers as Kowalskin wound up for the first pitch. A young guy with a green foam Rush finger two rows down let out an ear-piercing whistle, making her wince. The scent of popcorn and peanuts competed with the scent of the ball field, blending to create a heady mix.

The first pitch came and the batter for the Astros swung hard, connecting solidly. Dropping the bat, he sprinted toward first base. But he was too late. The ball made a line drive down the middle between second and third, straight toward the hotshot shortstop. Positioning himself with a shuffle, JP snagged the ball in midair and relayed it back to Drake, gaining the first out of the game.

Flashing a cocky grin that punched her in the stomach with potency even from across the field, JP pulled off his glove and adjusted the bill of his cap. Then he put it back on, smacked the inside with a bare fist, and crouched back into position, palms on knees.

Leslie tapped her on the shoulder just as the next Astro came up to bat. "Like I said, he's got some nice moves. Don't y'all agree?"

The smile she shot Sonny was full of camaraderie. Giving in to the good-natured probing, she ducked her head and looked at the blonde over the rim of her sunglasses. She could tell Leslie wanted the gossip bad.

Sonny caved and threw her a bone. "Totally."

Chapter Twenty

JP TOOK THEM to Red Robin per Charlie's request after the game. After walking into the restaurant he got a good look at the décor, and his eyes crossed and went a little blurry. Sonny couldn't resist teasing him and asked him what his problem was—all the primary colors or the posters taking up every square inch of wall space?

JP got into it though after he looked at the menu and saw the Towering Onion Rings. Then he got caught up trying to decide between that and the Buzzard Wings. Charlie bailed him out by convincing him to order both and then tell him which was better after he was done.

The kid already knew how to get a guy's back.

Sonny spent most of the dinner sitting back and watching the two of them interact. On and on they went about baseball and stats and the best ways to execute this play and that one. Their heads were together like they were conspiring on something.

And every time someone came by asking for JP's autograph, Charlie's chest got all puffed up with pride. It was obvious to anyone looking that her son was starting to fall for the ballplayer in a big way. Because it made her uncomfortable and kind of panicky, she desperately people-watched to distract herself from her feelings.

How could she live with herself if JP broke her boy's heart?

Her heart could be pieced back together, given enough time. But Charlie's? She refused to even think about it.

Instead she became obsessed with the geometric pattern on the bench seats and the framed posters on the wall. The one next to her was a black-and-white photograph of an observatory. She got real interested in the subtle play of light. Though she did usually try to be honest with herself, she was darn good at denial when she wanted to be.

There was a moment during dinner when she'd looked across the booth at JP and their eyes had locked and held. In that moment, emotions had churned in her like a hurricane. He made her feel so many things that she couldn't keep them all straight. And that was a hard feeling to have if you were the kind of person who always needed to be in control of them.

The shortstop had fixed those steady eyes on her and smiled like they were sharing the best secret. It hit her in the solar plexus like a punch. She was so in love with JP, but she just kept worrying over things.

How could she date him if it wasn't okay with Charlie? Even if it was okay, how could she date a celebrity knowing that her life would always be available for public scrutiny? That her son's would be too?

A part of her wanted to follow her heart and do it anyway—to take her happiness. Regardless of the problems. And it scared her because she knew that voice only too well. It was her mother's genetic legacy, that wild flighty side of Sonny she tried so desperately to keep under control.

But if she gave in and listened to that voice then she'd be no different than her mother. She'd be choosing a man over her child and she'd made a vow to never let that happen. But she'd never counted on falling for someone like JP.

Sonny's heart sank and she shook her head.

Was she really no different from her mother, after all?

When dinner was wrapping up and the check was getting settled, JP reached a large hand across the table and began playing with her fingers. "Is everything okay tonight, Sonny? You've been awfully quiet."

Not knowing how to share what she was feeling, she evaded. "I'm fine." His eyes narrowed with disbelief so she changed the subject quickly. "You looked good out there this afternoon. That muscle pull must not have hurt much."

Confusion clouded his eyes. "Pulled muscle?"

There was a lone strawberry at the bottom of her lemonade and she rooted it out with a fork. "Yeah." Then she shot him a pointed look and inclined her head toward her son. "You know, *that one* you had the other day."

Understanding replaced the confusion and he choked back a laugh. "Right. No, yeah, it was fine." He retrieved his wallet and threw some bills down on the table.

Something didn't seem quite right with that response and Sonny paused in the middle of retrieving the strawberry. "Am I missing something?"

"Not at all. Hey, I have something for the slugger here back at my place. I was hoping I could convince you to swing by before you headed back up to Longmont."

Charlie lit up like a Christmas tree. "You got me a present?"

If there was one thing that boy loved more than baseball, it was gifts. JP was scoring major points tonight.

"Sort of. You'll just have to wait and see." He shoved his wallet back into his butt pocket. "I'm ready when you are."

That's when what he said earlier registered and she got all giddy inside. JP's place. She'd been wondering what it looked like.

The one piece of advice worth its weight in salt that her grandmother had given her was "A man's place will tell you a lot about him. If he can't even scrub the damn toilet, dump his sorry butt."

Her Grams had been the kind and compassionate sort.

Sonny grabbed her purse and stood from the table. "I think we can manage the detour."

He rose, too, and glanced down at Charlie. "Who're you riding with, me or your mom?"

Her son looked from her to JP, a funny expression on his face. It took her a minute but she finally recognized what it meant. Charlie wasn't used to having adults to choose from. When he glanced at her again, she could tell which way he was leaning and helped him out. "You're not going to hurt my feelings, sweetie, if you want to ride with JP."

He scrunched his nose and asked hesitantly, "You sure?"

She nodded. "Totally sure."

Her boy whipped his head around to look up at JP and said real fast, "I want to ride with you."

"Cool." He ruffled his hair and pointed to the plastic kid's cup with the giant red bird on the side still sitting on the table. "Better not forget your drink."

Her boy snatched up the drink and the two of them headed toward the front of the restaurant, leaving Sonny to follow. Charlie had fused to JP and he didn't seem to mind. In fact, they looked just like two of a kind. And that gave her all kinds of mixed feelings.

Shaking her head, she fell into step behind them, feeling bemused until she noticed a man standing by a large carousel horse aiming a camera at them. When she passed he lowered it, gave her a greasy grin, and said, "Hello, Sonny."

She stopped dead and stared him down. "Excuse me? Do I know you?"

"I know *you*." He tipped his weak chin at her son and smiled like they were sharing secrets. "Must be a dream come true for you, finally finding Charlie a daddy."

Her stomach lurched and her blood went cold.

Now she wasn't bemused at all.

JP's APARTMENT WAS pitch black when he unlocked the door and stepped inside. Ducking his head back into the hall, he looked at his guests and said, "Give me a second and I'll be right back." The entry light bulb had burned out a few weeks ago and he hadn't found the time to fix it, so he had to turn on the lamp by the sofa.

Once the living room was lit with a warm glow, he headed back to the door and opened it wide. "Come on in."

Sonny ducked under his arm and he was surprised to find that he was nervous having her in his home. All the times they'd been together had been everywhere else but here. What if she didn't like it?

Charlie charged into his apartment and stopped, eyes huge. "Whoa."

JP gave his apartment a quick once-over. He supposed it was pretty cool. At least he'd thought so when he'd been traded to Denver last year. The place was in a renovated warehouse downtown and had hardwood floors and exposed brick. Duct work was exposed and left its original copper color. To his right were wood and metal stairs that led to his master bedroom and the kitchen was through the swinging door straight ahead of him on the other side of the huge living room.

The apartment was rustic and industrial and had tons of character. He especially liked all the storage space for his toys. If it weren't for that frigging neighbor cat it would be terrific.

JP gestured with a hand, indicating the room at large. "Have at it, kid. My place is yours to explore."

"Really?"

Yeah, really. "Adios."

With that the boy took off, making a dash for the swinging door that divided the kitchen from the rest of the apartment. Once he was on the other side he called out, "This kitchen is huge! And guess what, Mom? There's a TV in here!"

Sonny shot JP a questioning look and he shrugged. "I like to watch ESPN while I cook."

A cute little crease marred her brow. She looked surprised. "You cook?"

Of course he cooked. Exactly three things. "I make a mean Denver omelet."

"Is that so?" The woman didn't look like she believed him.

Charlie had vacated the kitchen for the spare room under the stairs, so he decided to take advantage of the privacy and snagged Sonny around the waist, pulling her close. "Tell you what. One of these mornings I'll make one for you." He liked the idea of waking up next to her and making her breakfast.

That reminded him of when he'd first laid eyes on her at the charity. He remembered thinking something very similar then. Like he'd instinctively known she was the woman he was meant to cook for. How about that?

Sonny snuggled into his embrace, her curves flush against him. When she looked at him with her beautiful blue eyes his brain went haywire and started sizzling. What had he just been thinking?

She leaned up and gave him a kiss that curled his toes, then pushed out of his arms when she heard Charlie coming out of the room. She cleared her throat and smoothed her shirt, and she looked so damn cute that he wanted to scoop her up and give her another kiss.

"Do you mind if I have a look around?" She was already scanning the books on the shelf behind him.

The boy waved her over. "You should see these pictures, Mom." He glanced at JP, his face scrunched in question. "How old were you in these?"

JP watched Sonny walk across the living room, open his linen closet, and peruse the messy pile of towels while his gaze lodged at the hemline of her shorts. She had the longest, silkiest legs he'd ever seen. And if Charlie wasn't there right now he'd take her to his bed and show her just exactly what those legs did to him.

"That one next to you with me posing is from fifth grade I think." Hell if he could remember. It was a long time ago.

Sonny traced a finger over the simple wood frame and darted a sideways glance at him. "Your place isn't what I expected."

He leaned a hip against the back of a gray chenille couch and crossed his arms over his chest. "How so?" His place was an average guy's pad. Lots of toys—mountain bikes, camping and climbing gear, giant flat screen. A fly-fishing rod was leaned in the corner. Even a pair of taped hockey sticks from his high school days hung on the wall.

"I don't know exactly. It's just that I'd pictured it differently, with less stuff. Especially all the pictures."

He loved his family. What could he say?

While he watched, she climbed the stairs, her butt swaying seductively with each step. His hands had been all over that ass recently and the knowledge made him hungry for a repeat. Shoving away from the couch, JP strode toward the stairs and was stopped by Charlie.

"Dude! That's such a big flat screen. Can I turn it on?"

Brilliant idea, JP thought. That'd give him a few minutes in his room with Sonny. "Sure thing, kid."

The boy beamed at him. "Sweet."

Turning his attention back to the woman in his bedroom, he darted up the stairs and stepped through the door. Sonny was in the middle of his room, a weird expression on her face.

When she spotted him she said, "I just heard the strangest thing." He opened his mouth to speak and she shushed him. "*Shhh.* There it is again."

JP closed his mouth and listened. Just as he thought, the neighbor's Siamese was at it again. "It's the cat next door."

Worry made her frown. "Is it okay? Do we need to call somebody?"

No, but he needed a new place to live. "It's fine. The cat's just in heat."

Sonny's glance skimmed over his bed and she blushed. "I've recently become acquainted with the feeling of sexual frustration. Poor cat."

Really now? That sounded promising. It was always a good thing to have the woman you were in love with hot and bothered over you. But, since they were on the topic, "It's been going on for a long time and isn't going to end any time soon. The neighbor refuses to get her fixed since she's a show cat."

Her blue eyes were filled with sympathy. "That sucks for you."

Yeah, well. "It's a situation." In fact, he'd been thinking about this situation some the past few days. He needed a new place, and things were going really well between the two of them. He was beginning to think that maybe they should have a talk, find out where Sonny saw the two of them heading. Because he was beginning to see them heading toward moving in together. And yeah, he knew it was soon to be thinking such things. But he couldn't help it. Thoughts like that just kept popping into his head.

JP took a step toward Sonny, distracted by the straps on her top and the way it bared her shoulders. She cleared her throat and gestured around her. "I like your space in here."

He liked her. "It works."

She waved at the wall. "Look at that brick. And I love the way you kept it minimal in here with the earth tones to keep the focus on the architecture."

The woman sounded like a decorating show. "I'm glad you like it." He bet that he could get that top of hers undone with one hand.

He took another step and so did she. In retreat. "You keep surprising me. Just when I think I have a handle on you, something new comes to light, completely throwing me."

He didn't consider that a bad thing. Here was something else for her to chew on. "I've got to find another place to live soon. The cat situation is out of control."

Sonny's gaze snapped to his face and she eyed him warily. "I'm sorry?"

JP studied her closely, searching for an inkling of her feelings. "Yeah, me too. But, I was thinking that maybe we should have a talk before I look for someplace new. You know, one of those 'where is this going' kinda discussions."

The woman took a keen interest in her cuticles all of a sudden. "Sure. Whatever." Her voice sounded off. Then her body tensed and he could tell he'd stepped wrong somewhere. She made a move past him. "It's getting late. We should be going."

Yeah, something was very wrong. He could tell by the way she'd closed up tight on him. Even the expression in her eyes was remote. "Is everything all right? Did I say something?" What was going on here? Was this about the stupid fame thing?

She ignored him and asked instead, "Didn't you have something that you wanted to give Charlie?"

Though his instincts were on high alert, JP nodded and took to the stairs. "It's down here." He glanced at her over his shoulder as he made his way down. "Are we okay?"

She tossed him a brief smile. "Of course."

He didn't believe that at all. Maybe he'd overplayed his hand with the moving. "I freaked you out, didn't I?" Her gaze flicked away. Yeah, he'd scared her all right. "Shit. I'm sorry, Sonny."

Suddenly Charlie called out, "You gotta see this, Mom!"

Sonny waved him off and avoided answering. "Let's

find out what he's up to." Then she practically leapt past him down the stairs, leaving him staring after her with a sinking feeling.

The boy's gaze was glued to the screen. It was JP on the evening news recap being interviewed. How about that for bad timing? "Eh, you don't want to watch that, kid. Why don't you put down the remote and come with me?"

Like it was a hot potato, the kid dropped the remote and dashed toward him. Sonny was busy pretending to stare at his family photos, so he led the boy into the spare room. Finding the right box, JP reached in and pulled out his old glove from Little League.

Charlie's eyes went round when he spotted it. "Can I hold it?" he asked.

JP handed the mitt to him, happy that the boy seemed excited. "You can do more than hold it, slugger."

"What do you mean?" He couldn't take his eyes off it.

"I mean that it's yours if you want it. I thought you might like to use my old mitt." He still couldn't believe that his mom had kept it around all these years.

The boy darted over and gave him a spontaneous hug. JP's chest went tight and hot and it was hard to breathe. "Thank you!"

With a throat suddenly too small and dry, he hugged the kid back and saw Sonny watching them from the doorway. She had the strangest expression on her face.

"Charlie," she said quietly. "It's getting really late and we need to get home."

The blond-haired boy hugged the mitt to his chest

after he turned toward the door. "Did you see what he gave me?"

Sonny nodded, her eyes unreadable. "I did and that's great. But we need to leave now."

For whatever reason she had pulled back and was acting distant. And he didn't like it one little bit. Tonight had not gone as planned, JP thought.

Not as planned, at all.

Chapter Twenty-One

SONNY STILL COULDN'T believe that she'd agreed to go to a barbecue at Peter Kowalskin's house. There was still so much that she needed to sort out. But Charlie had begged her to go after JP mentioned it and now, well, here she was.

On a Saturday no less.

Still off balance from what had happened at his place, she pulled her minivan into the neighborhood where Pete lived and chewed her bottom lip. She still didn't know how she felt about JP moving so fast. Well, okay, she did. It flipped her out. Totally and completely flipped her out. They'd only been dating a short while and their relationship was precarious at best. What had he been thinking?

More to the point, what was she thinking continuing to see him?

On an exhale she glanced over at her son. "We can't stay super long, kiddo."

Her boy gave her a cheeky grin. "Yeah, I know. It's our cleaning day."

Damn straight, Sonny thought as she located the address and found a place to park. JP's red Toyota was parked in front and she could hear voices from across the street. Nervous and jittery, she grabbed the rearview mirror and checked her make-up one last time. Satisfied there were no mascara smudges, she reached for her ChapStick and put some on. There, now she was set.

As much as she was going to be.

Turning to Charlie she asked, "You ready?"

He gave her an exaggerated wink. "I was born that way."

Laughter bubbled up and she gave him a kiss on the cheek. "I love you, kid."

"I love you too, Mom."

Opening the minivan door, Sonny smoothed her dress before she climbed out. Since she'd been invited to a pool party barbecue during high summer, she'd decided on a pale yellow cotton sundress that hit at her knees. And because it was a summer barbecue and she didn't know what else to do, she'd made a big bowl of potato salad. Professional ballplayers ate that, right?

Reaching for the large plastic bowl with the bright red lid through the sliding door, Sonny had to lean across the Honda to grab it from where it had slid during the ride. One foot rose as she balanced, very aware that she had on a short dress and skimpy panties. A flip-flop dangled precariously from her lifted foot.

From behind came a whistle. "Damn, woman."

It was JP.

Her heart did a little dance of joy even as her stomach dropped. Having such contradictory feelings about the shortstop had plagued her for days. One minute she was all over his cheese puffs, thinking to herself that he was the best thing ever and it was all going to work out amazingly well. The next she was battling her issues with the tired, inadequate tools she possessed and the desire to tuck tail and run was almost unbearable. It was an exhausting game of emotional ping-pong and she wanted it to end.

Emerging from the minivan with the salad, Sonny turned around to greet JP. When she saw him her heart overrode her stomach. She was just happy to see him. All the other stuff fell away.

For the time being. She wasn't fool enough to think that it would stay that way for good. "Hi." Why was she suddenly feeling shy?

"JP!" Came the shout from Charlie when he spotted the shortstop. "Look! Mom let me bring a water gun." He held up a neon and black mega soaker.

JP stood on the front yard grass barefoot and grinned at her son. "Nice. We'll fill that in a bit and get Pete with it, okay? First I have to talk to your mom."

Her boy gave him a mock salute. "Aye aye, Captain." He rounded the Honda. "Can I go inside and look for my friend?"

Sonny nodded, her gaze on JP. "Sure." The way he was looking at her was making her toes curl.

Once Charlie had made it to the door he asked, "Who's his friend?"

Sonny busied herself with the bowl and her purse and locked the Honda by pushing the remote. Not that she needed to set the alarm. Pete lived in a swanky neighborhood. Her car was the most beat-up one on the street.

With a hand she brushed her loose hair over a shoulder. "The one from the pizza party at Mark's place a few weeks back." He looked like he was drawing a blank. "They played Pokemon together."

Memory dawned. "Oh, right."

The way he was standing had her walking by him to get to the door. When she was within arms' reach, he pulled her close and kissed her lingeringly. By the time he was done, she'd forgotten her own name. And he knew it, too, by the self-satisfied smirk he wore.

"I'm sorry for the other day back at my place. I jumped the gun. Can we just forget that I said anything?"

Unable to resist, Sonny hummed softly and rose up on her tiptoes to kiss him again. His strong arms slid around her waist and he took her mouth hotly. She almost dropped the potato salad.

Five minutes ago she'd been thinking about Charlie's feelings and the best way to break up with JP. But the moment he touched her all she wanted was more of him. His laugh. His big heart and even bigger smile. Even his inflated confidence and swagger. What the hell was she going to do?

Releasing her mouth, he gave her another quick squeeze and escorted her toward the house. "So it's behind us then?"

Sonny gave a brief nod, not really meaning it. It wasn't

behind them, but she didn't know what else to do at the moment without causing a confrontation that she wasn't ready for.

He patted her butt briefly and grinned. "You are going to enjoy this. It's become a tradition for Kowalskin. Every season, at least once, he throws a backyard bash. Every player and his family is invited. It's loud and chaotic and you're going to love it."

The way he kept his hand on the lower part of her back made her feel sexy and protected—and so conflicted. JP's hand was so large that it practically covered her back from one side to the other. The heat of his palm felt delicious through the thin fabric of her dress.

Sonny discovered very quickly when the door opened that he wasn't kidding. People were everywhere, and the noise level was impressive. Kids of all ages ran in and out and from somewhere she could just barely hear the strum of an acoustic guitar.

It was loud and chaotic and she loved it, just like he said she would.

Charlie dashed by in front of them, immersed in a group of similarly attired boys. Sonny didn't even get a smile as he sped by. God, he was growing up fast.

JP leaned down and said against her ear, his breath hot and moist against her skin, "The food's out back, if you're hungry."

She nodded and he led her through the sprawling house to the huge kitchen in back. Ten or so people were milling around laughing, and a petite redheaded woman was bouncing an infant on her shoulder. Through the

French doors the back patio was visible. More people were out there, holding red plastic cups.

JP made brief introductions as they went, but he didn't stop until they were outside on the concrete. Leslie was there, plastic cup in hand, chatting with Lorelei and another woman Sonny didn't know. When they spotted Sonny, the blonde smiled and waved her over.

Though she didn't want to leave JP, she put on her game face and said to him, "I'll catch you in a bit."

As SONNY WALKED away from him, JP felt tightness grab his chest and rolled his shoulders to ease the ache. God that woman was beautiful. She did things to him he didn't think were possible. It was hard to watch her leave because he wanted to be close to her, but he figured he had to share her, and he looked around the yard for a place to sit.

Mark and Peter were sitting by the pool in plastic lawn chairs. The pitcher had a guitar in hand and was absentmindedly picking at the strings, teasing out a simple tune. Mark's brother-in-law Logan was sitting with them, his daughter Michelle in his lap. The little girl was growing so well since her heart surgery.

Picking his way through the crowd, JP looked out at the pool and laughed out loud. Drake was out there in a neon-pink Speedo, lounging on the back of a blow-up lobster. The skin on his chest was beginning to match the color of the inflatable plastic crustacean. One of the many kids in the water splashed him and he promptly lost his balance, going overboard. He came up soaking wet and sputtering.

Still laughing when he reached the guys, JP grabbed a drink from the cooler nearby and took a seat. "Did you just see that?" He tipped his chin toward the pool.

Kowalskin grinned and plucked a country tune. "That Susie Brewster is one tough six-year-old. Paulson's in trouble."

All three men turned their heads and looked at Drake. He was arguing with the feisty little redhead, all bluster. The girl knew it too and splashed him again before squealing and taking off. Drake shook a fist at her, though it was obvious by the look on his face it was all for dramatic effect.

JP spotted Sonny off to the side with Lorelei and felt something warm fill his chest. When she laughed he felt himself smile involuntarily and shook his head. That woman had a hold on him good.

Pete kicked his bare foot with a shoe. "Hey, hippie." He was referring to the lack of footwear. "Have you had a talk with the kid yet?"

JP leaned back in his seat and laced his fingers behind his head. "Not yet." He'd meant to ask Sonny about it when they'd been at his place, but things had gone off track after their conversation and had gotten tensely awkward, so it'd slipped his mind.

Mark leaned forward, joining the conversation. "Don't you think you should double-check with Sonny before you do?"

He had a point. "Probably. Look guys, I'm sure it's not even an issue. She's no doubt already talked to him."

Logan spoke up, his dark brown eyes confused. "Who's telling who what now?"

Pete stopped picking his guitar. "JP's been seeing a woman with a kid and he's not sure if the boy knows about it or not." As soon as he finished he started playing chords again.

There was a real serious quality to Lorelei's brother. He squinted against the sun and replied, "I reckon that's a tough spot to be in." Logan's little girl put her head on his shoulder and he cuddled her close.

JP agreed, but he also didn't want to worry about it and told himself that the guys were just being gossipy girls and getting all up in his Kool-Aid over nothing. Especially Pete. That guy needed a hobby.

He changed the subject. "Have you found a place yet, Mark?"

The catcher shook his head. "Nah. I haven't had much time. Lorelei though, she's been working with a real estate agent. Every few days she brings me a small stack of homes for sale and I go through them with her. But nothing's caught her eye so far."

JP thought about Sonny's modest place up near Longmont. He could see himself there. "When it's home you'll know it."

Just then Charlie raced by with the same group of boys and they all dove into the pool, drenching Drake again. The guy had just gotten resettled on the lobster too. He went over so fast he didn't even have a chance to catch his breath and came up coughing.

JP smirked and scanned the yard for Sonny. He found

her talking with the woman from the kitchen who had the infant. Her hands and face were animated, and she looked like she was sharing a funny anecdote. No doubt something Charlie had done that the kid would be totally humiliated if he knew his mom was sharing.

Standing up, he left the guys discussing Logan's chances at the next PBR bull riding final in Vegas and went to be with Sonny. It was like a compulsion, this need to be close to her. Every time she laughed or he heard her voice it beckoned him like a siren and he had to come.

When he came up behind her, JP slid his arms around her waist and pulled her back against his chest. At first she was tense, but after a few moments she relaxed against him. Deciding that he could read into it or not, he chose not to and said instead, "Are you enjoying yourself, sunshine?"

She nodded against him, her soft hair rubbing against his chin. "I am. Rita was just telling me about her latest adventures in parenting."

By the looks of the jelly-smeared kid she was packing around, JP figured she probably had some good ones. "Yeah? What's the latest?"

Sonny waved him off. "Oh, nothing you'd be interested in."

That comment nipped his feelings. Why wouldn't he be interested? "Surprise me."

Again she dismissed him. "Don't worry about it, JP. It's stuff you wouldn't get."

Now he was outright offended. "Try me. There were six of us kids, remember?"

She patted his hand, seemingly oblivious to his feelings. "But you weren't their parent. It's different."

What the hell? Suddenly he didn't have any credibility?

JP pulled away and let his arms drop. It didn't sit well with him, this feeling that he had something to prove. Especially when he wasn't being given a choice in the matter. That, in addition to the unease he was beginning to feel over what Charlie did or didn't know, was making him feel insecure.

Did Sonny even see him as parent material?

Because her comments made it sound like she'd decided he couldn't possibly understand what it meant to be a parent. Screw that. Whether or not it was true, didn't he deserve the chance to figure it out?

She belatedly noticed he'd stepped away and glanced over her shoulder at him. "Are you okay, JP?" Her big blue eyes were full of innocence.

He swallowed around the lump in his throat. "Yeah. Just fine." Out of the corner of his eye he spotted Charlie and his new group of buddies, and the frustration he'd felt moments ago began to churn in his gut. Needing some distance to calm down, JP kissed her briefly on the cheek. "I'm going to see what Charlie's up to."

Her reply barely registered. He was already cutting across the yard after the kid. By the time he'd reached the boy the other kids had taken off, leaving Charlie sitting on an oversized boulder in the shade.

"Mind if I join you?"

Charlie patted the bare rock next to him. "Nope. You

can sit here. The rock's super warm from the sun and feels awesome."

Planting his butt on the granite, JP's eyebrow shot up in surprise. He hadn't been kidding about the rock. It was hot enough to fry an egg on. "You having a good time?"

Soft blue eyes sparkled at him. "Yeah, totally! Did you know that Peter has samurai swords and ninja stars in one of his rooms? They're so cool!"

Why didn't that surprise him? "You didn't play with them, did you? I'm not sure that's safe, slugger." That was a good parenting call, right? Responsible and cautious.

Charlie ducked his head and muttered, "Couldn't. They're in a glass case that's locked." JP opened his mouth to reply and the kid rushed to add, "I didn't try it. Another kid did. Mom would kill me dead."

No doubt. "Speaking of your mom, she's pretty fantastic." Even though he was frustrated with her at the moment, it was still true. And it was becoming more and more obvious that they needed to talk. A plan was beginning to brew in his mind on how to make that happen. It involved getting a few days alone with Sonny—an idea which he liked more and more the longer he mulled it over.

Scrunching his nose, Charlie tipped his head at JP and asked, "You like my mom, don't you?"

A squirrel chattered at them from a branch above their heads. "Of course I do. What's not to like?"

The boy shook his head vigorously. "No, I mean you, like, *like* her. Like girlfriend and boyfriend."

JP narrowed his eyes and focused on Charlie. "What are you trying to say, kid?"

"You and my mom are dating." The way he said it sounded like a statement.

So he knows, JP thought, and he felt tension that he hadn't known he'd been carrying uncoil in his shoulders. Until that moment he hadn't realized how much he'd been stressing over it. But he should have known Sonny would say something. "Is that all right?"

"I knew it!" Charlie said and jumped off the rock. The boy's shoulders slumped and he looked away. "What's gonna happen now?"

Alarm darted through JP. "What? Wait. Did you know already, Charlie?" He hoped like hell the kid already had, otherwise he'd really fucked up.

"Sure," the kid said.

JP wasn't convinced, but he saw the frown worrying the kid's brow and had the strongest urge to say the right thing to smooth out the wrinkles. He wasn't sure what the right thing was, so he settled for, "I was thinking about joining your guys' team, if you'll have me."

He held his breath waiting for the answer. It didn't take long. "Are you guys gonna kiss and stuff in front of me?" The kid looked totally grossed out by that thought. "I don't want you to do that."

JP could respect that. It was going to take time for the kid to get used to the new situation. But no kissing *ever*? That wasn't going to happen. "How about I promise to try not to do anything that makes you uncomfortable?" That was the best he could do because swearing to never touch Sonny was an impossibility.

"Okay."

He didn't look okay. "What's wrong, Charlie?"

The boy was quiet for a moment and then the words came rushing out. "Is she gonna stop wanting me now?" Big blue eyes got all watery as they held steady on JP.

Where was that coming from? "Of course she's not going to stop wanting you. Why would you say something like that?"

Before Charlie could answer Lorelei came into view waving a magazine in the air, her face pinched and full of concern. Even though she was still halfway across the yard, she spotted JP and called, "You need to see this."

Clearly using the interruption to avoid answering, Charlie gave JP a quick hug and headed off. "I'm going to find my friends," he said over his shoulder.

"Wait," he called after him. "When's your next game?"

Charlie hollered back, "Next week!"

His mind made up, he replied, "All right. I'll be there."

The kid pumped a fist and said, "Sweet!" as he passed Lorelei.

"What're you waving at me, Lorelei?" Whatever it was had her pretty upset. JP let out a sigh. Shit. Things just weren't going his way lately.

Stopping right in front of him, the brunette planted a hand on her hip and thrust the magazine at him. "Here, take a look. I found this today at the grocery store. Sonny had a hard enough time with Charlie's stint on the news.

She said as much to me. But this"—she waved it in his face—"she's going to be so pissed."

Apprehension crept up his spine as he took it from her outstretched hand. Looking down he scanned the name and swore. It was that fucking *Beat* tabloid.

And right there, front-and-center on the front page, was a picture of him and Sonny from the day they'd gone tubing. *Together.* He had his hand on her breast and they were kissing on the riverbank. Son of a bitch.

Lorelei was right. Sonny was going to be pissed.

Chapter Twenty-Two

SONNY SEARCHED THE crowd for JP with a frown. What she'd said earlier had set him off. And she'd done it on purpose. It had been her chance to put some distance between them and send the signal that he was pushing too hard too fast. She was hoping he'd get the message and back off a little. She hadn't expected him to get so upset though.

Men. They called themselves the less complicated sex, but they were dead wrong. Some of the things they did made absolutely no sense. No frigging sense at all.

And they called women irrational.

With a big sigh, Sonny excused herself from Rita and started off in search of JP. If she'd hurt his feelings, she was going to feel bad about it. And she wouldn't be able to relax until she knew if he was okay or not.

But why, oh why, did he have to be so temperamental? She wasn't used to it. For the past ten years she'd had relative peace and quiet in her life. With just her and Charlie there wasn't much frenetic energy or drama. Even when she'd been facing finals at college while she'd had the flu. Although, that had just sucked.

Still, JP was so very different than what she was used to, and it was making her shifty and a little nervous. Like he was a big powerful presence and he was planting himself in the center of her life. And it was such a polarizing feeling because on the one hand it was incredible and wonderful and made her feel like the most precious thing. But on the other hand, he wasn't a gentle energy that could be controlled. The man was cocky and temperamental and big-hearted as a bear.

And he just did things. He didn't wait to ask permission.

It was how he'd won her.

There was so much to JP, she thought as she entered through the French doors to the kitchen. Being in his apartment the other night has made that clear. There'd been so much there that she wouldn't have guessed of him in a million years.

Like fly-fishing. Who would have figured that he liked fly-fishing? Or that he had a well-used gourmet kitchen and a not-at-all tidy linen closet?

What about all the family photos? She never would have guessed that he would have so many. Seeing them really brought home to her how loyal to his family JP really was. It was clear for anyone to see just how much he loved them.

And that alone made her feel off and self-conscious.

Her family had been a joke. The only real family she'd ever had was Charlie. She didn't know what it was like to be a part of a large, loving family. The idea of it created an almost panicky feeling in her chest actually.

That was just so many people up in your business, judging and telling you what to do, she thought. Who wanted that?

A voice inside her said, "You."

Sonny ignored it. It was wrong anyway. She'd decided that a long time ago. It was just her and Charlie.

She stopped cold in the middle of the open kitchen. It hit her that it wasn't just her and Charlie anymore. Now there was JP. That's why she was going after him, wasn't it? Because he was a part of something.

Mulling over the information, Sonny glanced around the empty kitchen in search of a bathroom. She needed to make a detour on her way to JP. Spotting a short hall off to the left by the fridge, she made her way across the tile and saw a door.

Feeling hopeful that she'd guessed right, she went to the door and pushed it open. And came face to face with Leslie and Pete in a very compromising position. Not believing her eyes, she blinked hard and tried again.

Nope. Still there.

"Oh my Lord, Sonny! I'm sorry y'all. Wait. Stop! This isn't what you think." Leslie's voice was a little shrill—and a lot breathless—as she tried to back away.

Really. Because it looked a whole lot like she had her bare legs spread wide while Pete kneeled before her. At least that's what it looked like to her from this angle. Her shorts were so skimpy that if they were doing what it looked like they were doing, he wouldn't have to work all that hard.

Wait a minute . . . wasn't Leslie dating that other ball-player?

Though she pushed hard against Pete's shoulders, he didn't budge. Instead, while Leslie blustered and stammered and tried to explain herself, he just hung his head and laughed silently. Sonny could see his shoulders shaking hard from restraint.

What the heck had she walked in on?

Leslie gave up shoving against Pete and gave him a sound whack on the back of his head. "Stop it!" she cried indignantly. Her feline eyes were big and panicked like a cornered animal. But Sonny had been around her enough already to know that Leslie was no genteel little dove. That woman had teeth.

Peter let out a snort and all the laughter he'd been holding inside burst loose. He placed his palms on his knees and hung his head, laughing so hard he had to take big gulps of air.

Slapping his shoulder again, Leslie hissed, "Damn it. Get up."

Peter looked at Sonny with sparkling eyes. His humor was infectious and she found herself grinning back at him. There was something incredibly alluring about the guy, though it was hard to put her finger on it. He just oozed charm and bad-boy fun.

With a roll of her tawny eyes, Leslie said frankly, "I got a bee sting, y'all, right on my lady bits. Peter was getting the stinger out because John had to leave."

It was true. He held up a pair of silver tweezers, the light of the devil in his eyes. He wasn't even trying to hide how much he was enjoying her predicament.

Leslie now, on the other hand, was downright miserable. Her normally flawless face was flushed, and her eyes were red and puffy like she'd been crying. Frustration pulled the skin tight around her eyes.

Taking pity on her, Sonny dropped the teasing and asked, "Would you like some ice to put on it?" That was the second time recently she'd said that exact thing to someone. Weird.

Finally relenting, Peter stood up, stretching to his full height. He was still having a grand time. With a wicked grin he slapped the inside of Leslie's thigh, making her hiss like a viper and shoot him a glare. "This filly gets real pissy when she's riled, sweetheart, so I've got her covered. She needs a man to settle her down."

Taking a step in retreat, Sonny bit her lip to keep from laughing when Leslie snapped, "Get your hands off me. And I'm not a fucking horse, Kowalskin." But with her gentle southern accent all that angry just sounded so pretty.

The sound of Peter's laughter followed Sonny down the hall as she backtracked and renewed her search. She couldn't wait to tell JP. Shaking her head at the scene she'd witnessed, she made her way through the house and came up empty. There was no sign of him anywhere.

Come to think of it, there was no Charlie either. Where could they be?

She hadn't looked out front, so she went down the

stairs and out the front door. On the way through she made small talk and kept an eye out for either of them. But she had no luck.

Next stop was the huge front yard with the stone and wood fence. Sonny stepped out onto the grass and took a slow turn, looking for clues about where they might be. About to give up, she finally spotted her boy with Lorelei, running shirtless and barefoot over the grass on the far side of the lawn. He tossed a quick wave over his shoulder and she looked behind him, finding JP sitting on a rock holding something.

Deciding to find out what was up, Sonny kicked off her flip-flops and strolled easy across the cool green grass. The closer she got to him, the faster her heart beat. Emotions played tug-of-war inside her, and by the time she was standing in front of JP her stomach was tied in knots. Everything between them seemed to be happening so fast.

Sonny didn't think she was wrong for feeling uncertain and a little shaky. In a few short months she'd gone from closed off single mom to falling in love with a sports celebrity.

If she felt like it was all spinning too quickly, who could blame her? And it wasn't her crazy saying that either. That was just calm logic. She was pretty sure anyway.

"Hey there, pretty lady." His watchful gaze was positively sinful. It made her unease lower a few notches. How could things be wrong when he looked at her that way?

"I just saw the boy head off that way." She pointed over her shoulder toward the house.

He set down a magazine and said, "Yeah. We were agreeing on a day for me to make one of his games."

She tipped her head and glanced down at him. "Really?"

"Why wouldn't I?"

A good answer evaded her. "You're just so busy."

JP shrugged a shoulder and changed the topic. "I can make the time. You look pretty in that dress." His gaze was steady on her chest. Sonny could feel her nipples get hard from his attention.

Trying to ignore the way her breasts had plumped and gone achy, she tucked a wayward curl behind her ear and studied JP. He was so darn good-looking. No wonder the tabloids liked to take his picture. With his strong features, full lips, and gorgeous eyes, he was a natural-born cover model.

And right now he had those sinner's eyes on her. "I've come to apologize if I upset you earlier."

His gaze warmed and he reached out a hand for her. Sonny took it and he pulled her between his legs. "No worries. I got over it."

He had too. She could see it in the way he was sitting. He was so much less tense than earlier. "Oh. That's good." It was too, but now she didn't know what to say. She'd built up a speech in her mind. But, then she thought about what she'd seen in the bathroom and she jerked in his arms. "Oh my God! I forgot to tell you."

He feigned surprise. "Oh my God, what did you forget to tell me?"

Sonny made a face. "If you keep making fun of me I won't tell you."

JP's hands crept down her back and squeezed her butt. "'Kay."

She narrowed her eyes at him. "Promise?"

He squeezed again. "Promise."

Because she still could hardly believe it, Sonny opened her mouth and nothing but a giggle came out. She tried again and was overtaken once more by a fit of giggles. It was just too good.

"What's so funny?" She could tell that he really wanted to know.

Sonny waved a hand in front of her like a fan and said through the giggles. "I walked in on Pete and Leslie in the bathroom."

His eyebrows shot up. "No shit?"

"It looked like that, but he was actually helping her get a bee stinger out of her bikini line." She could still picture Leslie's face and fell into laughter again.

JP smirked. "I'm sure Pete took his sweet time getting it out."

Yeah, she'd had that thought too.

Smiling down at him, Sonny felt her heart get all wobbly when his amber eyes went soft on her. He had a way of looking at her that made everything else disappear. And because he made her want to, she leaned into him and wrapped her arms around his neck. Then she pulled him close for a slow, lingering kiss, knowing that there were still issues between them. That knowledge made her a little panicky and she rejected it, diving into the kiss and losing herself in the feel of him.

A peal of laughter came from their left and Charlie

suddenly appeared, skidding to a halt. "They're getting ready to play chicken in the pool, JP. You gotta help me!" He spotted them and his eyes went round. "Whoa."

Sonny yanked away from JP so fast she pitched off balance and almost landed on her butt. "Charlie! I didn't hear you coming." She tugged her dress down and smoothed her hair as JP pushed away from the rock and stood up.

Her son gave her an unreadable look. "I wasn't being sneaky."

Shit. She wasn't ready for Charlie to know about this. Oh God, how was he going to handle it?

Charlie tipped his chin up and said to JP, "Do you want to play chicken with me? It's us against Drake and Susie."

Considering the first baseman outweighed JP by a good forty pounds, she figured the age gap between the two kids made things even.

Her stomach dropped when Charlie wouldn't even look at her. He kept his gaze on the man currently standing next to her, and anxiety started to claw at her throat. What had she done, being so careless? JP spoke casually, "I'll be there in a minute, champ, and we'll wipe the pool with them."

As soon as he heard that, her boy spun on his heels and took off. The second he was out of sight, Sonny sighed and rubbed her eyes. "I have to go talk to him." She was so not looking forward to it. This was one discussion she'd never thought she'd have to have with Charlie.

JP stayed her with a hand. "Easy, Sonny. Don't get

stressed and upset. Didn't he already know?" Something in the tone of his voice sounded off when he asked that question.

Sonny spread her fingers and peered at him, suspicion creeping into her tone. "What do you mean?"

He rocked back on his heels and crossed his arms, looking uncharacteristically edgy. "I had a talk with Charlie a little bit ago. He said he knew."

JP did *what*?

Indignation slammed into Sonny and all rational thought flew right out her ears. "You talked to my son about us?" How dare he!

JP nodded, "Yeah. You mean he didn't already know?"

Sonny kept her voice very calm. Inside she was raging. "No, he didn't already know."

Something changed in JP. His eyes shuttered and his body grew tense. "Why haven't you told him about us?"

Sonny completely missed the edge in his voice. "He is *my* son, JP."

He set his jaw stubbornly. "Yeah, and you're my girl-friend. You didn't think he had a right to know that?"

Didn't he get it? "When it comes to Charlie you don't get to call the shots, Jason." It felt good using his full name. She was mad as hell. "What made you think that you could just take the decisions about how I raise my child out of my hands without even talking to me? Are you always this controlling?"

The look he shot her was lethal. "Wait. What are you talking about? What the hell is going on here?" He raked a hand through his hair and swore.

Her mad was building up steam. Maybe it was from hiding all her fears about their relationship. It had just been building under the surface, getting ready to erupt like a volcano this whole time. "I'm talking about you, JP. And how you think you can just saunter into my life, taking over everything, because you want it a certain way. You're not in control of me. You're not in control of what I tell my own child." He opened his mouth to speak and she wouldn't let him. "Damn it, you don't get to dictate."

That made him mad. "Now hold on a minute. I didn't tell Charlie."

"No, *you* hold on." Every ounce of edgy insecurity she'd been fighting came flooding out. "Charlie and I were perfectly happy before you came along and decided it was all going to be on your terms."

He held up his hands incredulously. "*My* terms? You think all this has been on *my* terms?"

If it hadn't, that said a ton about JP. "You came at this thinking that you knew what was best for everyone involved. When you didn't, and you don't. And you certainly don't get to make parenting decisions for me."

He stared at her hard, his jaw set tight. "Right. Because me trying to show you that I can make capable parenting decisions is such a horrible thing." His gaze went cold. "Why were you hiding us from him?"

"Because he wasn't ready!" And because telling Charlie made their relationship real. She wasn't ready for real. "I knew this was going to happen."

JP scowled. "What exactly did you know?" He raked a hand through his hair and paced a few steps away. He stopped and turned around, his gaze searching her face. "Is this fight because I talked about us moving in together?"

"I don't know what you're talking about." The denial was instant.

His long, muscular legs ate up ground as he came back to her. "I scared you when I talked about it. I know I did."

Emotion welled in her and she threw up her hand, declaring, "Of *course* you did! I'm a single mother, for God's sake! You don't just up and talk about moving in together after a few weeks. What the hell were you thinking? Why would you say something like that?" She'd wanted to ask him that from the moment he'd first mentioned it to her.

Pain flashed in the amber depths of his eyes and he jerked. "Because I'm falling for you, Sonny, that's why!"

The world ground to a halt and everything inside her went still. "You're what?"

His voice went soft. "I'm falling for you."

She went from still to chaotic in a heartbeat. Emotions pumped through her with violent force, and that part of her she didn't trust leapt up and started screaming at her to take Charlie and run away. Just run away and ignore everything that frightened her.

It was so, so tempting.

But she didn't do it. Instead she reached down deep inside herself for control. "Do you swear you didn't tell Charlie about us on purpose?"

He held out both hands palms up. "I didn't tell him. Not like you think."

She blew out a breath and tried to calm down, tried to trust him. "How did he find out then?"

"He's a smart kid, Sonny. Maybe he just figured it out."

The logic behind it made sense. Charlie was too damn smart for his own good sometimes. "Okay. You're probably right."

JP took a step toward her, his eyes dark and his voice soft. "Are you going to respond to the other thing I said?"

Not if she could help it. She wasn't ready. She was way too wound up inside and unstable. "I don't know what to say, JP." Hopefully he'd let it be for now, until she'd sorted through her feelings.

He took another step. "You could say it back." His voice was barely more than a whisper.

Right then she couldn't do what he wanted, wasn't sure if she ever could, so she stepped to the side and tried to put some space between them. When she did, her eyes landed on the magazine JP had been holding. "What were you looking at?" She asked and pointed to it, trying to change the subject.

All of a sudden his face went pale. "Sonny, wait. Don't look at that. Let me explain—"

But it was too late. She'd already snatched the magazine off the rock and glanced at the cover. What she saw made her blood run cold. On the front page was a photo of her and JP from their day of tubing, kissing, and touching intimately on the riverbank, their private moment plastered across the front of a tabloid for all the world to see. The headline read: BASEBALL STAR SCORES BIG OFF THE FIELD.

Something inside her snapped. Oh, that was it. That was just fucking *it*.

She couldn't do this anymore. Taking a step in retreat, she waffled her hand between the two of them, still holding the magazine. "This was a mistake."

His eyes narrowed to a terrifying degree. "Are you serious?" His voice was eerily calm.

Desperate to regain a measure of control, Sonny nodded. "I was foolish to think a relationship with you would work, that I could deal with who you are and your life. But I can't."

He stood there staring at her, his eyes hot and dark and angry. "So you're just going to walk away from what we're building together because of some goddamn gossip magazine?"

She turned to go find Charlie so they could leave and tossed the offensive thing on the ground. "That's exactly what I'm going to do."

JP swore behind her. "Fuck. You're making the wrong choice. We have something special happening here."

It wouldn't be the first time. She could make a whole blasted career out of them. When would she ever learn?

Leaving JP behind, she headed for her flip-flops in the grass by the house. Suddenly a thought occurred to her, and she threw up her hands. "Of *frigging* course!"

It was Saturday.

Everything bad in her entire life happened on that damn day. Holding her head up high, Sonny fought for composure as she spotted Peter nearby. Just what she needed. He'd witnessed the whole frigging thing.

He looked past her toward JP and shook his head as she stormed by. "Man, I gotta stop throwing parties."

Chapter Twenty-Three

A WEEK HAD passed and JP was still mad. Damn her stubborn ass, he thought as he hung up his phone. Why wouldn't she answer her cell? He'd been trying to call her for days now and she hadn't picked up once. The woman was avoiding him like a pro.

As he walked into his kitchen at the crack of dawn in a pair of plaid boxers, grumpy from no sleep, he scowled and yanked open the refrigerator door. Didn't she understand yet that he hadn't done anything wrong? He hadn't planted the fucking paparazzi. But you wouldn't know it by the way that woman had tore into him, her anger cold and bitter. The way she'd looked at him, her eyes so remote, still made his blood freeze up. Who knew that she had that side to her?

Sonny went as cold as an Alaska January when she was mad.

JP grabbed the jug of Florida orange juice and slammed

the refrigerator door shut. Twisting off the top with more force than necessary, he brought the half-empty jug to his lips and took a long, long drink. He'd been trying everything since their fight a few days ago to cool the fire in his gut. But he couldn't do it because the fact was that he was just plain pissed off about the whole thing. He'd thought Sonny had more trust in him than that.

Apparently not though. She'd simply shut down when she'd seen that goddamn photograph. He had never seen a person climb back up inside themselves and shut down faster than Sonny Miller.

One minute she'd been warm and soft and present, and the next she'd been gone like the wind, staring at him with chilly, distant blue eyes. As if the intimacy they'd shared had done nothing to merit more from her than that.

"Damn!" JP slammed the orange juice jug on the counter. He *did* deserve more merit than that. And that was just what he was going to tell her.

Leaving the jug there, he stomped out of the kitchen and up the stairs to his room. Why was it always this way? Why did nobody see the rightness of a situation without him spelling it out for them?

Yanking open the top drawer on the bureau against the far wall that he shared with the neighbor, JP reached inside and pulled out a clean pair of socks. Through the wall he heard the Siamese next door begin to stir. Her yowling started slow and increased in volume and frequency until she was caterwauling like she was the last cat on earth.

Just frigging fed up with listening to that goddamn cat every minute of every day that he was home, JP pounded a fist against the wall and yelled, "Shut the fuck up!"

Miracle of miracles, the cat shut up.

Glaring at the wall for good measure, JP grabbed the rest of his clothes and headed to the shower. It wasn't until the hot water was pouring over him that the stress released from his shoulders and he was able to see a glimpse of the silver lining he'd been taught by his parents to look for. Lathering his hands with soap, a few swipes of the suds, and he was rinsing clean.

Maybe since she wasn't answering her phone he should hop on in his truck and go pay her a visit. It was so early that he'd be back in plenty of time for the game that evening. Besides, this was important. It was their future on the line.

It just sucked, though. With baseball he knew what he was capable of and that there was nothing he couldn't do if he put his mind to it. Always a matter of determination, JP had the deeply ingrained knowledge that whatever the sport threw his way, he would come out on top.

But this. This was different.

There were so many moving parts and Sonny was a real live person with feelings. His hard-nosed persistence was all he had to use with her. JP closed his eyes as he tipped his head to the ceiling and felt the spray massage his shoulders. With any luck that would be all he needed.

Because the fact was he couldn't change who he was. He couldn't change the fact that people knew his name. In all honesty he didn't want to, even if he could. Ever

PLAYING THE FIELD   263

since he was a kid, he'd dreamed of being a famous baseball player. Granted he hadn't envisioned how much of an annoyance paparazzi could be, but then again he hadn't expected to fall in a love with a woman so hell-bent on keeping herself off the radar.

Maybe if he showed up at Sonny's place she'd be ready to talk. Yeah. She was a logical person. Of course she'd be ready.

Eagerness jump-started his pulse and he finished his shower quickly. That had to be it. She wasn't answering her phone because she felt silly for overreacting. All she needed was a little face time with him and everything would be set back to rights.

In much better spirits by the time the shower was over, he dressed and headed back down stairs just in time to catch the tail end of his phone ringing. Thinking it had to be Sonny, JP leapt over the banister and fell the few feet onto the wood floor barefoot.

As soon as he touched the smooth surface he dashed to the kitchen and snagged his phone. "Hello." Anticipation had him short of breath.

"Well now, what has my kid brother been up to that's made him so out of breath?" Damn. It wasn't Sonny. It was his brother Ray.

"Not the fun stuff that you were imagining, I can guarantee you that." If he didn't make up with her soon there wouldn't be any more fun stuff in his future. And that thought was hugely depressing.

His brother chuckled quietly. "Why, do you have an infant wreaking havoc on your sex life like I do?"

Ray's wife Breana had given birth to their daughter six months ago, and the lack of sex had been a frequent topic of commiseration. JP figured that Ray should be satisfied right now with getting anything beyond a testy "Don't touch me," but that was just him. What did he know about having a baby? Kids Charlie's age were way easier to figure out.

"Why are you calling, Ray?" He was happy to hear from his brother, but when he called JP, there was usually a reason. Chatting for the sake of hearing their own voices wasn't something that the Trudeau boys were big fans of doing.

A muffled sound came over the line and a baby cried in the background. He could hear his brother cooing to his little girl for a minute or two before he said to JP over the airwaves, "I wanted to talk to you about Mom and Dad's upcoming anniversary. Do you know if you're going to be able to make it?"

JP shook his head like his brother was standing there in the room with him and could see. "I'm not sure. It all depends on what happens with the playoffs. As it stands, we're in good shape to take the division title. If that's the case then I won't make it. Sorry."

He hated knowing that too. It was their thirtieth anniversary. It was pretty damn significant. But if he couldn't be there, at least he could send his mother a ridiculously expensive bouquet of flowers like he did last year when his team was in the postseason. Sometimes there were drawbacks to being a professional athlete. All the family events he missed were frustrating.

Ray cooed again and made his daughter giggle this time. "Keep me posted, all right? I've got this idea to send Mom and Dad on a thirty-versary to Ireland. You know how Mom has been hounding Dad to take her there for years. What do you think?"

He thought it sounded like a great idea. "Sounds good. If you guys can get it researched and organized, I'll pay for it." *That* was one of the perks of being a professional athlete. It did his heart good to know that he could take care of his family.

Ray chatted with him for a few more minutes. His oldest stepdaughter interrupted them with some tween drama that had unfolded at school recently and that she'd decided couldn't wait until he'd gotten off the phone to share. JP smirked, thinking it funny that even though Ray had given up the farm life for the cushy bene-fits of the corporate capitalist way, his kids woke up early like they were in rural America instead of suburban Des Moines.

About to wind down the call, it hit JP that Ray was probably the perfect person to talk to about his situation with Sonny. Not that he was asking for advice really. It just might be nice to get some perspective from the guy who'd successfully dated and married a single mother. "Hey, Ray. Before you go I have something I wanted to run by you."

It took a few minutes, but JP got the story out. When he was done the phone line remained silent. It stretched on long enough that he started wondering if the call had been dropped. Pulling the phone from his ears, he checked the reception and found four bars. "Are you still there, Ray?"

"Yeah."

Impatience nipped him. "Then why aren't you saying anything?"

Ray let out a long-suffering sigh. "Because I can't believe that you actually told her son about your relationship without her consent. How big of a dumbass are you?"

Their relationship had been smeared across a tabloid and that's what he was zoomed in on? "Focus, Ray. Charlie already knew. And that's not the big deal."

It didn't take ESP to know that Ray wanted to punch him. He could hear it in his tone. "The *big deal* is your ego."

That wasn't the first time he'd heard that recently. Sonny had mentioned something a lot like it before she'd told him it was over. And it was so damn frustrating that it made him want to pull his hair out. "Fine. Okay. How did my ego cause this mess?"

Ray wasn't one to pull punches. "It made you act like an ass."

JP raked a hand through his hair. "Can you be more specific?" Being an ass was such a generalized condition.

"Look JP. You're involved with a single mother. She already naturally feels protective of herself and Charlie. Especially since you say she's had a rough go and crappy upbringing. It's been her all by herself holding the boogeyman at bay, taking on the world, ready at the spur of a moment to slay dragons or anyone who might possibly pose a threat to her and her son. And you're a professional athlete—a celebrity. You live your life wide open for anyone to see. That's got to be scary for her, man. I mean, think of the potential risk from her point of view. It probably goes against every protective instinct she has just to *be* with you. And then you went and told her kid about the relationship. Even if it was an accident, you did it without even discussing it with her or knowing her thoughts. You made her feel defensive. Plus, you pushed her way too soon with your apartment situation. Between those screw-ups and the tabloid it's no wonder she's not answering her phone."

The sinking feeling in his stomach indicated that he understood what Ray was spelling out. "Damn it, Ray. It's a clusterfuck, isn't it?"

"Yeah it is."

"I just saw what I wanted and didn't pay attention to any warning signs or really anything else, period. I was completely insensitive to her needs."

"You're a good guy, JP. But you've always been the golden boy who never did anything wrong. You're life has been nothing but roses and you've always been told your shit don't stink."

"Gee, thanks." His brother was such a sweetheart.

"Shut up and let me finish." Irritation made Ray short. "You're cocky, J, and you know it. You have good reason. But sometimes that arrogance clouds your judgment and you get pushy or step on people. We've all gotten used to the way you work because we know you have a big heart and we love and trust you. But this woman you're dating doesn't. Not yet. Add into the mix that you actually like being famous, and you can be a whole lot to take."

JP pressed his lips in a flat line. What his brother was saying rang true, and he suddenly felt like the biggest horse's ass. "I love her, man."

If anybody understood that it was Ray. "Then go get her back, dumbass. Use some of that hard-headed persistence you prize so much and show her that she and her boy are safe with you no matter who's watching."

Sounded like a plan.

He ended the conversation and tossed his phone on the counter. That's just what he needed to do. JP had to go to Sonny and he had to win her back. Even if she was resistant, he couldn't give up. Because they were meant to be together.

Yeah.

Racing around his apartment, JP got his stuff together in almost no time. Surely Sonny had calmed down in the week since they'd seen each other. That alone would make the conversation he was planning go a whole lot smoother.

Heck, maybe she was sitting at home hoping to talk to him, but she just didn't know how and that's why she wasn't picking up the phone. Yeah, maybe.

With one last glance around the apartment, JP grabbed his wallet and keys and headed out the door, locking it behind him. He was pretty sure that once he explained his side of things, she would forgive him immediately. Then they could get back to the way they were before she'd flown off the handle.

As he drove up the interstate a feeling of apprehension buzzed at the back of his neck. It was just the unusually dreary weather, he told himself. He was a sun lover and the clouds were making him depressed.

When the sky opened up and it started pouring buckets, the apprehension grew. It was like the universe was giving him a great big sign. Question was what was it? And, was he willing to listen?

JP turned on the wipers and kept going. Not a chance.

Chapter Twenty-Four

RAIN POUNDED AGAINST the windows of her workspace as Sonny set giant pots of goat milk boiling. She'd been up working since about four in the morning, having been unable to sleep. This thing with JP was really getting to her.

Still hurting from the way things had gone down, Sonny reached for the mug of coffee she'd brought from the house and took a bracing sip. It just figured that she'd fallen in love with a guy who was fundamentally wrong for her. Right from the get-go her intuition had warned against getting involved with him. She'd heard it plain as day. But she'd ignored it because he'd made her feel wanted and so very alive. And now she was dealing with the consequences of following her hormones instead of her head. Hadn't previous experience taught her anything?

Rain raced down the windows, making a rhythmic

patter on the glass. The sound usually soothed her, but her emotions were so jagged this morning that it only succeeded in not making her feel worse. It certainly didn't help make her feel better.

That made her even madder about JP. He'd ruined the rain for her. And here she'd thought that wasn't even possible. Just showed how much she knew.

Big fat jerk.

Snuggling into her oversized dark blue sweater, Sonny wrapped her arms around her waist and stared blindly out the window. It was raining so hard she couldn't see anything out there anyway. At any other time she would have loved this morning's weather. Rain was one of her very favorite things, and it was definitely in short supply in Colorado.

But this morning all the rain had accomplished was to make her feel isolated and alone.

She'd let herself down.

Tears sprang to her eyes, making them sting at the thought. She'd known the risks, known what could happen. But she'd done it anyway. Anger seized her and she bit back a sob. Typical.

She really knew how to pick them, didn't she? When was she finally going to understand that she was a relationship failure and just give up?

"Starting now," she sniffed. She was done with men.

It was for the best anyway. Every single time she ventured from the safety of the sidelines she got hit hard. Not once had a relationship with a guy brought anything but heartbreak.

Now she could go back to the way it had been before JP had swaggered into her life. Just her and Charlie. The two of them against the world. It was right—the way it should be.

So why did the thought of it feel so bad?

Sniffling again, Sonny padded in her monkey slippers to the pantry and stuck her head inside, searching for something—anything—to distract her. The door creaked open behind her and she said without looking, "What's up, Charlie?"

"Sonny."

Her heart stopped beating. JP. Every emotion imaginable slammed into her solar plexus at the sound of his voice. Anger and sadness dueled for top billing while she tried to brace herself.

When she was reasonably confident that she wouldn't start blubbering, Sonny closed the pantry and rounded slowly on JP. When she was facing him and saw him standing there dripping wet, the bottom dropped out of her stomach. "What are you doing here?"

"Can we talk?" He sounded uncharacteristically subdued.

Emotions dueled and anger won out. It was safer to feel angry than get her heart stomped on. "I don't want to talk, JP." Why did she have such poor judgment when it came to men?

This whole thing was all her fault really. She'd chosen to sleep with him. Even knowing that this very thing could happen. That she could find her private life flung wide open for public viewing. But she'd just had to go and get naked with him and now look at the mess they'd made. Charlie was acting all weird and distant since the day he'd caught them kissing.

JP was wasting his time. "Go home."

His face was set in a grim line. "I want you to hear me out, Sonny."

She held up her hands. "Why?" She shook her head. "There's nothing you can say that will make it all right." The shortstop opened his mouth to speak and she cut him off, her heart aching, "Look. We both knew this wouldn't last anyway."

Eyes loaded with emotion pinned her. "I didn't know that."

Sonny snorted humorlessly. "Then you were a fool."

"Maybe, but I have some things to say, and I won't leave until you hear me out." He planted his feet and braced his legs apart. His arms were crossed over his chest.

There was no point in arguing. She knew it. JP could say all he wanted to, but it wouldn't change anything. "I won't listen."

Frustration ripped through him and his voice went gravelly. "Christ, you're a stubborn woman." He shoved his hands through his hair and swore. "How am I supposed to reason with you when you refuse to be reasonable?"

"You're not." Sonny inclined her head toward the door. "You know the way out."

What she guessed could only be sheer obstinacy held him rooted to the spot. "I said I'm not going anywhere."

One look at him proved he was serious. Fine. Let him

stay there all day. She turned off the stove, biting her tongue. She'd consider the pots of milk casualties of the fallout.

Sonny grabbed her jacket off the giraffe and walked around JP and out the door. Rain was soaking her before she heard, "Where are you going?"

She didn't even look back. "Home. I suggest you do the same."

"I'm not leaving. I'll stand here in the rain all damn day if that's what it will take to get you to hear me."

Against her better judgment she glanced back and saw him standing there in the downpour, his clothing plastered to his fit body. "What's to hear, JP?" Seeing him like that made her heart squeeze tight. But it was best this way.

With muscular legs spread and rain pounding his shoulders, he shouted to be heard over the downpour, "That I'm sorry and I want you to come on the next road trip with me so that we can spend time together and talk things out."

She narrowed her eyes on him. "What about Charlie?"

JP shrugged his broad shoulders and strode closer. "Can't he stay with a friend or something? We need some time, just the two of us, without him."

Ghosts from the past rose up and swallowed her, the fear of abandonment she'd struggled against her whole life suddenly overwhelming her. Her mother had dumped her because her boyfriend hadn't wanted Sonny. Having a kid around had been a real drag. And now it seemed JP was saying something very similar.

It hurt.

But unlike her mother, she loved her child more than freedom. "Charlie and I are a package deal." And he deserved to be wanted every bit as much as her.

He quickly shook his head, water shedding. "Christ, Sonny. That's not what I meant."

Maybe it wasn't. It didn't matter either way.

JP and his life were just out of her league.

"I can't do this." On those words she turned her back on the only man she'd ever loved and left him standing in the rain.

It was the hardest thing she'd ever done.

Charlie was standing in the kitchen when she came inside, dripping water on the floor. "Was that JP, Mom? He's coming to my game later, you know. He promised."

Sonny clamped down hard on her emotions and watched through the window as JP drove away. "Not now, Charlie."

His eyes grew sullen, "You really are going to forget about me now, aren't you?"

Frustrated and emotionally tapped out, Sonny snapped, "I don't know what you're talking about. How can I forget you when you're my entire life, kid?"

His thin shoulders rounded defensively. "I thought you liked it that way."

She had. Before JP. And that realization was sobering. She really was her mother's daughter.

Suddenly weary, Sonny scooped Charlie up in a bear hug and ignored the stiffness in his posture. "I love you, big C. And I do like it being just the two of us."

He held his body rigid against her. "Then why are you so upset? Before we met JP you never got this sad, not that I remember."

Before JP there'd never been anything that could make her feel that sad. That was the complexity of love.

But she didn't want Charlie to worry. "I'm upset because he's my friend and we had a big fight. Just like I get sad when Janie and I argue."

He snorted against her shoulder and began to relax. "But you don't kiss Janie."

Good point.

Sonny sighed into her son's hair, grateful that he'd thawed out and was hugging her back now. "Look, baby. Grown-up relationships are complicated, and sometimes they hurt. But I love you and I will never ever forget about you. You're my heart."

"Promise?"

"Promise."

Letting Charlie take up all the space was the best thing she could do. It kept life simple that way. Just her and Charlie and no temptations that could lead her astray.

If her heart wept a little at that, she was the only one to know.

By the time Sonny had pulled into a parking spot near the ball fields at Sandstone Ranch she had a splitting headache. It had started with all the tension she was holding. But then it'd been compounded by Charlie's endless chatter about JP and how excited he was to have him come to his game.

She wasn't so sure. For one, it was Saturday again. And two, it was yet to be determined if he would actually show up or not. Odds were against, she was guessing. Because a guy like JP, who was so wrapped up in himself he couldn't see daylight, probably wouldn't bother coming to some kid's game now that they weren't dating.

She was okay with that, but JP had made promises.

Sonny put the minivan in park and pushed the automatic door opener. The passenger side door slid open and Charlie jumped out, his uniform sparkling clean and pressed. Though she abhorred ironing, the kid deserved to look his best for every game.

"Do you see his truck, Mom?" Her boy craned his neck and scoped the parking lot. "I bet he's here already."

Much more skeptical, Sonny rounded the back and popped the trunk. A medium-sized box sat on the floor filled with a huge plastic bag of orange slices and Nalgene bottles full of fresh water. Lifting the box out, she slammed the trunk door and winced. Her brain hurt.

"I don't think he's here, kiddo." She hadn't actually looked. Talking to JP again today was about the last thing she wanted to do. She'd rather have her teeth pulled.

But because she couldn't help it, Sonny scanned the parking spaces for a red Tacoma as they made their way to the correct ball field. Though there were quite a few trucks, JP's wasn't one of them. Bitterness welled within her.

It figured.

"Did you notice that I brought his glove? I bet it brings me extra good luck 'cause it was his and everything." His slim shoulders were barely wide enough to hold on to the strap of his duffel bag. The poor kid had to keep jostling it back on and his shoulder notched higher and higher until he was comically offset. "I bet I make tons of outs today."

Listening to her baby go on and on about JP was hard. The kid had so much invested in him. He was going to be devastated when he found out that JP wasn't going to be around anymore. He already should know the truth, but she hadn't had the heart to tell him. And yeah, she knew she was being a sissy. But breaking her boy's heart wasn't something she was just rushing to do.

Damn it. That's why she had stayed away from getting involved. It had kept her boy from being hurt. How was she going to be able to let him down like that?

Sonny dug the heels of her hands into her eyes and rubbed as she waited for Charlie to catch up. *Ugh*. They would have been so much better off if she'd never met JP.

Sometimes she could be so stupid.

"Sam and his mom are supposed to meet us by the field and I was wondering if it would be all right if we had a sleepover tonight?"

Why not? It's not like she had something more pressing going on. "That will probably be okay, but let's see how everyone feels after the game."

Charlie nodded and adjusted his duffel again. "Cool." The kid looked back over his shoulder. "You don't think JP will have any trouble finding us, do you?"

Not if he actually showed up. "I'm sure he'll be fine,

honey. But you shouldn't be worrying about him. Your mind should be on your game, Charlie."

The blond-haired boy ducked his head, busted. "I know, Mom. It's just I'm so excited."

If he said that one more time her heart was going to break. Wanting to guard him against potential heartache, Sonny warned, "Something may have come up for him." Like they were no longer speaking. "You shouldn't get your hopes up so much, honey. I'd hate to see you get hurt."

The minute the words were out of her mouth she had an intense feeling of foreboding. If JP hurt her son she would never forgive him. Hurting her was one thing.

"I'll be okay, Mom. JP would never let me down."

Famous last words, Sonny thought cynically. Not that long ago she'd said the very same thing. Look where it had landed her. "Hmmm," was her only response. Time would tell.

Charlie saw his team up ahead and dashed off, leaving Sonny to bring up the rear. Which was fine by her because she was moving slowly from lack of sleep. By the time she'd found a spot and set up temporary camp, the game was starting and Charlie was too busy playing to obsess over the ballplayer.

But he hadn't forgotten about him altogether. Every so often she could see him peruse the crowd looking for JP. Though it pained her to admit it, she did the same thing because deep down in her heart she really hoped that he wouldn't do that to her baby boy. But by the time the last inning had come to a close and he was nowhere in sight, Sonny had to admit the truth: JP had stood up her boy.

Glancing back over to Charlie, she could tell he knew it too. Her boy yanked off the glove he'd adored mere hours before and threw it in the dirt, his face tight and angry. Her heart ached for him.

Waiting for Charlie was horrible. It was plain as day that her baby felt terrible. The ballplayer that he idolized and who he'd thought of as a friend had broken a promise to him and his little heart was bleeding. Guilt rose in her when she thought that it shouldn't have been that way.

Today was just one more example of why she was the reigning queen of bad decisions. Because of her, her son had become emotionally involved with a guy who'd just ended up hurting him. Exactly like she'd feared he would do.

It seemed like forever before her boy walked over to where she was waiting. He'd taken a few good slides into bases and his jersey was covered in dirt and he had a scrape on one of his elbows. His hat was pulled down low over sad, sullen eyes.

Sonny tried for cheerful. They both needed it. "Great game! You did a fantastic job at shortstop. I was super impressed by how you covered second and got that kid out on a relay."

"Thanks." He was so bummed out, poor kid.

Tossing her arm over his shoulders, Sonny gave him a reassuring squeeze. "Hey, I'm sorry JP didn't come."

Anger distorted his face. "He lied to me!"

It was like a knife in the heart. "I know, baby." Why she felt the need to defend the giant jerk she didn't know. But it came rolling off her tongue before she could stop it.

"Maybe something came up. Something really important that he couldn't avoid."

Charlie scowled off into the distance. "Or maybe he just didn't care."

She knew the feeling. "I'm sure he cares. But he's a professional ballplayer and it's the middle of the season. Things come up that get in the way of even the best of intentions." Whether or not that was really true Sonny didn't care. She was trying to mend a boy's bruised and battered heart. Charlie felt rejected and she couldn't stand it. "Hey, are you still wanting that sleepover with Sam?"

Her baby snuggled into her side and shook his head. "I'd rather go home."

Damn you, JP.

Something caught her attention as they made their way back to the parking lot, and Sonny whipped her head around, her heart skipping a beat. For a split second she thought she caught sight of a figure before it disappeared behind some cars.

What the hell? Sonny shook her head and looked again.

There was nothing.

Great. Just frigging terrific.

She was so mad that everyone looked like JP.

Chapter Twenty-Five

FOR THE NEXT week JP brooded over Sonny. Then he spent some time being real honest with himself over a lot of things. Old things that he should have had a handle on a long time ago. And by the time the week was done he'd come to a conclusion.

He needed advice.

And there was only one place in town where he could go and get what he needed. Only one place where someone had messed up as bad as he and still managed to make it right.

JP needed Mark Cutter.

So, on a sunny and quiet morning when he couldn't stand being away from Sonny for one more minute he found himself knocking on the catcher's condo door with a tray full of coffee. Mark's fiancée was a notorious coffee fiend. The cups were his way of apologizing for barging in on them at eight in the morning.

A big part of him couldn't believe that he was standing there either. Him. Jason Patrick Trudeau. The natural born winner at just about everything had lost the only woman he'd ever loved due to stupidity. The guy who never asked for advice because he was so damn sure of himself was asking for advice.

It was humbling.

JP sighed. Life, meet irony.

The door opened and Mark appeared in the doorway, a gleam in his eye and his hair kind of messy. "Sorry to keep you waiting, brother. Lorelei needed help with something. Come on in."

By the look of him JP could figure the kind of help she'd needed.

"No worries." He held out the tray of to-go cups. "I brought coffee."

The catcher's eyes lit with humor before he threw a look over his shoulder. "The fiancée is going to love you for this. We just ran out."

Anything to help out a friend. "Glad I could help."

Mark led the way into the living room, his bare feet muffled on the thick rug. "Lorelei will be out in a minute." He put the coffee on an end table and took a seat. "What's on your mind, man?"

It was weird sitting there asking for an opinion. JP figured he ought to know himself well enough to have a sound idea of what was going on, but the truth was he didn't. This thing with Sonny had him in way over his head. Sure people had been angry at him before. But not like this.

This was serious.

He wanted Sonny back. He wanted Charlie back too. It had been days without them and he had never been more miserable. Nothing felt right. Even playing baseball, which he lived for, didn't hold the same appeal that it had just a few short weeks ago.

They were meant to be together. After she'd walked out on him the other day and left him staring at empty space he had stood there steaming and indignant. Hell, he'd been there to apologize to her and what had she done? Kicked him out.

And when he'd refused to leave she'd stomped out on him, giving him no opportunity to change her mind. For long minutes he had debated whether or not to follow her into the house. Finally he'd convinced himself to leave well enough alone for the time being and he'd left without saying another word to her.

It had been the better part of two weeks since that day and with the time and space his emotions had settled out. Enough time had passed that he wasn't angry at her anymore. No, now he just wanted her back. The time apart had given him ample opportunity to see just how empty his life was without her and Charlie.

The only thing he had waiting for him when he got home was the damn neighbor cat.

JP wanted more.

Shifting on the couch, he stretched out his legs and reached for a coffee cup. He took a near scalding sip and thought about what he wanted with his life. Playing baseball was all well and good. It was a part of how he expressed himself, who he was. But there was more to life than the sport and those were the things he was missing.

Things like having the love of a good woman. Cuddling down on the couch with her after dark, kissing and watching a movie. Being able to share the details of his day with someone who actually wanted to listen. It might sound lame, but things like that mattered. They mattered a whole hell of a lot.

With Sonny he'd captured a glimpse of the life he had envisioned—life with love, laughter, and friendship. And that's what he wanted. He didn't give a rat's ass about dating gazillions of brainless women. No, what JP wanted was a strong, intelligent woman who could be his best friend and his lover. Someone who would challenge him and never leave him bored.

He'd found all of that in Sonny. And he'd been such an arrogant douche that he'd really screwed it up. So he was at Mark's about to ask him how to make it up to her. Because he wanted Sonny and all of her baggage. No exceptions.

Lost in his thoughts, JP took another sip of the hot coffee and burned his tongue. "Son of a bitch."

Mark was all sympathy. "You're having a tough run, aren't you?"

He bent his knee and set the cup on it. "That's an understatement."

The catcher laced his fingers behind his head and assessed JP. "Woman troubles."

"Is there any other kind?"

"Not that gets under your skin the same way."

"True that."

Mark leveled his pale gray eyes on him. "So, you going to tell me what's up or do I have to guess?"

JP always appreciated his straight talk. He never minced words. It was nice. "I told Charlie about my relationship with Sonny."

Mark stilled and nailed him with a stare. "Did you talk to Sonny about it first like I mentioned you might want to do?"

Feeling sheepish like a schoolboy, he braved another sip of coffee and shook his head. "Nope. It just sorta came out by accident. But that's not the worst of it. We were fighting about it when she came across a tabloid picture of the two of us making out—the one that Lorelei gave me."

Just then Lorelei walked into the living room and said, "Let me guess, she got pretty irate over that."

JP nodded. "You could say that."

Mark asked, "Why?"

Because he was a dumbass. "Because she hates that I'm a celebrity. I didn't know how much because we hadn't talked it over," he saw Lorelei open her mouth to speak and hastily added, "*which* I know is a problem. I'm seeing the value in communication now, trust me." She smiled and he continued, "She took one look at that stupid gossip magazine and said it was over."

The curvy brunette settled on her fiancé's lap, giving his cheek a kiss. "Given the few things she's said to me, I can see her doing that."

Frustration made his tone sharper than he had intended. "Why?" Realizing it, he apologized with a softer voice. "Sorry. I'm just up to here"—his hand was at eye level—"with the whole thing. I even went to her after she got mad about it and tried to apologize."

Mark leaned his head around Lorelei to look at JP. "What happened?"

He got his ass handed to him. "She shut me down, man. Didn't even give me a chance to explain my side of things."

Lorelei began playing with Mark's hair absentmindedly, her fingers tangling in the waves. "I hate to say it, but I can see why."

JP raised an eyebrow. "You can?"

She nodded. "Well, yeah. Sonny's a single mom and Charlie is all she's got, right?" JP agreed and she continued. "You telling her son about an intimate relationship with his mom was like putting a wedge between them. Suddenly it wasn't just her and her boy anymore. Because you spilled the beans, it became her and Charlie and you. She no longer had the security of being that exclusive little unit anymore. Just you being there changed all that. And then suddenly this major change that she's making in her life is slapped all over a magazine for everyone to see. I think anyone would freak out."

JP had never thought of it that way. He frowned into his coffee. "The life change was supposed to be a good thing."

Lorelei took pity on him. "Honey, it *is* a good thing. It's also really scary for her too. But she'll come around."

He wasn't so sure of that. "Any advice on how I could go about making that happen?" He missed her. Missed the feel and sound and smell of her. He even missed the way she blew her nose when she was sick with a cold, all delicate and polite-like.

Mark piped up. "You could try skywriting."

He didn't follow. "What?"

The catcher chewed on his idea and grinned. "Skywriting. You could tell her sorry or that you love her or something with a big message in the sky." He looked questioningly at his woman. "That should do the trick, don't you think?"

Lorelei smiled weakly and patted his shoulder. "Sure thing, baby." To JP she shook her head as she spoke, green eyes round with warning and then silently mouthed, "No."

Yeah, he didn't think so either. "I'll keep that suggestion in mind."

He could tell Mark really liked his idea. "You should, bro. Even if you don't use it this time, there's bound to be others."

Not if he could help it. One thing JP didn't do was make the same mistake twice. "Will do."

Lorelei spotted the tray filled with coffee just then and practically leapt off Mark's lap for it. "Hot damn, there's coffee." She rubbed her hands together and said to him, "If you tell me that one of those is a triple-shot then I promise to name our first born after you."

The woman really wanted that coffee. "There's a triple-shot mocha in there. It should be marked on the side if you look."

Snatching a cup, she read the side and smiled like a woman reunited with her long lost love. "Oh, dear coffee, how I love and have missed you." Turning the topic back to Sonny, JP said, "Mark does raise a good question, Lorelei. Do you think she would respond well to an overblown gesture?" It wasn't really his style, but he'd give it a shot if there was the chance it would win her back.

She considered while she sipped her triple-shot mocha. "I don't know, honestly. I've only been around her a few times, but she didn't strike me as the over-the-top kind."

JP agreed. "She's not." Sonny was natural and sweet and simple in the best way.

Lorelei inhaled the rich aroma and sighed dreamily. "Then maybe you should consider it."

What? Wait. Why would he do it if Sonny wasn't that kind of woman? She wasn't Mark's sister Leslie. "Back up there a ways. You think I should do something big and overblown to win her back?"

She replied, "Do you think anyone ever has for her?"

Good point.

Mulling it over, JP was about to stand when Mark spoke up. "Mostly, dude, you just need to be honest with her. Let her know what your motivations are so that she doesn't continue thinking that you were just being an asshole."

Right. Okay. Not an asshole and big gesture. Got it.

There was just one tiny little problem. He grimaced. "I was kind of an asshole, though."

Mark shot him a look, one eyebrow arched. "Aren't we all sometimes, man?"

Lorelei held up her hands. "Amen to that."

The catcher snagged her around the waist and pulled

her in for a kiss. "That's what makes us so great, sugar. If a guy isn't an asshole once in a while then it's because he's a pussy."

JP had to agree with that assessment. "Sounds like you're saying that I shouldn't let that stop me."

"I didn't let it stop me." Mark pointed out. "Do you see where I am now?"

Yeah. In a plush-ass condo with a beautiful fiancée. It didn't suck to be Mark Cutter.

Didn't suck to be him either. He just needed to work on the whole getting-Sonny-to-forgive-him thing.

"Well, thanks for letting me crash your pad, Mark." It was time to get going so he could think on what was said.

"Anytime, brother."

About to stand up, JP felt the phone in his pocket vibrate and frowned. He didn't remember turning the volume off. Reaching into a front pocket, he pulled out his phone and saw that he'd missed a call. He was about to put the cell away when he noticed the number.

It was Sonny.

The woman hadn't spoken to him in two weeks and he'd been calling regularly. Looks like she'd finally decided to talk to him. Maybe she was already starting to forgive him.

JP glanced at Mark. "Do you mind if I check a message? Sonny just called."

Lorelei waved a hand. "Of course not."

Quickly connecting to voicemail, JP felt the leap in his pulse at the announcement that he had one new message. Maybe she wanted to talk. The important thing to note was that she'd broken her silence and had reached out. That meant something.

Placing his free hand over his exposed ear, JP strained to listen as the message began to play. What he heard took him by surprise. It wasn't Sonny. It was Charlie.

What he heard made his heart sink. "I thought we were friends." The boy started angrily and defiant. "You said you were my friend and that you wanted to be in my life, but you're nothing but a liar."

JP frowned and continued listening. "You told me you would come to my game. You *promised.* I looked for you the whole game and you never showed up."

The kid took a breather and he thought the message was ending, but then it went on. "We were supposed to be a team. Isn't that what you said when you told me about you and my mom? That you wanted to be a part of our team? I believed you."

The pain in Charlie's voice made his chest ache and grow hot. "You were my role model, you know. Now you and Mom don't talk, so you don't want to see me." The boy's voice began to waver, crushing him. "Well guess what, JP? I don't want to be like you anymore."

There was rustling and shuffling and then in the background came Sonny's voice, and it was the last straw. JP broke. Tears burned the back of his eyes and he pressed his lips together hard as he listened. "Have you seen my phone, Charlie?" the love of his life asked. And then the line went dead.

JP lowered the phone from his ear, stunned. Swallowing around the lump in his throat, he blinked the tears back hard as clarity came to him in a painful epiphany.

He had blown off and dumped a ten-year-old kid.

God, he really was an asshole.

That ball game he'd promised to go to had obviously meant everything to Charlie and he'd forgotten all about it because he had been so wound up over the fight earlier that day with Sonny. And then because he and Sonny weren't talking he hadn't made any attempt to talk to Charlie. Why the hell hadn't he realized that his relationship with Charlie was its own thing? That he couldn't just walk away from it if or when things didn't work out with his mom?

The kid deserved better than that.

Taking a deep breath, JP looked over to find two worried faces watching him carefully. Now he had two hurt people to win back.

"Is everything okay?" Lorelei asked, her voice colored with concern.

Not in the least. "I need to do that big gesture."

Compassion softened her green eyes. "I'm sorry."

So was he. For a lot of things. His brother was right. He really was cocky. And it had hurt the people he loved very much. Knowing that made him feel terrible. He didn't blame Charlie for going off on him the way he had. He had deserved it. But just because he deserved it didn't mean he was going to leave it this way. Hell no.

Resolve began to flicker to life in his gut. He was going to make it up to them. He was going to make everything right. They needed to know that they hadn't put their trust in the wrong man.

Mark stood up and walked to the glass doors that led out to the balcony, saying as he went, "You need to think of the one thing you could do that would show them how much you care. Something important that they would recognize." He glanced over his shoulder at JP. "You're a ballplayer. What's your superstition?"

Not following the catcher's logic, he thought about it anyway and came up with an answer after a few minutes. He wasn't the most superstitious guy around. "I never wash my ball cap during the season."

Mark shook his head. "No one does that. Give me something better."

Did he have something better? "I use a different deodorant for away games than home ones."

"Nuh-uh."

Crap. This was hard. JP knew that there were lots of baseball players with really far-out-there superstitions, but he wasn't one of them. He didn't wear the same underwear for months or refuse to shave. He certainly didn't abstain from sex like some players he knew. Those guys swore the sexual frustration improved their game, but he thought they were just dumb.

There wasn't really anything he was weird about. The closest thing he could think of was his walkout song.

JP went still. His walkout song.

Bingo. He had his big gesture. "I've got it."

A memory came to him of a conversation he and Charlie had had on one of their drives about game songs.

It had happened during the ride over to Mark's house for the game recap. Charlie had asked him if he could change the station.

"I really like 95.7 The Party," the boy had said. Grinning at JP, he'd found the station and cranked the volume. "It has the best music."

JP completely disagreed. "I don't think so."

Charlie looked at him, eyes all round and earnest. "It's true! They even play my favorite song on there lots."

JP reached over and ruffled the kid's hair. "What's that?"

"If I tell you, you got to promise not to laugh. None of my friends at school like it, except Sam, so they tease me." Charlie slid a glance over at him. "No teasing, 'kay?"

JP's chest went tight. Of course he wouldn't tease him. "I promise."

Charlie hesitated. "I got to trust that you won't." He held up a hand. "Shake on it?"

Eyes full of innocence looked up at him, and his heart tripped in his chest. "Deal." JP held out his hand and felt Charlie's small one slide into his. "Now tell me."

The boy leaned across the seat and whispered the song in his ear. JP's eyebrow shot up at the title, though he'd never heard the song. He was just playing along. "Good call."

Charlie grinned sheepishly. "Yeah?"

JP nodded. "Yep." He had no idea honestly, but was already planning on Googling it when he got home.

Leaning back in his seat, Charlie had resumed playing

with the radio knobs. Then he stopped, turned to him and said with feeling, "I really like you, JP."

His chest went tight again. "I really like you too, kid."

Now he remembered Charlie's favorite song with a sinking feeling. But this was about winning back the hearts of the ones he loved. There was no room for sissies. Still, he flinched. He couldn't help it. This was going to be painful.

But it was time to go big or go home.

Chapter Twenty-Six

"TELL ME AGAIN what happened so that I get the big picture, Sonny." Janie leaned back in her seat at the kitchen table and pulled off the top of a blueberry muffin. Popping it in her mouth, the pregnant woman waited for Sonny to answer.

She grabbed a muffin out of the bakery box on the table and went in search of a plate. "I've told you most of it."

Around a mouth full of carbs her best friend replied, "I know, but I want to hear it again. With every telling of the story new information comes to light."

What was there to recap? It was over with JP. So much for her short-lived jaunt into relationship-land. "I'm not sure where to even begin."

Janie pointed at her with a piece of muffin top. "I'm still confused about why you blew up at him so bad over him telling Charlie. I mean, I get that it was wrong and all. He shouldn't have done that without talking it over with you first. But to have lost your shit like that and not give him a chance to at least try and explain confuses me."

Sonny picked at a blueberry imbedded in the top of her pastry. "Does it matter? He stood up Charlie at his ball game. That's inexcusable."

Her best friend put a hand on her rounded belly. "Is it? Ben's missed stuff of the kids' and I haven't left him over it."

A bird landed on a tree branch just out the window and Sonny watched it. When it began to sing she looked back at the brunette. "That's different, though. For one, you two are married. And that means that he did a lot of stuff really right at the beginning or you wouldn't have gone down the aisle with him. So when he screwed up later he'd already earned himself some street cred."

The bird kept singing, the sound drifting toward them on a rose-scented breeze. Janie looked confused. "Have I never told you about the time he messed up with Michael when we were first dating?"

Umm, nope. "I think I would remember if you had."

Her friend nodded. "I think so too."

Sonny stood up and went in search of some glasses for water. "What happened?"

With a hand still on her belly, Janie wiggled her bare toes on the braided rug. "We'd only been together about three or four months. I'm not sure. But, I do recall that we'd been together long enough that I had felt comfortable asking him to pick up Michael from basketball practice after school. I had something come up and couldn't make it in time." She took another bite and chewed. "I got a call from the coach an hour after practice had ended asking me why I hadn't retrieved my son. Poor Michael had been sitting outside in front of the school building waiting for Ben."

That must have been terrible for the boy. "That's awful. What happened after?"

Janie took a sip of water. "I was livid by the time I had picked up Michael and got a hold of Ben. I reamed him a new one and promptly broke it off."

Seemed about right. "I get that. I mean, he let Michael down."

Her friend nodded. "He did, it's true."

"So then how did you forgive him?" That was what she really wanted to know.

"I forgave him because I remembered all the good things he had done, too. I didn't let one failure override all the successes." She ducked her chin and gave Sonny a pointed look.

Okay, she got it. "I hear you. Really I do, but what JP did with Charlie was a big transgression."

"Did you ever stop to think that maybe something important came up?"

Of course she had. She wasn't heartless. "I did."

Janie reached for another muffin. "And? Did you ask him?"

Why would she go and do that? That would have been the mature thing to do. Sonny wasn't winning any points in that category lately. "We haven't spoken about it, no."

"Why not?"

"Because he hurt Charlie. What's there to talk about? He can't take it back and unhurt my son. Even if he could somehow rewind the clock, he's still a celebrity. Where he goes, a camera soon follows, and I hate it. You saw that picture. It's invasive and feels like such a violation of my privacy when I'm with him and some paparazzi starts snapping away." She squared her shoulders, resolved.

Her friend got quiet and thoughtful. "I hear you, Sonny. I was merely asking on the off chance that he did have a valid reason for not making the game."

Why did Janie have to go and be pragmatic all of a sudden? She was pregnant. It was her God-given right to be irrational as hell. "Even if he did have a valid reason—and I'm not saying that he did. But even if he did it wouldn't matter. I don't want to live my life under a spotlight." She didn't want to be judged by a world of strangers.

"Okay." Her friend decided not to push the subject. "How is Charlie holding up?"

Restless suddenly, Sonny hopped out of her chair and went to look for dishes to wash by hand. It was a great outlet for her nervous energy. "He's still upset, last I knew. You know, I think he called him the other day."

Janie's aqua eyes grew big and round. "Really? Why do you say that?"

A plate was in the sink and she went to work on it. "I couldn't find my phone the other day and then when I went looking for it, he had it. And JP's number was in the outgoing calls log."

"Do you think that he misses him?"

Absolutely. And it pissed her off. Her boy had really cared for JP. "I think so. He hasn't said anything, but he's started using the mitt he gave him again."

A loud thump came from the far side of the living room. "Speaking of boys. I think Michael and Charlie found the old mini-trampoline."

Earlier, after Janie had arrived with Michael, her boy had asked to play with the small trampoline outside. He'd mentioned something about it and water balloons. As long as it went down outside, she'd told them to have at it. By the sound that just came from the living room the boys couldn't wait for outside.

Janie started to push out of the chair and Sonny stopped her. "Stay. I'll get this."

Leaving her friend in the kitchen, Sonny found the boys jumping on the trampoline. "I told you that you had to play with it outside, Charlie. I didn't mean right here in the house. You two boys need to take it where it belongs before I change my mind about letting you use it."

Unwilling to risk it, Charlie grabbed one end of it, apologizing. "I'm sorry, Mom. We just wanted to see how high we could go."

"That's fine, but you need to do it in the yard where there's space." She did not want to be replacing anything.

"All right." The boys lifted the metal frame and began carrying it toward the door. A foot or two from the door they set it down and Charlie said, "There's a Rush game on in a little while. Will you come get me before it starts?"

Sonny cocked her head to the side and studied her

boy, instincts on sudden alert. This was new. "You want to watch, buddy?"

Charlie brushed hair out of his eyes and shrugged, "Why not?"

Umm, because JP was a jerk and he didn't like him anymore? "Just asking. I'll let you know when it starts."

Returning to the kitchen, she found Janie holding her phone. Her friend looked up, mild amusement in her pretty eyes. "You got a text."

Sonny sat back down and reached for the cell. "Why is that so newsworthy?"

The brunette handed it over. "Because it was from JP."

Her hand froze in midair. "What?"

Janie waggled the phone. "You heard me. The text came from JP."

Bracing herself with a deep breath, Sonny took the phone and opened the message. It read simply:

Don't argue. Just watch the game with Charlie.

What the heck?

Frowning even though her heart had started pounding the minute Janie had told her who the text was from, Sonny handed the phone over for her friend to see. "What do you make of that?" More importantly, why should she care?

She was still so angry at him for what he'd done. And yes, she could admit that there'd been a part of her that had panicked and looked for an excuse to shut things down. Oh, all right. A big part had.

But he'd been way more wrong than her.

Janie snagged her attention. "I think we should watch the game."

The clock on the wall said that they had twenty minutes until it started. "Why? What's the point?"

Janie gave her a look like, "Duh" and replied, "To find out what he's up to."

Yeah, that might be a good idea. She was about to say so when something occurred to her. "I wonder how he was able to text down on the field so close to the game starting."

Janie tapped the table with a hand, making a soft, sharp rap. "Another reason to watch!" she declared with a bright chirpy smile.

Okay, fine. She would watch, but she sure as hell wasn't in the mood to forgive him. He didn't deserve it.

Moving into the living room, Sonny turned on the television and found the channel. There were still a few minutes before the game started, so Sonny decided to make something to drink.

She turned to her friend who had curled up on the couch with a pillow between her legs for support and asked, "Do you want something to drink? Maybe some tea?" As soon as the words were out she thought of the first night she and JP had been together after she'd invited him to stay and have a drink.

A small ache surrounded her heart. Maybe she missed him a little bit. But only a little, and certainly not enough to try a relationship with him again. She didn't want to put Charlie through that. Being the kid of a single parent could be tough enough at times. Trading that for a life in the public eye wouldn't be any easier. Her boy deserved more than that.

But what about you? her heart whispered. *What do you deserve?*

Something that just wasn't meant to be.

Looking radiant from pregnancy, Janie smiled appreciatively and arched her back to momentarily ease the strain. "That would be great. I'll take chamomile if you have it."

Of course she had chamomile. It was a staple. "I'll be right back."

In the kitchen alone, Sonny let down her guard some and sighed wearily. Now she was about to watch him play baseball on the tube. It made her jittery with nerves and anticipation. She wasn't sure how she was going to feel, seeing him for the first time since their fight.

Why did he want them to watch the game?

Through the windows over the sink she could make out her son and Michael using the trampoline to try to reach a branch on the large maple nearby. They weren't doing such a good job, but she figured the fun was in the process and not the end product. She sent a brief prayer to the universe that nobody broke anything. But the game was about to start.

Rapping her knuckles on the window to get their attention, Sonny pointed to the living room once they'd looked her way. The boys shared a smile and raced to toward the house. Satisfied they wouldn't miss anything, she turned back to making tea.

The kettle had just finished heating and the tea was

brewing in cups when she heard Janie call out, "You need to get in here, Sonny. The game is about to start."

Excitement that she didn't want to admit she felt jangled her nerves and made her hurry. Why did he want her and Charlie to watch the game? What could he possibly do that would matter or make a difference?

Trying so hard to cling to her anger at the shortstop, Sonny squeezed the honey bear fiercely and dumped way too much into a cup. "That'll just be mine," she muttered quietly and eased up on the poor plastic bear. So many emotions had gone through her the past few weeks. Everything from anger to depression to outrage had taken up temporary residence at one time or another. Other feelings like sadness and heart break she'd tried her best to hide from. She'd told herself she was doing it for Charlie. He needed her to be strong.

But the truth was she was hiding from herself. Because if she acknowledged how much she hurt, then she had to admit how much JP mattered. And if he mattered, and she couldn't be with him, then the pain would be too much to bear. She was better off shutting down.

How could somebody so perfect, so strong and reliable, turn right around and do something so thoughtless? She just didn't get it.

Charlie ran into the kitchen, startling her. "Me and Michael want drinks." If she wasn't mistaken, her boy had an extra spring in his step all of a sudden. It couldn't be because they were about to watch JP, could it?

She decided to ask. "Hey there, kiddo. You look awful chipper. Any particular reason?"

Her boy shrugged his shoulders. "I'm just excited to watch the game. That's all."

Sonny set down the tea mugs. "I thought you didn't want to see JP anymore after him not making it to your game." That was correct, wasn't it? Or had he thrown a change-up and felt differently and she just hadn't noticed because she was too wrapped up in her own inner drama?

Probably.

Charlie raided the fridge for drinks. "I'm getting over it."

Well now, how very mature. She wished she could say the same. "I'm glad, honey."

Coming back out with his arms loaded, he kicked the refrigerator closed with a grunt. "Can we have popcorn too, Mom?"

She didn't see why not. "Sure, babe. You finish getting the drinks and I'll make it."

Her son flashed her a grin. "Thanks, Mom. You're the best!"

She tried like hell to be. "You too, big C." Walking over to her boy, she dropped a kiss on his head. "We're a good pair."

And they were going to stay that way. Just the two of them. That's the way it was meant to be.

Michael poked his head into the kitchen, searching for her son. When he spotted him, the fifth grader beckoned. "Hurry up already, Charlie. The game's about to start."

The two of them took off and Sonny busied herself with the popcorn. By the time it was done and she had it in a large bowl, the game was under way. It took some finesse, but she managed to carry the bowl and both mugs of tea out to the living room.

The boys had taken up residence on the floor in front of the television. As soon as she got close enough, Charlie grabbed the bowl and filled his hand with popcorn. "Thanks," he said, his eyes already glued to the screen.

Finding a spot next to Janie, Sonny handed her the tea and sat. She tucked her bare feet underneath her and took a sip. Her lips puckered and she cringed. Wow, that was sweet.

On the screen the Rush put down two outs almost immediately, Peter burning up the field with red-hot pitches. The camera flashed over JP out at shortstop and Sonny's heart climbed into her throat. There he was, gorgeous and intense out on the field, his ball cap pulled low over his eyes.

Emotions slammed into her as she watched him catch a grounder and sail it off toward first for the third out. She hadn't expected seeing him to make her feel like this. But she felt like she'd just been sucker-punched in the stomach.

Was that why he'd wanted her to watch? So that she'd feel bad?

Charlie turned his head and looked at her over his shoulder, bare feet crossed at the ankle and bent up behind him. Though his eyes were a little sulky, she could see that he was feeling conflicted just like her. "Did you see the way JP got in front of the ball, Mom? I've been working on that at practice."

"That's good." It was hard to yank her gaze from the

flat screen. They'd just shown a shot of JP's butt as he jogged off the field.

Janie made a little hum in her throat. "Dang, Sonny," she drawled with appreciation.

True that.

First up to bat was JP and it seemed like everyone in the room tensed up with anticipation. The announcers went on and on about his batting average this season and other significant stats that she tuned out while he warmed up. She just ogled JP, eating up the sight of him. Something changed in the way they were speaking and she tuned back in.

Just in time too.

The announcers on the television said as JP stepped on to the field and headed for the batter's box, "And would you listen to that everybody? JP Trudeau has a new walkout song. The shortstop has used the same song religiously since the minors. I wonder what spurred this decision." The announcer paused and then added, "You tell me, folks, if Trudeau has made a mistake and this will affect his performance for the remainder of the season."

The sound rose and suddenly Charlie leapt to his feet and exclaimed, pointing at the TV, "That's my song! That's my song!"

Sure enough, her son's favorite song, "Tonight Tonight" by Hot Chelle Rae was blaring through the stadium speakers. As JP walked toward the plate the boy band rocked their little pop music hearts out, singing about there being a party on the roof top, top of the world.

Halfway to the mound, JP stopped and started dancing, mimicking the way she'd been dancing the night he'd walked in on her. Then he pointed to the Jumbotron just as the announcer cut in, "Would you look at that, folks? The shortstop is clearly sending a message."

Charlie was dancing in front of the TV along with JP until the Jumbotron came on the screen. Then he stopped and yelled, "Mom! Mom, look!" pointing at it.

Sonny leaned to the side and looked around her son, her pulse racing and her stomach doing jumping jacks. When she saw what was on the giant screen her heart opened wide up and she started to cry. It read in red, flashing letters:

Sorry, Charlie. This one's for you.

Janie gasped. "Oh my God, Sonny. Do you see that?"

She did. She so did.

The announcer cut in again. "Whoever Charlie is, they must be extremely special to the shortstop for him to pull this kind of stunt." Another pause. "And will you look at the crowd? They're going nuts out there, imitating Trudeau's moves."

They were too. JP had stopped shaking it and was walking the rest of the way to the plate, but the crowd was having a grand time rocking out to the teenybopper song, ignoring the game. Because, as the song said, whatever—it didn't matter.

The camera zoomed a close-up on JP's face and he looked directly into it, his eyes penetrating and intense. Then he held up a hand, palm facing out, and she could see writing on it. The camera focused further until the words became clear. Sonny read them and had to choke back tears. On his hand in black marker was written:

I need sunshine.

The man was very obviously sending her a message. And it was most definitely received. Sonny felt it clear down to her toes. It vibrated inside her.

No, she didn't want to be with a celebrity. Everybody knew him and everybody had something to say about what he was doing. Being with him extended that attention onto her and Charlie. She had already discovered what that felt like with the tabloid photo. It sucked. Really, really sucked. Just the thought of it still made her want to hyperventilate and hide under a rock.

But there was JP on national television, larger than life, making a complete ass out of himself. Dancing and writing messages and declaring his feelings. All for her and her son because they mattered more to him than what anyone else could possibly say or think.

That creepy tabloid photographer was on screen in the background snapping away like crazy. And she didn't care. Because JP clearly didn't. He made her feel safe—even with the whole world watching.

Suddenly it all became very, very clear. Opinions were just that. Opinions. And fame was nothing more than an illusion. What she and JP had was real.

And it had taken the media for her to see it.

That's when she knew. Beyond a shadow of a doubt and it stunned her.

She was still in love with JP.

Chapter Twenty-Seven

THE SATURDAY MORNING dawned clear and beautiful and JP was in his truck and on his way to Sonny's before breakfast. He'd made his play and was going to see if it had paid off. With any luck she had decided to not be obstinate and had watched the game. It was a gamble with her stubborn streak though.

The sun had just risen as he headed up the interstate, casting the Front Range in a peaceful light. August had come on strong, drying out the grasslands and turning the foothills golden brown. But even in the dead of summer he could still make out tiny pockets of snow up on the Rocky Mountain peaks.

It was one of the things he really liked about living in Colorado. No matter the season, there was always a view. Back home in Iowa, though it was pretty, there was a whole lot of flat. And he liked his landscape bumpy.

Reaching out to hit the power button on the radio, he

thought better of it and pulled his hand back. Nah, he thought. The quiet was good. It felt right. The whole way up, JP spent some quality time thinking about himself— who he was and who he wanted to be. Then he thought on how he behaved in the world and how that behavior affected other people. Other people that he cared for deeply.

He'd been wrong to be so insensitive to anyone else's feelings, to steamroll simply because he'd assumed everyone was on the same page as him. And he'd been wrong to be so self-involved that he'd stood up a boy who'd been counting on him. Every time that message from the kid popped in his head he flinched. It was the most humbling dressing down he had ever experienced.

But he'd deserved it. Because the truth was he had been expecting the relationship to unfold in a particular way. His way. He'd decided that he wanted Sonny and that was that. Any opposition or reluctance he'd just bowled over without even blinking.

He did that sometimes. Most often he didn't find fault with that particular character trait. But now he could see the flaws and drawbacks. Could see how his tunnel vision had a way of pushing everybody else's feelings off to the side.

JP didn't like what that said about him. For the most part he considered himself a good guy, but when he was slapped in the face with a big ol' character flaw and its consequences, it made him recognize his shortcomings.

Personal growth was always damn humbling.

Catching sight of the turnoff to Sonny's place, JP adjusted in his seat, feeling nervous. Last night he'd pulled out all the stops and done his best to make a huge gesture that she would recognize. And if she'd watched the game then he was sure she got it.

The questionable part was if she'd actually watched the game. Knowing that woman and how hard-headed she could be, she might well have not watched it out of spite. There wasn't anything he would put past Sonny. And he'd thought of a contingency plan in case she hadn't watched. It wasn't nearly so good, but he still had a plan B, and that's what mattered.

He just hoped to hell he wouldn't have to use it.

The arching sign that spanned Sonny's driveway entrance came into view and his gut tightened with anticipation. He liked her wood SONNYSIDE FARMS sign. On each end a sun rising over a vivid green pasture had been hand-painted, the sun's golden rays stretching off into the horizon.

She'd made a good life for herself and Charlie, JP thought as his pickup passed underneath the sign. A life that focused on the things that really mattered, that were at the heart of living. Love, comfort, stability.

What she'd made wasn't flashy or artificial. And because of that she had a terrific kid who she could be proud to call hers. All on her own, with nothing but her own determination and iron will, she'd created something wonderful.

Sonny was a hell of a woman.

As JP came to a stop at the end of the driveway, he felt a pressure bear down on his chest. He played baseball for a living and had never felt this nervous before a game.

But this wasn't a game. It was his life and he was there to claim it.

Vader came ripping around from the side of the house, wagging his tail. It was kind of silly, but he liked that the dog recognized the sound of his pickup and didn't bark. Instead he dropped his butt in the gravel and wagged his tail so hard his whole body was swaying. The Australian shepherd looked at him with a huge doggie grin. It was nice to be welcomed.

Climbing out of the truck, JP gave the dog a good pet and scratch under his chin. "Hey there, pup. Where's your mom?"

He'd half expected her to come running out with a broom to shoo him off as soon as he'd pulled up.

The dog flopped on his back and held up a paw begging for a belly rub. Unable to resist, JP crouched down and gave him a good rub down. A hind foot started motoring as he found a tickle spot. "There you go, Vader. That's the spot."

While he was crouched there giving the dog some affection, his gaze took in Sonny's property. Mature trees were scattered around the yard, flowers blooming happily in well-tended flower beds. The brick house sat simple and unadorned in the middle of it. Sonny's workspace with its flowering vine cover sat off to the right and back of it, the small red barn just visible behind. The doors were cracked, which probably meant that she was inside milking her goats.

It was so peaceful here. All he could hear were the sounds of nature and the occasional roar of a far-off tractor. It was a nice change from the constant noise of the city.

JP inhaled the fresh country air, filling his lungs. Sonny had busted her ass and made a good home. He could be happy there with her and Charlie.

All she needed to do was agree.

For that to happen he had to stop procrastinating like a wuss. He played ball for a living and took on badass men all the time without a second thought. And yet he was terrified of one strong-willed woman's rejection.

How was that for love?

Deciding to get it over with, JP straightened and wiped his hands on the front of his old jeans. No use waiting any longer.

Vader righted himself and nudged his hand with a cold nose, looking for more pets. "Not now, dog." He bent and retrieved a broken stick. "Here. Fetch." The stick flew through the air and landed in the grass halfway across the yard. The dog took off after it happily, his tongue lolling out of his mouth and off to the side.

Going in the opposite direction, JP was just passing the porch when Charlie opened the screen door and stepped outside. He took one look at the kid and felt his heart fling wide open. That boy was a gem and he wanted to be the one to help him grow in to a man.

If he would have him.

"Hey, Charlie." But for that to happen, he owed the kid a huge frigging apology.

The boy stood there silently staring at him for what felt like an eternity. He didn't speak, just stared hard at JP with big blue eyes and it felt like getting kicked in the gut. What if the boy didn't want to forgive him?

While he waited for Charlie to respond, JP felt an acute self-consciousness, like he was in a lineup waiting for inspection. For a guy who'd never questioned anything, it was damn disconcerting to feel nothing about himself but uncertainty.

Anxiety built in him until he couldn't take it anymore, the wait making him crazy. If the kid hated him, he just needed to come out and say it, because he couldn't take the suspense anymore. And if the kid did hate him, it would be flat-ass devastating. Because as he stood there looking at the blond-haired boy with the giant blue eyes and freckles, he fell head over heels.

Clearing his throat, JP was about to speak when the boy shifted. Snapping his mouth shut, he waited for him to say something. But he didn't. He didn't speak at all.

Instead a slow, brilliant smile spread across the boy's face. It started soft and ended up blinding and JP exhaled sharply. Hot damn.

Relief flooded him as the kid leapt off the porch and came running, his face lit with happiness. "I knew you would come!"

JP opened up his arms and Charlie flew inside for a hard, encompassing hug. Feeling his lips tremble, he pressed them together and held the boy tight. "I'm so sorry I let you down, Charlie."

The kid had his head buried in his chest and his voice came out muffled. "It's okay."

No, it wasn't okay. But it was a mistake he wouldn't be

repeating. "I was selfish, Charlie, and I hurt you. If you'll forgive me I can promise it won't happen again." He'd make damn sure it didn't.

The boy nodded against his chest, his arms still holding JP tight. "I forgive you."

Thank God. "You're an all right kid, slugger. I'm lucky to have you." He meant it. The kid was one in a million.

Now if he could only get Sonny to forgive him too.

Charlie pulled back and looked up at him, blue eyes bright with unshed tears. "I saw the game last night."

JP arched a brow. "And?"

The kid broke out giggling, "I can't believe you used my song!"

Neither could he. And the hell of it was, he'd played an exceptionally good game last night. Part of him was real worried that he'd landed himself a new walkout song permanently. But, if it made the kid happy then he'd just have to deal. Seeing him smile was worth it.

Behind him came the sound of someone clearing their throat and JP looked over his shoulder to find Sonny standing there, her arms full of cut herbs from her garden. Just one look at her had his stomach coiling with need and his heart thundering heavily. He loved that woman so much it was downright scary.

"Sonny." Her name was the only thing he could say. Only thing he could think.

With unreadable eyes she approached. "JP."

Charlie pulled out of his embrace and said, "I'm going to go make some breakfast." The kid turned to leave but spun back around, his face worried. "Don't leave without saying goodbye, okay?"

"You got it, slugger." Never again.

JP HELD HIS hands out, palms up. "Look, I'm really sorry."

Sonny sent Charlie inside and stared at JP, swallowing against the tightness in her throat. Seeing him holding her boy had brought all kinds of feelings to the surface, and she was real close to crying. Nobody besides her had ever hugged him like that. And seeing the shortstop do it made her realize how much her son deserved that kind of love.

And not just from her.

Charlie needed to be loved by JP.

All this time she'd been trying to protect her baby from hurt and all she'd succeeded in doing was keeping him away from experiencing love. With JP standing in front of her, his brown eyes earnest and unsure, all of her misgivings fell away.

Every reason she'd ever thought of and every excuse she'd told herself fell by the wayside and her heart filled up with hope. JP was the one for her and she had to have the courage to take that next step—in spite of all her insecurities. The only thing they were going to do was keep her from having what she wanted the most anyway. But he was here now and she wasn't going to let him get away.

Setting the bundle of freshly cut basil on the hood of JP's pickup, Sonny straightened her shoulders and walked right on up to the ballplayer. "I was really mad at you for standing up Charlie."

The shortstop inclined his head. "I know it." He shifted his feet. "And I'm sorry for it. I was so wrapped up over us that it slipped my mind. It's inexcusable."

She agreed. "Yeah, it is. If we're going to do this thing, JP, then we've got to try harder. Relationships are a team effort."

His eyes narrowed and went dark with emotion. "Are you saying that we're going to do this? You're okay with everything?"

That was the exact question she'd stayed up all night pondering. For so long she'd hidden from taking chances, afraid of what might be inside her if she did. For so long she'd used her old issues as an excuse to stay safe and alone. But then he'd come along and showed her how good it felt to be with someone who made her excited with possibilities. Who made her want to go beyond her walls and build something that would last.

Someone who made her feel more love than she'd ever thought possible. And that someone was JP. World-famous baseball player and amazing human being.

He was standing there in the shade of an oak tree, his eyes uncertain, and Sonny found that she didn't like seeing that look in them. It didn't belong there. JP was a cocky, self-assured ballplayer with a heart of gold. He simply wasn't the man she'd fallen in love with without his swagger.

Sonny took a few steps until she was standing directly in front of him and tipped her head back. Everything she felt for JP she let show when she looked up at him and smiled slowly. As she watched, the uncertainty left his eyes and was replaced by something warmer and a whole lot more confident.

And because she missed him and his smile more than she'd ever missed anything, Sonny said, "I'm saying that we can do this, but you have to do one thing first, Mr. Celebrity."

JP stared at her mouth and murmured, "What's that, sunshine?"

Reaching out a hand, she traced a finger over his chest and heard him inhale sharply. "You have to do that dance for me."

He frowned, confused. "What dance?"

This was going to be fun. "The one you did last night. I hear it's pretty popular. They're calling it The Trudeau." She and Charlie had watched it on YouTube about a thousand times. She'd laughed every single time. Sometimes the media did good things too.

His eyebrows shot up in disbelief. "You're kidding me."

Sonny shook her head and traced her finger across the flat of his belly. "Nuh-uh."

He was silent for a moment and then said, sounding pouty, "You really want me to do it again?"

She nodded and wrapped her arms around his waist, biting back a smile. "Yeah. Then I'll know you really love me."

JP pulled her in tight. "I do love you, Sonny. More than I ever expected to love anybody." He started rolling and grinding his hips and his eyes lit with naughty humor. "But, if this makes you hot . . ."

JP grabbed her butt and dipped her so low her hair touched the grass. It made her laugh from the exhilarating feel. "I love you too, JP." And it felt so good to finally say it out loud.

His hand was at the back of her neck when she straightened and he held her there, his expression suddenly serious. "I screwed up and I'm sorry."

He didn't mess up any worse than she had. Only he hadn't blamed anybody else. That'd been her doing. "I'm sorry too. I warned you about The Crazies."

JP smiled. "Yeah you did." His lips brushed her temple and he said against her ear. "I've grown fond of them. They keep things interesting."

His mouth was heaven. "How handy for us then."

He laughed softly. "So we're good?"

If by good he meant amazing. "Yeah."

Without warning JP tossed her over his shoulder and clamped a hand across the backs of her thighs, making her squeal. "JP! What are you doing?"

He patted her butt and headed toward the house. "It's time you got over this phobia, Sonny. It isn't good for your health."

His butt was right there and she gave it a good pinch. "What are you saying, huh?"

He laughed and pinched hers back. "That I'm taking you inside and making you love Saturdays."

And he did. He made her love the hell out of Saturdays.

Twice.

*See how Jennifer Seasons's Diamonds
and Dugouts series first started!
Keep reading for a sneak peek from*

STEALING HOME

Available now from Avon Books.

An Excerpt from

STEALING HOME

When Lorelei Littleton steals Mark Cutter's good
luck charm, all the pro-ball player can think is
how good she looked . . . and how bad she'll pay.
Thrust into a test of wills, they'll both discover
that while revenge may be a dish best served cold,
when it comes to passion, the hotter the better!

RAISING HIS GLASS, Mark smiled and said, "To the rodeo.
May you ride your bronc well."

Color singed Lorelei's cheeks as they tapped their
glasses. But her eyes remained on his while he took a long
pull of smooth, aged whiskey.

Then she spoke, her voice low. "I'll make your head
spin, cowboy. That I promise."

That surprised a laugh out of him, even as heat began
to pool heavy in his groin. "I'll drink to that." And he

did. He lifted the glass and drained it, suddenly anxious to get onto the next stage. A drop of liquid shimmered on her full bottom lip and it beckoned him. Reaching an arm out, Mark pulled her close and leaned down. With his eyes on hers, he slowly licked the drop off, his tongue teasing her pouty mouth until she released a soft moan.

Arousal coursed through him at the provocative sound. Pulling her more fully against him, Mark deepened the kiss. Her lush little body fit perfectly against him and her lips melted under the heat of his. He slid a hand up her back and fisted in the dark, thick mass of her long hair. He loved the feel of the cool silky strands against his skin.

He wanted more.

Tugging gently, Mark encouraged her mouth to open for him. When she did, his tongue slid inside and tasted, explored the exotic flavor of her. Hunger spiked inside him and he took the kiss deeper. Hotter. She whimpered into his mouth and dug her fingers into his hair, pulled. Her body began pushing against his, restless and searching.

Mark felt like he'd been tossed into an incinerator when he pushed a thigh between her long, shapely legs and discovered the heat there. He groaned and rubbed his thigh against her, feeling her tremble in response.

Suddenly she broke the kiss and pushed out of his arms. Her breathing was ragged, her lips red and swollen from his kiss. Confusion and desire mixed like a heady concoction in his blood, but before he could say anything she turned and began walking toward the hallway to his bedroom.

At the entrance she stopped and beckoned to him. "Come and get me, catcher."

So she wanted to play did she? Hell yeah. Games were his life.

Mark toed off his shoes as he yanked his sweater over his head and tossed it on the floor. He began working the button of his fly and strode after her. He was a little unsteady on his feet, but he didn't care. He just wanted to catch her. When he entered his room he found her by the bed. She'd turned on the bedside lamp and the light illuminated every gorgeous inch of her curvaceous body.

He started toward her, but she shook her head. "I want you to sit on the bed."

Mark walked to her anyway and gave her a deep, hungry kiss before he sat on the edge of the bed. He wondered what she had in store for him and felt his gut tighten in anticipation. "Are you going to put on a show for me?" God, that'd be so hot if she did.

All she said was "mmm hmm," and turned her back to him. Mark let his eyes wander over her body and decided her tight round ass in denim was just about the sexiest thing he'd ever seen.

When his gaze raised back up he found her smiling over her shoulder at him. "Are you ready for the ride of your life, cowboy?"

Hell yes he was. "Bring it, baby. Show me what you've got."

Her smile grew sultry with unspoken promise as she reached for the hem of her T-shirt. She pulled it up leisurely while she kept eye contact with him. All he could hear was the soft sound of fabric rustling, but it fueled him—this seductively slow striptease she was giving him.

He wanted to see her. "Turn around."

As she turned she continued to pull it up until she was facing him with the yellow cotton dangling loosely from her fingertips. A black, lacy bra barely covered the most voluptuous, gorgeous pair of breasts he'd ever laid eyes on. He couldn't stop staring.

"Do you like what you see?"

Good God, yes. The woman was a goddess. He nodded, a little harder than he meant because he almost fell forward. He started to tell her how sexy she was when suddenly a full-blown wave of dizziness hit him and he shook his head to clear it. What the hell?

"Is everything alright, Mark?"

The room started spinning and he tried to stand, but couldn't. It felt like the world had been tipped sideways and his body was sliding onto the floor. He tried to stand again, but fell backward onto the bed instead. He stared up at her as he tried to right himself and couldn't.

Fonda stood there like a siren, dark hair tousled around her head, breasts barely contained—guilt plastered across her stunning face.

Before he fell unconscious on the bed, he knew. Knew it with gut certainty. He tried to tell her, but his mouth wouldn't move. Son of a bitch.

Fonda Peters had drugged him.

About the Author

JENNIFER SEASONS is a Colorado transplant. She lives with her husband and four children along the Front Range, where she enjoys breathtaking views of the mighty Rocky Mountains every day. A dog and two cats keep them company. When she's not writing, she loves spending time with her family outdoors exploring her beautiful adopted home state. You can find her online at www.facebook.com/jennifer.seasons.3.

Visit www.AuthorTracker.com for exclusive information on your favorite HarperCollins authors.

Give in to your impulses . . .
Read on for a sneak peek at four brand-new
e-book original tales of romance
from Avon Books.
Available now wherever e-books are sold.

THE MAD EARL'S BRIDE
By Loretta Chase

WANTED: WIFE
By Gwen Jones

A WEDDING IN VALENTINE
A VALENTINE VALLEY NOVELLA
By Emma Cane

FLING
A BDSM EROTICA ANTHOLOGY
By Sara Fawkes, Cathryn Fox, and Lauren Hawkeye

An Excerpt from

THE MAD EARL'S BRIDE
(Originally appeared in the print
anthology *Three Weddings and a Kiss*)

by Loretta Chase

Gwendolyn Adams is about to propose to an
earl. On his deathbed. Because she comes
from a long line of infamous heir breeders,
she is being offered up as the last chance to
save a handsome aristocrat's dying line.

The Earl of Rawnsley is in for the shock of
his life: a surprise bride. No one asked him
what he wanted, but if he may die, he most
certainly does not want to spend his last
days breeding . . . no matter how tempting
and infuriating Gwendolyn may be . . .

"The name is Adams," she said. "Gwendolyn Adams."

He scowled. "Miss Adams, I should like to know whether you are trying to convince me to marry you or to kill myself."

"I merely wished to point out how pointless it is, in the circumstances, to quibble about our respective character flaws," she said. "And I wished to be honest with you."

A wicked part of her did not wish to be honest. She realized he was worried about his male urges clouding his judgment. The wicked part of her was not simply hoping the urges would win; it was also tempting her to encourage them with the feminine tactics other girls employed.

But that was not fair.

They had turned into the narrow drive leading to the stables. Though the rain beat harder now, Gwendolyn was aware mainly of the beating of her own heart.

She did not want to go away defeated, yet she did not want to win by unfair means.

She supposed the display of her limbs—however much her immodest mode of riding had been dictated by the need for haste and the unavailability of a sidesaddle—constituted unfair means.

Consequently, as they rode into the stable yard, she headed for the mounting block.

But Rawnsley was off his horse before she reached it, and at the gelding's side in almost the same moment.

In the next, he was reaching up and grasping her waist.

His hands were warm, his grasp firm and sure. She could feel the warmth spreading outward, suffusing her body, while she watched the muscles of his arms bunch under the wet, clinging shirtsleeves.

He lifted her up as easily as if she'd been a fairy sprite. Though she wasn't in the least anxious that he'd drop her, she grasped his powerful shoulders. It was reflex. Instinctive.

He brought her down slowly, and he did not let go even after her feet touched the ground.

He looked down at her, and his intent yellow gaze trapped her own, making her heart pound harder yet.

"The time will come when I will have no power over you," he said, his low tones making her nerve ends tingle. "When my mind crumbles, little witch, I shall be at your mercy. Believe me, I've considered that. I've asked myself what you will do with me then, what will become of me."

At that moment, one troubling question was answered.

He was aware of the danger he was in. His fears were the

same as those she felt for him. His reason was still in working order.

But he continued before she could reassure him.

"I can guess what will happen, but it doesn't seem to matter, because I'm the man I always was. A death sentence has changed nothing." His hands tightened on her waist. "You should have left me in the mire," he told her, his eyes burning into her. "It was not pleasant—yet Providence does not grant all its creatures a pretty and painless demise. And I'm ready enough for mine. But you came and fished me out, and now . . ."

He let go abruptly and stepped back. "It's too late."

He was in no state to listen to the reassurances, Gwendolyn saw. If he was angry with himself and didn't trust that self, he was not likely to trust anything she said. He would believe she was humoring him, as though he were a child.

And so she gave a brisk, businesslike nod. "That sounds like a yes to me," she said. "Against your better judgment, evidently, but a yes all the same."

"Yes, drat you—drat the lot of you—I'll do it," he growled.

"I am glad to hear it," she said.

"Glad, indeed. You're desperate for your hospital, and I'm the answer to your maidenly prayers." He turned away. "I'm desperate, too, it seems. After a year's celibacy, I should probably agree to marry your *grandmother*, Devil confound me."

He strode down the pathway to the house.

An Excerpt from

WANTED: WIFE

by Gwen Jones

TV reporter Julie Knott has been dumped
two weeks before the wedding. But when she
follows a story to the backwoods of New Jersey,
she finds a new marriage proposal, one born
of logic. Can they keep their relationship
simple, or will love come crashing in?

Andy Devine Seeks a Wife
Landed, Financially Secure 40-YR-Old Male
Seeks Healthy, Athletic Female
For Marriage and Family.
Must Submit to Full Disclosure and
Be Willing to Work Hard.
Generous Monetary Compensation
If Terms of Contract Are Not Met.
Interviews Will Be Held at the Iron Bog Firehouse,
Main Street, Iron Bog,
Friday, 27 August, 1:00–4:00 PM.
Please Bring ID.

"You," Andy Devine said. "I want you for my wife."

As that statement traveled the neuron pathway to the part of my brain that would absorb, interpret, and decide how to answer, I couldn't help but think of all the bizarre things I've seen. A dog on a high wire balancing an egg on his nose, a three-legged goose, a woman who ate nails, a man surgically altered to look like Chewbacca, a woman living in a refrigerator, an old man who hoisted a truck when it rolled atop his grandson's leg, a couple whose house had two rooms filled to the ceiling with pennies. I've seen heroism and lunacy, oddity and insanity, but up until that moment, none of it had made my jaw drop. Because up until then, none of it had involved me.

So "*What?*" was all I managed to reply.

To which he reiterated, "I want *you* for my wife."

I smiled, clearing my throat. He had to be playing with me. "I'm flattered, Mr. Devine, truly I am, but what's your real answer?"

He leaned in, his proximity sending numbing signals to my brain. "The same."

I laughed. "You're joking."

"When I'm joking," he said, moving even closer, "you'll know it."

Denny lowered his camera. "Excuse me," he said to Andy Devine, "but are you for real?"

"Pardon?" he answered, unblinking.

"Okay, never mind," Denny said, realigning the camera. "Go on."

I slapped my hand over the lens. "Shut that thing off. Are you insane?"

Denny lowered it. "I ought to be asking you the same thing. It's the best offer you've had in years."

I scowled at him, returning to the subject at hand. "Mr. Devine—a word." Then I promptly crossed to the other side of the room. When I turned, Denny had sunk into a folding chair and my would-be suitor was standing before me.

"Yes?" he said, calmly attentive.

A part of me was so flabbergasted I hardly knew where to begin, but I retained enough professionalism to override anything. "I'm a TV reporter, Mr. Devine, not a candidate for your fiancée. I'm here to cover a story, not to become one. So as tempting as your offer may be, I have to decline."

He lifted a brow. "Why, Ms. Knott, are you patronizing me?"

That threw me. "What? No!"

"Because I detect a hint of condescension."

"Then you're imagining things." My hands were sweating. I swiped them on my skirt. "I'm just stating a fact."

His gaze dipped seductively. "So you don't think I'm worth considering."

"Mr. Devine, don't take—" Suddenly I was struck by the line of his jaw, so angular and forthright that I swear he could be a judge or a juror or anyone who's supposed to be capable of impartiality, and yet . . . there was something about it, in his emerging beard and how it sloped toward his mouth, that was so indefinably sexy it knocked all sense out of me. I was fighting a losing battle, and I knew it.

I cleared my throat and began again. "Look, I don't want you to take this personally, but—"

"I won't," he said. "In fact, I've gone out of my way to make sure personalities have nothing to do with it. I need a wife to help run the farm and have our children. And if she does, she'll share equally in all the rewards and benefits. All I ask is that she's healthy, able to have children, and willing to work hard. You, Ms. Knott . . ."—he looked me over—". . . appear to meet all the criteria."

The man was astounding. "But you know nothing about me!"

"What do I need to know beyond what I can see?"

"How about what's inside me, what my interests are, if I'm honest, how I take my coffee—Christ!" I stabbed my fingers into my hair, a comb tumbling out. "Why, if I even *like* you, for Pete's sake!"

He plucked the comb from the floor. "Do you like me, Ms. Knott?" he said with the barest of smiles, the bit of tortoise-shell plastic pinched between his fingers.

I snatched it from him, shoving it into my hair. "That's not the issue and it never was."

He leaned in. "My point exactly."

An Excerpt from

A WEDDING IN VALENTINE
A VALENTINE VALLEY NOVELLA

by Emma Cane

It's the wedding all of Valentine Valley has been
waiting for, and once again the town works its
magic in this brand-new novella by Emma Cane.

Heather Armstrong is looking forward to
a weekend away at her best friend Emily's
wedding, but when she learns that her
previous one-night stand is Emily's brother,
the weekend takes an unexpected turn.

Heather Armstrong gasped as the plane dropped down between the Colorado mountains, which were painted myriad shades of green below the tree line, barren and brown at the top, awaiting the next winter's snow. The ground seemed to rush up, and only when they touched down at the small Aspen airport did she let her exhilaration at her first mountain landing subside back into wedding excitement. She was about to be a bridesmaid in the June wedding of an old friend, Emily Murphy.

As she waited for a call from Emily, she wandered the airport. It bustled with people dressed casually for the outdoors, many carrying cases for fishing equipment, a pastime this valley was known for in the summer. She'd always preferred being a people watcher, observing from the background rather than commanding attention herself. It was one of the reasons she'd never enjoyed being in charge of a restaurant's kitchen and had opened her own catering business. But now her people watching skills made her halt in her tracks as she caught a glimpse of a familiar figure.

A man wearing a cowboy hat slouched in a chair near the main doors, as if he, too, was waiting for someone. His head was bent over a book, and she couldn't quite see his face. A feeling of unease shivered up her spine and made her so wary that she backed up to where she was partially hidden around a corner. Peeking out again, she studied his pale blond hair beneath the hat, the checked Western shirt that snugly outlined his broad chest, the long legs encased in faded jeans above worn cowboy boots.

The bang of dropped luggage drew his attention, and he looked up. Heather recognized him instantly, and with a gasp, she retreated behind the safety of the wall. His name was Chris, and that was all she'd known when they'd been snow-bound together in the Denver airport seven months before. Late-night drinks at the bar and mutual attraction—make that lust—shared with Chris had turned her into a person she'd never been, a daring flirt who'd ended up in bed with a cowboy. They'd spent two wild days together, exploring and laughing and connecting on an intimate level that had surprised her with its depth, considering they'd been strangers and all. Though she'd left him her number, assuming they'd see each other again, he'd never called. She'd felt like an idiot, a slut, and whatever other bad names she'd called herself over the following months. Gradually she'd accepted the "adventure" as a risk she'd obviously wanted to take, and had learned from. She wasn't cut out for one-night stands. She felt too much, expected too much. A man pursuing such a brief affair wanted only that and nothing else.

Today had been the first day airports hadn't made her think about him, she thought bitterly. Tough luck for her.

To find some peace, she'd chalked the experience up to a valuable lesson. Other women had done stupid things in college, but not her. She'd been too focused on her business degree, and then culinary school, the future her goal. She was little lured by frat parties and wild drinking. She'd had a boyfriend or two, of course, serious engineering and business students, and that same pattern had continued throughout her twenties. Never time for an intense relationship—until Andrew four years before. She'd thought everything so perfect, so wonderful, and hadn't even seen that he was pulling away from her, that their sex life was full of desperation more than real passion. Everything on the surface had been too good to be true. The breakup with him was probably what had launched her recklessness that snowy night in Denver.

But Chris's face had haunted her a long time, lean and sculpted, his blue eyes almost startling in their intensity. She hadn't been with another man since him, had been ready to change her life, find a new place to start over, to forget her past and find more peaceful surroundings.

FLING
A BDSM Erotica Anthology
by *Sara Fawkes, Cathryn Fox, and Lauren Hawkeye*

Welcome to Fetish Week

Unleash your kinky side with three tales of BDSM
romance in an exclusive Mediterranean sex
resort from three hot erotica writers, including
New York Times bestseller Sara Fawkes.

Take Me by Sara Fawkes
The minute sexy hotel manager Alexander Stavros spots shy,
sweet Kate Swansea at the Mancusi resort, he can tell she's
begging for release. This Dom is the perfect man to help her
. . . if she's willing to let go of her inhibitions and enjoy the
ride.

Teach Me by Cathryn Fox
There's nothing Luca Mancusi loves more than lingerie. So
much so, he's made it his business. Fashion design intern Josie
Pelletier is supposed to be negotiating a deal with him, but as
talks heat up, he can't wait to teach her the ways of business
. . . and BDSM.

Tame Me by Lauren Hawkeye

CEO Marco Kennedy can't help being drawn to Ariel Monroe. When he follows the pop star abroad to the Mancusi resort, she agrees to a deal: He'll win her as a sub through pleasure . . . or he'll disappear from her life. Ariel's game . . . just as long as she doesn't lose her heart too.

Available now from Avon Red
Wherever e-books are sold